Mystery Young X
Young, Sherban,
Double talk : a Warren Kingsley
mystery /
$20.00   ocn968745671

DOUBLE TALK

By Sherban Young

THE ENESCU FLEET SERIES

Fleeting Memory
Fleeting Glance
Fleeting Note
Fleeting Chance
Fleeting Promise

THE WARREN KINGSLEY SERIES

Five Star Detour
Double Cover
Double Tak

MORE BOOKS

Opportunity Slips
Dead Men Do Tell Tales

DOUBLE TALK

A WARREN KINGSLEY MYSTERY

SHERBAN YOUNG

MysteryCaper Press

Columbia, MD

ISBN-10: 0-9912324-8-8
EAN-13: 978-0-9912324-8-2

MysteryCaper Press
Columbia, Maryland

www.mysterycaper.com
www.sherbanyoung.com

1 — OPEN COMMUNICATION

"**W**e all talk too much."

Frederick Abbott scowled. As the recipient of this succinct observation, he was frankly nonplussed. "What did you say?"

"I said we all talk too much," clarified the speaker, making himself comfortable on the other's office sofa. "As a society, we talk and talk, and then we talk some more. It bugs me. Nobody knows how to have an unexpressed thought anymore. The older I get, the more I realize one simple truth in life: most things are better left unspoken."

Abbott scowled a second time. He was a tart and crusty little man, 5'4" in height and impeccably dressed. He had a round belly and a face like a squashed pecan nut.

He refused to accept that his visitor could have recognized any simple truths in life, just as he rejected the notion that the latter could be getting any older. One look at those placid features and that long, powerfully built frame—the exact inverse of Abbott's own build—and he couldn't think of a person getting any less old. Abbott, meanwhile, felt like he had aged several years in the last ten minutes alone.

"Most things—?" he hazarded.

"Are better left unspoken," agreed the supine thinker, shutting his eyes in meditation.

The older man wriggled; his puckered brow darkened. "But you're my speechwriter!"

His associate sighed. It was a sigh that bespoke many well-considered thoughts, the thoughts of a man who truly thought about the things that he thought about. He opened his eyes. "I am aware of that, Mayor, well aware."

"Are you? Because you're acting like you aren't."

"Well, I am. I've just come to the conclusion that none of it matters, really."

Abbott glared. This kind of talk didn't put votes in the ballot box. "What's going on with you today?"

His speechwriter remarked that nothing was going on with him that wasn't going on with the rest of a sad and purposeless mankind.

The elder member of this mankind grunted. He turned from his listless pen jockey and emitted a sigh himself.

Through the gigantic balcony window behind his gigantic desk, the poor politician gazed out at the Frederick Abbott Baseball Stadium. It was a very nice baseball stadium, made even nicer, in Frederick Abbott's opinion, by its new title. He had bought the ball club last winter, and ownership had its privileges.

Like most residents of Kilobyte, the mayor was not content with one profession alone. He was a public servant, a team owner, a restaurateur and the majority stockholder of half the companies in town. The term *conflict of interest* held no meaning in KB.

Founded in 1976 by a prosperous vitamin salesman who dabbled in computer science, the modern-day municipality continued to embrace the eclectic—none more than its present leader. In Kilobyte, your plumber might also be an advertising executive, and the mortgage brokers at the intersection of Chesterfield and Eighth could, in fact, turn out to be purveyors of quality running shoes and athletic apparel, but it was the mayor who raised the bar for all of them.

Of course, being multifaceted wasn't everything. Abbott was already beginning to regret hiring a certain mix of perfect male specimen and brooding philosophizer as his new wordsmith.

He rotated back around. It was raining now, and the grounds crew had started tarping the field of play. Abbott hated when the grounds crew tarped the field of play. He picked up a chunk of petrified oak off his desk—a souvenir from his timber firm—and stared down at it dully.

"About this debate on Monday," he tried again.

The chunk of wood did not immediately answer, and neither did his new speechwriter.

Abbott frowned. He could be wrong, but this lack of reply signified a shift in occupancy in the room: a change in the number of men discussing a sad and purposeless mankind. He peered around and found that his supposition had been correct. His employee had vanished without a word (not a trait you appreciated in an employee and especially not in a speechwriter).

* *

While the mayor continued to snort and sputter to himself about the abominable cheek of his staff, his well-built and undeniably cheeky advisor made his way down the hall, down the elevator and across a short corridor into the lobby of the Kilobyte Municipal Building—also known, in full, as the *Frederick Abbott Kilobyte Municipal County Legislative Building/Corporate Headquarters of the Kilobyte K's (Independent League Baseball Team)*. It was a building name the town council had spent considerable time deliberating on, for there was always a danger of it becoming too wordy.

Abbott's brawny new employee repaid their efforts with blank indifference. He strode by the length of brass-plated letters and polished cherry veneer with nary a glance. He had more important things on his mind than endless signage.

He was brooding still. He was a born brooder, and he did it well. People who think they know the strong, silent type have never met Warren Kingsley on one of his reflective mornings. He could make the most rugged ponderer look reedy and unattractive.

On the surface, there was nothing for him to be so pensive about. He was handsome without being excessive about it. He had a tall and muscular physique that required little to no dieting or exercise to maintain. And about a month ago, a nice, comfy job had landed squarely in his well-hewn lap. Yet was it enough? He would say no. Not even stumbling upon a town ideally designed for his disposition could buck his spirits.

He and Kilobyte seemed to be made for each other. He fit the town work ethic like a laser-cut sprocket. Others dabbled—Warren preferred to wander from one activity to another, usually at the expense of whatever he was supposed to be doing in the first place. He was the enemy of follow-through and the god of short attention. That god had found his Valhalla.

His present position was cushier than most and had the added attraction of paying better than it deserved. He should have been doing cartwheels to the office every day, even if such an action would have wrinkled the crease of his designer suit. But he did no cartwheels, and the folds of his Armani no longer amused him. Why? The answer was simple enough.

He was brooding on something.

Why should he let it bother him? (he brooded). What did it matter what some random person said to him—or anyone said? People (especially female people) talk too much. That was his motto.

But it did bother him. It did matter.

During this run of internal Q&A, the Prince of Preoccupation gazed vaguely around the lobby, taking in this and that.

On his third pass, he hesitated, as something worthy of his notice had captured his attention. It wasn't the twelve-foot-long building name, nor was it the guard at the reception desk, a man Warren was pretty sure had come by his place the weekend before last to clean out his rain gutters. It was something more intriguing than that.

It was a person from Warren's past: a person who might well be curious to hear what he had been doing with himself these last few years and what others might have said to him in that time which shouldn't bother him but did.

He picked up his feet, passed through the line of metal detectors separating the lobby from the elevators and cut the guy off at the decorative fountain. The man was in an elite category for Warren and, therefore, worth the extra exertion. He was someone Warren had worked with once who hadn't actually ended up dead.

He might as well say hello.

**

Four floors above this joyous reunion, Frederick Abbott was still making strange vibrating sounds with his lips. An expert on human communication might have called these sounds speech, but to us laymen, it simply came across as so much noise.

He had no sooner completed an impressive round of grunts and grumbles—marching from one side of his office and back again—than a voice spoke to him from the doorway, frightening the bejeebers out of him.

"Talking to yourself again, boss?" asked the voice.

Abbott snarled something under his breath and glared hotly. He was in his shirtsleeves now, his tie slightly askew. "What do *you* want?" he spat.

It wasn't a very nice greeting for a person to receive, but this was not a problem. The new arrival wasn't actually a person; merely Abbott's intern for baseball operations, "Telly"—short for—well, no one really knew what it was short for. Nor did anyone care. He had been hired a couple weeks earlier as a favor to Abbott's sister, Clarisse, wife of the team's general manager and aunt to Telly (on her husband's side). It was not one of the owner's finer acquisitions.

"You're late," Abbott told him, consulting his watch. "Seventeen minutes, ten seconds. You've been late every day since I hired you."

Telly considered this. He was an amiable young man with a scattered mane of near-black hair, a wisp of beard under his chin and the appearance of too many teeth. He had no watch himself, but he had a working knowledge of what one looked like. "Did we say nine?" he asked.

"We said nine. Your workday starts at nine o'clock sharp."

"Really? Thought we said nine thirty. 'Nine-ish' I think you said at one point."

"I have never said 'nine-ish' before in my life."

Telly said "K," an expression he was very fond of. "Have it your own way, boss."

"I will," Abbott asserted. "Now what do you want?"

"Nothing, just passing by and wondering if you were talking to yourself or not."

"Well, I was."

"K."

"Now go away."

"K." The intern did not go away. "Were you saying anything in particular," he went on, "or just speaking aloud to the universe?"

Abbott scowled. That made three and counting. "I was speaking to Mr. Kingsley."

"Now?" Telly was familiar with the dimensions of his boss's new speechwriter and failed to see how the former could have concealed the latter anywhere in the office.

"Not literally now," Abbott growled. "Before. I was in the middle of a conversation with the man when he made some flippant remark about simple truths and vanished."

Telly said ah. He thought he had smelt a hint of the dude's after-shave: robust with a touch of smoked hickory. Since becoming colleagues, Telly had often found himself admiring—in a purely heterosexual way—the characteristic Warren smell. "You must have been reviewing the finer points of what he said." He nodded knowingly. Telly knew from personal experience that you often had to talk it out before you could appreciate the full brilliance of one of Warren Kingsley's brainwaves. He was that kind of dude.

Fred Abbott had yet to reach that level of saturation himself. "You still here?" he asked.

Telly reassured him on that point.

"Are you growing a beard?"

The young man made a vague, noncommittal gesture. He replied that it would be more appropriate to say that he was not *not* growing a beard. "So how was your meeting with the other indie-team owners?" he wondered, referring to a trip his employer had taken the day before yesterday. As nephew to the general manager, practically next in line to the throne, it was natural that Telly would take an interest in the machinations of the back office—especially when those machinations affected overall team growth. (In other words, he wanted to be sure that, as many a fan before him had put it, the owner didn't bitch everything up.) "Did you have a pleasant and productive journey?"

His employer resented the question and responded to it only reluctantly. Much as a crime boss resents getting probed by a junior DA, Abbott preferred not to open up to his new intern under any circumstance, and certainly not after his nerves had already been jangled by Warren Kingsley and his vagaries.

No, he did not have a pleasant journey. The train was late, the seats were uncomfortable, and on his way up the platform, he was pretty sure he swallowed a bug. Did that answer Telly's question?

Telly felt it had. "Didn't they feed you on the train?" he quipped.

A low, grumbling noise, not unlike distant thunder—or the sound a paper shredder might make should someone stuff an intern into it—indicated that the older man was not amused.

"Well, think of it this way," said the youth, "it was probably a lot more traumatic for the bug."

Abbott sniffed. "And I could hardly get in the door at the hotel without some slimeball sports journalist hounding me about that ex—right fielder of ours, Hector What's-His-Name. As if this was the first time a minor league superstar has crapped out after making it to the majors. And how is it my fault? We're not an affiliate—what does what someone does in the major leagues have to do with me?"

Telly agreed that the question was a tough one. "If anyone asks me about interleague development, I got my quote all ready. Wanna hear it?"

"No."

"What I would say is—"

"Would you bug off, please?"

Telly repeated the phrase amusedly. " 'Bug off.' Bug on the plat-form, bug in the office." He laughed heartily, which made one of them. "And, by the way, it wasn't Hector, boss. Hector is still on the team. The name of the player who crapped out was Javier. Javier Clark—"

"Bug off!" insisted the team-owning mayor.

A short silence followed, on Telly's part a thoughtful one, as he struggled to put the proper construction on his employer's words.

"No, wait," said Abbott.

Telly hadn't moved. Given his cue, he didn't miss an opportunity to say K again—he seldom did—but in honor of his boss's request he said it with an unbridled fervor that suited him well. It might have been the K of an eager squire answering the summons of his knight.

"I want you to do something for me."

Telly responded with another of his knowing nods. He could guess what that something was. Despite his crotchety exterior, the old man clearly needed moral support. "You're all worked up about that

debate on Monday, aren't you? Did I tell you the one about the Swed-
ish milkmaid and the jackhammer? It's hilarious, and you can open
with it."

"No."

"No—I didn't share the one about the milkmaid? Or no—you
aren't all worked up?"

"Both."

Telly said right. He didn't think that was it either. "It's the hole in
our lineup, isn't it? You and my uncle have been seeking a power-hit-
ting right fielder to fill the void, but you continue to seek in vain. Is
that it?"

"We aren't seeking anything of the sort," Fred Abbott informed
him.

"A power lefty for the bullpen, then?"

"We don't need a power lefty for the bullpen."

"Everyone needs a power lefty for their bullpen," said Telly. He
spoke austerely, for he felt strongly on the topic. "Take Kansas City—"

"Never mind Kansas City!" snapped the weary executive, taking a
lap around his colossal desk. "I didn't call you in here to discuss Kansas City."

Telly withdrew into another silence, this time a wounded one. He
was all for doing his part for the team, but he resented getting jerked
around and having his time wasted. He was a young man with plenty
of friends to tweet and no shortage of naked women to download
from the Internet. He frowned at his boss impatiently.

"Do you know Ms. Henrietta?" Abbott asked him.

"The human-resources lady or the office-supply lady?"

"They are the same person."

Telly nodded. He supposed they were. "What about her?"

"I want her to get me everything she can on our illustrious new
speechwriter. We must have run a background check on him. I want
to see it."

"On Warren Kingsley?"

"On Warren Kingsley."

Telly was confused. "You want info on Warren?"

"That's what I said."

"Why?"

"Why? *Why?* I desire it, that's why! It occurs to me that I know absolutely nothing about the man."

"He looks good in a suit," Telly offered.

"I know he looks good in a suit!"

"And he's always pondering stuff. Seems like enough qualifications to write political blather to me," said the intern/community-college attendee (minor in communication). "Besides, didn't you hire him yourself?"

Abbott had the good grace to avert his glare. "Yes. Yes, I suppose I did. It seemed like a good idea at the time."

Telly could see that. He frowned. "Why?" he asked.

Abbott lowered his gaze farther still. All these questions had broken down his reserve. "He bedazzled me, I suppose. One day, about a month ago, I left a copy of one of my speeches at the diner. When I came back to retrieve it, a man sitting at the next table had picked it up and revised it. Kingsley was that man. His revisions were good. Damn good."

"Put some clever lines in, did he?"

"Mostly he cut three-quarters of it and told me not to be such a blowhard. I should have known then," said Abbott, shaking his head. "As I say, he bedazzled me."

Telly could see that too. Warren had the sort of peculiar charm that could easily bewitch a person. (In a purely heterosexual way.)

Abbott waxed on. "He was such a change to the swarms of smarmy yes-men I had on staff before then. I hired him as my new speechwriter on the spot. Not that he's written any speeches yet," the mayor sighed. "He mostly lays around and spouts philosophy at me." He sighed again. He could do with some of those smarmy yes-men now. Smarmy yes-men wouldn't know a philosophy if you showed it to them in a four-part PowerPoint presentation.

"And so now," Telly presumed, "you want to know who it is you hired. Is that it?"

Abbott agreed that was it.

"Well, I can help you out there, boss. I know quite a lot about Warren. I find him fascinating. In a purely—"

Abbott frowned to himself. A battle raged within his barrel chest. It was fought between ridding his office of his pesky intern—admittedly, one of the reasons for sending him on his errand—and learn-

ing something about the oddball Kingsley sooner rather than later.
His natural curiosity beat out his desire for tranquility. "What do you
know?" he said.

The intern answered promptly. "He used to be a bodyguard, for
one."

"A bodyguard?"

"One of the most sought after around, Warren tells me."

"He was competent?"

"He was the best," said Telly simply. "I mean, with a name like
*King*sley he'd have to be good," he remarked—wondering, after he
said it, whether he was perhaps confusing him with Smucker's jam.
"All I know is, he was totally awesome, always thwarting assassins and
throwing himself on grenades and junk." (Unless that was Polaner All
Fruit.)

Abbott found these rave notices doubtful. No one, to his mind,
was awesome, much less totally awesome. They might be acceptable
perhaps, even satisfactory at times, but then they just go and wander
off when you're in the middle of a conversation.

"It was quite a lucky break landing him," Telly continued. "From
what I understand, normally you have to have an 'in' to work with
Warren Kingsley."

Abbott, though baffled by this requirement, replied that he did
own an inn. Also several motels and a B&B in Rhode Island. The
mayor was big into commercial real estate.

Telly realized that his meaning had been misapprehended. "An
'in,' boss. *I* single *n*. Not *i* double *n*. You gotta have one. An in. *I* single *n*."

At this point, Abbott said something coarse about not giving an
f about *i* single *n*'s or *i* double *n*'s, and something even coarser about
blithering *a* double *s*'s.

"You don't care?" Telly asked.

"I don't care," Abbott assured him.

Telly said K. "Of course, if you're unhappy with his speechwriting, you could always hire him as your muscle."

"I don't need any muscle."

"Of course you do. Everyone needs muscle. Take the mayor of
Kansas City—"

Abbott had no wish to take the mayor of Kansas City. "I've never had a bodyguard, and I have no need for one now. No one is trying to kill me."

"What about your opponent in the election?"

The other frowned. "That was only talk," he said quietly.

Talk or not, Telly remembered enjoying it. "What did he say again?"

The mayor blenched. "The last time we saw each other, he said he would like nothing better than to see my dead body laying on a slab."

"Lying."

"What?"

"It would be *lying* on a slab, boss, not *laying*. If he were to put it on the slab himself—after murdering you, let's say—then he would be *laying* it there. However, if your dead body was there by its own accord, it would be *lying*. Now, *lain*—"

"Would you shut up, please? Go talk to Ms. Henrietta."

Telly did not go talk to Ms. Henrietta. He was too busy thinking deep, Kingsley-esque thoughts. "This sudden impulse to check up on Warren," he inquired delicately, "it wouldn't have anything to do with your wife, would it?"

Abbott's eyes bugged out. "My wife?!"

"Your wife—Sheryl."

"I know my wife's name!"

"I know you do. And I thought I sensed something there, is all. A sort of seething fury on your part whenever the little lady and Warren speak to each other. Pique," said Telly, demonstrating that the Internet also had a Word-of-the-Day page. "Ire."

Abbott, though he would have denied it, seethed with pique and fury now.

"I know how overly attuned you are to her, boss, her being so much younger and prettier than you are. Aunt Clarisse is always talking about that. Warren would be pretty steep competition in that area, although I'm not suggesting anything funny is going on. That's all in your head."

Abbott rejected the notion that anything could be in his head except for pure, unadulterated thoughts and empty space. "I'm not overly attuned to anything," he said, "and I'm not jealous of Warren

Kingsley or anyone else. I simply want info. Now, for the last time, GO!"

Telly went. It meant calling their meeting to a close a little early, but he thought it best. Already, he was beginning to sense a thinly veiled hostility in his employer's manner.

* *

Five minutes after Telly had left—a blissful, soothing five minutes—Abbott was still pondering what his intern had said. He was pondering the bodyguard question. He had never thought of hiring one before, but perhaps the kid had a point. Everyone needed muscle.

It was nothing to do with his opponent's rants. In spite of what the younger generation might think, Abbott did not concern himself there. Kilobyte was quaint and unassuming, not a hotbed of mayhem like other towns—perhaps Kansas City. In Kilobyte, men like himself were not in constant danger—at least not from their political rivals. It was for this reason, and others, that the mayor was beginning to question whether Kilobyte was truly the path to glory he had once thought it.

That notwithstanding, there could still be some purpose to hiring a security consultant. It would look good for Abbott's image, for one. And Warren—should they choose to go that route—was already on staff, so they wouldn't have to pay him anything more. That would save meeting with Ms. Henrietta on the issue. Abbott hated meeting with Ms. Henrietta on issues, whether in her capacity as human-resources manager or Empress of Thumbtacks and Staples.

He had made up his mind. He slipped his pinstriped jacket back on, ran his hand through what remained of his hair and nodded. He would do it. The die was cast.

The mayor's bodyguard. It had a ring to it. Mayors *did* have bodyguards. They were important men, mayors, and important men should be protected.

Abbott was an important man. He had always said so.

* *

Not far away—perhaps fifty feet, as the dust particle flies—another man, soon to become very important in the mayor's life, prowled the shadows of the third-floor conference room. He was searching a potted fern. He was no horticulturist, and it showed. His gloved hands were covered in soil, and his polyester uniform, emblazoned with the emblem of a courier company that did not exist, was moist with perspiration.

He glared peevishly. There was nothing here. A thought occurred to him, and he took his prowling over to the outer doors. He continued out onto a partially covered balcony, and there he smiled. There were plants here too. Plants and a steady rain.

He went to the pot at the far end, an azalea, and almost immediately his efforts bore fruit. He pulled out a bedewed semiautomatic pistol, complete with silencer.

Turning, he crept back inside to locate the private office belonging to one Frederick Abbott, very important man.

2 — REINTRODUCING THE STRONG, SILENT TYPE

ownstairs, at a tiny café table in the lobby of the Kilobyte Muni Building (etc.), John Hathaway stared across at the smiling, clean-shaven face of his one-time friend and associate Warren Kingsley.

"What in God's name are you doing here?"

It was a question that could have easily been uttered by either man—but, in this case, Hathaway beat out Warren by a nose.

"I work here," he answered, and once again Hathaway stared.

"Since when do you know anything about baseball?"

Warren knew hardly anything about it. He was curious how this should prohibit him from working in the sport. "Anyway, I'm not working for Frederick Abbott, baseball-team owner. I'm working for Frederick Abbott, mayor at large."

Hathaway nodded slowly. "Are there two Fred Abbotts in the building?" he wondered.

Warren said no, and Hathaway nodded again. Why would there be? he agreed.

He wrinkled his brow. He was a slim and mild-looking man of forty, although many would have mistaken him for thirty. Like most men his age (who weren't Warren Kingsley), he had a growth of stubble on his innocuous face, and his light-brown hair stood up in several places on his head, no matter how much product he used on it.

Though born in the US, he had a faint British accent, having spent his formative years in the UK.

"Working for the Man again, eh?" he said. "Amazing. And a mayor minder to boot. Very nice. I guess I should feel in elite company there." He paused, thinking about the elite company he had once been in and how he had ever managed to get away from it with his life. "But I thought you had given up full-time bodyguarding?"

The one-time full-time bodyguard looked up from a riveting spot on his knuckle. "What was that, Hathaway? Were you saying something about Roy Orbison?"

Hathaway said he was not.

"No? Well, someone was."

"No one was talking about Roy Orbison, Warren. I said you were working for the Man."

"Ah. Well, be that as it may, I'm not guarding him. I'm his speechwriter."

Hathaway breathed a sigh of relief for the unseen politician. Lucky stiff—rich, powerful and free of the burden of having Warren Kingsley responsible for his well-being. Some guys had it all.

He leaned back and pondered the man across from him. Contrary to popular intern opinion, Warren was not a bodyguard worthy of the name. Hathaway had plenty of experience with that simple truth. The only person Warren had ever kept out of harm's way was Warren, and the only assassin he had ever thwarted had done more to thwart himself than any bodyguard could. As far as he was aware, he—John Hathaway—was Warren's only surviving client.

After years of contemplation and several meaningful therapy sessions, he had concluded that Warren's track record was more about a lack of interest than a lack of courage. Warren was not uncourageous when he needed to be. He simply had to care, and Warren seldom cared. As he liked to say, if your life is in danger, the smartest thing you can do is blend in and try to avoid getting killed. These were words to live by, from a professional who knew.

"Speechwriter," Hathaway repeated. "I didn't know you knew anything about politics."

"I don't," said Warren.

"And yet you write about them?"

"Not so much write, as think. There's a lot of thinking in politics, Hathaway."

This was news to his friend. As far as he could make out, there wasn't any thinking there at all. (His uncle, the congressman, was a case in point.) "So how'd you land this gig? Were you in charge of guarding your speechwriting predecessor?"

Warren shook his head. It was nothing like that. It just sort of happened.

Hathaway understood. "One minute you're minding your own business, going about your day—the next, you're hunched over a bunch of index cards, scrawling out gibberish about points of light and a chicken in every pot?"

Warren peered up from his untasted low-fat chai. "Were you saying something about Colonel Sanders, Hathaway?" Hathaway said no, not so you'd notice, and Warren furrowed his brow. "Thought you were saying something about 'a pot of lightly fried chicken.' At any rate, I couldn't tell you how I got this position as speechwriter. The mayor took a liking to me, I suppose."

Hathaway had observed this phenomenon before. Warren's last client, British electronics magnate Sir Roger Banbury, had succumbed in much the same way. It was hard to deny that Warren had a certain magnetism, the chiseled lunatic. "So whatever happened with Sir Roger? The last time I saw you, you were ensconced at Rangeley Manor as bodyguard to a man who liked his security personnel to be seen but not heard, and not really seen all that much. You were on easy street. Semiretired, on full pay. How'd you manage to muck it up?"

Warren said he would rather not talk about it.

Hathaway looked concerned. "Don't tell me you applied the characteristic Kingsley method to him? I would have thought a nice old industrialist like Banbury—kind, enemyless, eminently guardable—would be the one person you could keep alive."

"I said I'd rather not discuss it, Hathaway."

Hathaway did not press him. He felt bad for Sir Roger, though. He had been a pleasant old duffer. "So what's eating you? You seem distracted, even for you. I know it can't be over Banbury. You've never given your client failures a second thought. What's up?"

Unfortunately, what was up with Warren, and possibly even what was eating him, would have to wait for an explanation. At the exact moment of Hathaway's question, the security guard from the front desk arrived at their side. He laid a package on the table between them and said, "I saw you were over here and thought you might want this."

The offer confused Warren. He was acquainted with Earl as a stalwart of the reception desk: a fan of jelly-filled pastry, a good nodder hello and a helpful guy to have on your speed dial should you have an overabundance of gunk in your rain gutters. This new Earl, however, this Earl of unexpected parcel deliveries, he wasn't so sure about. "What's this package?"

"A package of some sort," said the guard. He was a man who liked to call them as he saw them.

"Yes, but why bring it here?"

"It's for you."

Warren gave it a suspicious squint. He wasn't expecting any deliveries. For that matter, he wasn't aware that anyone had this address. When you've made the sort of enemies Warren has, you prefer to remain off society's mailing list. "Where'd it come from?"

"A delivery guy dropped it off. Some company I've never heard of. I told him deliveries all had to go through the back, but he said his firm only makes special kinds of deliveries, the kind that have to be signed by the principal, so I said fine and told him the box would have to be X-rayed—security reasons. Funny thing is, he disappeared while I was looking up your phone extension."

"That is funny," Warren agreed.

"Whadda ya gonna do?" said Earl.

Hathaway peered back and forth between the two blank faces. He sighed. If no one else was going to say it, he might as well: "What did the X-ray show?"

"Not a thing," said Earl. "Thing's busted." That seemed to settle the matter.

"That was Earl," Warren remarked, as Earl departed with a quick bob of the head. He was right; the man was a good nodder.

And then there were three: Warren, Hathaway and a package of questionable origin.

Warren took the initiative. "You wouldn't want to give this box a peek inside, would you, Hathaway?"

"No, Warren, I would not."

"It's probably not a bomb. Better than a sixty-forty chance, I would say."

"Nevertheless."

"Come on, Hathaway. This is right up your alley. Are you a free-lance courier, 'The courier you call when you're in a pinch,' or aren't you?"

Hathaway said *aren't*. He hadn't been a freelance courier, one you called in a pinch or otherwise, for years (and even if he had been, couriers don't generally look in other people's packages—not unless they have a really good reason).

As it turned out, he had a whole new profession now, one not entirely alien to some of Warren's past dabblings. The latter listened patiently and without interrupting while his friend gave him full and complete details on his exciting new career path, what he was doing in Kilobyte this weekend, and everything in between. Once the narrative had concluded, Warren frowned thoughtfully and said, "So what you're saying is, you won't open this box for me?"

"That is what I'm saying."

"Very well, Hathaway." He pushed the box off to the side. "It will be here if you change your mind. So do you still live in Maryland?"

Hathaway shook his head. "As I said, I moved to Maine a few years ago. It made sense with my change of work."

"Really?" Warren wondered what that work was. "I was in Connecticut once," he said, pausing in remembrance. "So are you still mooning over that British chick?" he asked. "Brittany or Grace or whatever her name was?"

"Her name is Lesley," answered Hathaway stiffly, "and I married her almost a year ago."

"So no, then," Warren replied.

There had been a time when he and Hathaway had competed rather rigorously for the affections of Grace or Brittany or possibly Lesley. "Mooning over her," as Warren liked to call it. Although, he would have called Hathaway's efforts more mooning; his own were dignified and discreet.

Alas, it was not to be. She had chosen Hathaway over him. It was the story of Warren's life. "Do you know what Gladys said to me last week?" he asked abruptly.

"Gladys?" Hathaway knew no Gladyses.

"My tiny neighbor," Warren explained, "the middle of five girls. Very cute, the lot of them, exactly like their mother in appearance. They look like Russian nesting dolls. Only they're not Russian; they're French or Greek or something. Or the mother is. She's a peach, Hathaway. There are two types of women in this world, those who reach out and touch your arm when you say something witty and those who do not touch. I like touchers. Are you listening?"

"Two types of women," said Hathaway.

"Exactly. Touchers and non-touchers. Gladys's mother is a toucher. Anyway, I was telling you what her daughter said to me last week. Meeting me as I was carrying in my groceries, she said she had seen the pizza girl bringing me a small pie a couple times recently and wanted to know if this pizza girl was my wife. Keep in mind, she is only four. Gladys, I mean, not the pizza girl. I told her no. As much as I would relish having a wife who brought me pizza, she was no wife of mine. I didn't have a wife. This shocked and disturbed Gladys. 'You don't have a wife!' she gasped—'no wife or kids or anything!' I said no, no wife or kids or anything, and she slapped her forehead, as if to say Gadzooks! Or the Greco-Franco equivalent. She thought *ever-y-body* had a wife. Her dad had a wife. Then she asked me what was in the bags, and I told her groceries. 'You bought groceries!' she gasped, with all the old astonishment, and I went inside and took a nap."

Hathaway reflected on the Warren-Gladys epic. The interview had obviously made a strong impression on the man, though Hathaway was at a loss to see why.

Warren took a step toward clearing up that mystery. "You know I'm turning forty this month? Just like the town we're in. Kilobyte and Kingsley. A couple of life's forgotten old geezers."

Hathaway admitted that he did not know about his friend's ruby anniversary, no.

This shocked and disturbed Warren. His female neighbors all knew, and he wouldn't have expected Gladys to have kept these details to herself. Normally, she was quite the little blabbermouth, that one.

Hathaway reminded him that he did not know Gladys personally—although Warren's description of her had done much to bring the character to life.

Warren acknowledged this. He supposed the little one's social circle was rather limited in scope. "It makes you think, turning forty," he went on. "I mean, there you are, not forty—you're thirty-nine or thirty-eight or something reasonable like that—and then someone throws a switch, and you're forty. Forty, unmarried and utterly alone in the world. The sad old bachelor, the ridicule of happy couples and outspoken munchkins everywhere."

Hathaway gave his empty coffee cup a sympathetic twirl on the top of Warren's package (he hoped this wouldn't cause the bomb to explode). He knew nothing of this munchkin ridicule of which Warren spoke. "I sympathize about getting older, though," he said. "I turned forty myself recently, and it sucked. Of course, it didn't help that Lesley was pushing for children. If you really want to feel ancient, try picturing yourself as a father."

Warren waved aside these feelings as overly self-indulgent and superfluous to their discussion. As usual, people loved to talk about themselves and nothing but themselves. "It's not that I need someone to make me happy," he remarked. "I simply want someone in my life I can make happy again."

It was Hathaway's turn to be amazed. He wouldn't have credited Warren with this level of emotional generosity. "You mean you've made someone happy in the past?" he said.

Warren ignored the dig. "I'm always saying witty and interesting things to myself—in my head—and I can't help feeling that by the time I meet that special woman, I will have used up all these witty and interesting things and won't have anything witty or interesting left to say."

Again, Hathaway was surprised. "You've said witty things?" he asked.

Shortly thereafter, the two men parted ways. John Hathaway, vaguely depressed by the general sadness in the world, went off to continue his exciting new career elsewhere. Warren Kingsley, meanwhile, headed back up to the fourth floor to brood some more.

And maybe, just maybe, find someone to open his package for him.

* *

Upstairs, one such possibility—the mayor of Kilobyte and owner of the Kilobyte K's—was back at his balcony window again. It was coming up on ten o'clock—9:58 to be precise—and already Abbott felt he was behind his time. Never enough hours in the day...

No stranger to unwanted deliveries, he had a packet of scouting reports on his desk. He had been wearing the unmistakable team-owner glare since they arrived: the glare of a man who feels that no matter how much he spends, the other teams will always outpitch his hitters and outhit his pitchers.

And this was merely his normal mode of self-expression. What with Warrens and Tellys and everything else, it was amazing, he felt, that no one had fitted him for a designer straightjacket and sent him off to one of those exclusive spas for the rich and eccentric. The kind of places you have to have an "in" to frequent. Abbott was fairly certain he owned one such in Minnesota. Or perhaps that was another of his B&Bs.

Turning his view from the window—the grounds crew had started smoothing out the tarp they had recently laid, and he hated when the grounds crew smoothed the tarp—he took a sullen stare at his desk—he hated his desk—and grunted. This done, he produced a toy rabbit from one of the bottom drawers—a gift for his wife's dog, Butter-scotch—and shifted his stare to its face. He grunted again.

For those who like to keep track of these things, Fred Abbott was, as Telly suggested, very attuned to the attentions paid his attractive, much-younger wife. Attuned like the dickens. But in hinting that he suspected Warren Kingsley of stepping out of line in that way, the intern had only been correct up to a point.

True, there had been a time when Abbott suspected Warren of flirting with Sheryl, but he only suspected him in the vague sort of way that he suspected all men of flirting (in short, every player on his roster, every player on the visiting teams' rosters and the guy who delivered the bottled water). Like commercial real estate, Fred Abbott was big into suspecting. Having had, in his life, more wives than Henry VIII and a Mormon traditionalist combined will do that to a person.

Sheryl Abbott, the newest member of this not-so-exclusive club, deserved special attention in this area. Not just because of her overwhelming beauty, but also her carefree attitude when it came to flaunting this beauty. These flaunts bred rancor in the mind of her husband, and a rancorous brood was precisely what dominated his thoughts now. Varying a touch from their normal trend, they did not dwell on rugged youth or hairy-chested bottled-water men. The star of his rancor since six o'clock this morning was someone else altogether.

Abbott ruminated on this unnamed mystery man with even more rancor than before.

How could he not have foreseen this? he asked himself. In his defense, few would have suspected *that* particular snake in the grass. Sure, the snake and Sheryl enjoyed many of the same things—things Abbott couldn't care less about, dogs, the great outdoors—but what of it? Lots of people enjoyed things.

Of course, there was the baseball perspective. The snake had been a ballplayer. One of the finest. And Sheryl made no secret that she loved ballplayers—like a sister, Abbott had always thought, but now he wasn't so sure.

Do sisters wriggle with ecstasy every time their brothers take the field?

Ever since getting remarried a year ago, Fred Abbott had been asking himself questions like this nearly every day. And he didn't usually care for the answers. There were times when something in Sheryl's manner could be enough to disturb him, like her manner last weekend when they ran into the snake at a health-food store outside of town. Sort of evasive. Or if not evasive, sort of embarrassed. Evasive and embarrassed, that's how he would describe it.

It was rather like her manner when he found her in the pool house with her dog groomer, Enrique, the Sunday before last. (Just to keep the record straight, the Enrique incident had all been cleared up. Far from any hanky-panky, Sheryl was simply asking Enrique's advice on some trendy spots to see in Acapulco for the Abbotts' upcoming vacation. A compelling explanation, had Enrique hailed from Mexico instead of the Dominican Republic.)

Abbott took up the bunny again. "Oh, Sheryl, Sheryl," he might have said, or something equally revolting, had another interruption at the door not nipped this soliloquy in the bud.

The troubled mogul gave this new addition a look no person, not even a Latin dog groomer, could ever truly deserve. "And who might you be?" he asked.

The newcomer did not answer. He stepped fully inside the office with an air of mystery, wearing a strange and unknown delivery-company uniform. He looked very serious and a little damp (some of this rain, but much of it his own personal moisture).

He raised the gun in his hand and pulled the trigger.

3 — KEYNOTE ADDRESS

With a breezy chime, the elevator doors opened onto the fourth floor, and Warren Kingsley stepped out.

He sighed as he emerged. It seemed like he was doing a lot of that these days—sighing—and so was everybody else. It only confirmed what he had already said about mankind: a pack of sad and purposeless sighers if ever he saw one.

And now he had this parcel to deal with. But *how* to deal with it? That was the question he kept asking himself. Most people open their parcels, but when you've lived the life Warren has, you're not most people. He could still remember that client he had a few years back; "The Episode of the Client and the Basket of Exploding Fruit" he planned on calling it in his memoirs. If only he had been more careful, that guy.

Ankling across the tile, he set the parcel softly on the receptionist's desk, her station currently unmanned, and looked askance at his little bundle. The return label struck a chord with him. There was no name attached to it, but he thought he recognized the street address.

He realized why. It mirrored the delivery address. This address.

Only it didn't. The floor number was off by one level. But it was close. Too close for Warren's comfort.

It raised an obvious question: *Why should someone downstairs send him a package?* It didn't make any sense. Why not simply amble up and hand it to him? It was weird. He didn't like it. It bugged him.

Resolved to examine this conundrum from every angle, he picked up a letter opener from the receptionist's illustrated desk blotter, currently displaying kittens at play, and gave the box an inquisitive poke.

He wasn't getting anywhere like this. He needed a deputy in this enterprise. One of his fellow sighing mankind. A sucker, in other words. The only problem was, none of his fellows were among those present at the moment, sighing or not. The entire fourth floor was deserted. Warren found this very atmospheric, all alone with the neatly stacked stationery and the silently blinking switchboard. He also found it quiet. Too quiet for Warren's tastes.

He was just considering taking the parcel back down to the lobby to see if Earl would like another go at it, when a noise arrested his attention. Apparently, the floor was not as deserted as he had thought it. Another human being—or some such equivalent—skulked about in the vicinity. Warren could hear it sniffing. Sniffing and skulking.

Scooping up his package, he proceeded around the bend toward the source of the racket.

The skulker was humming now. The tune he hummed—for it would seem to be a male skulker Warren had gotten a bead on—was not a melody Warren was familiar with, and he didn't care for it. He didn't care for where his trek had taken him either. He found himself in the tiny recess belonging to the intern of baseball operations. Telly's recess.

It was a small and curiously decorated space, chock-full of baseball memorabilia, film memorabilia and action figures manipulated into a variety of unnatural poses. Warren's office was nicer (even if it was too cold in the afternoons and lacked a proper southern exposure).

He gave the legions of bobbleheads surrounding him an appraising glance, then turned his gaze on their life-sized leader. The head bobblehead appeared to be listening to music—or some such equivalent.

Stepping up behind his chair, Warren gave him a cautious jab in the headphones with the letter opener.

Telly sprang forward in his seat, scattering pita chips in every direction. He whipped off his headphones and said, "Bleck!"

That was Warren's opinion of things as well. Bleck. He surveyed the music fan anew. He had never been clear who Telly was exactly. He also didn't care.

Telly's jumpiness had subsided now. He was only too glad to shoot the breeze with his best office bud. "It's you!" he guffawed. "I was just talking about you."

Warren was not surprised by this. He was a complex and fascinating subject.

Telly offered him a pita chip. Politely refused, he chomped down on it in Warren's place. Suddenly, the intern's face lit up. More than it already had. "Hey, you got one too," he said.

"Got one?"

"A parcel." He reached across the pita crumbs on his desk and snagged a package very much in keeping with the one in Warren's hands. "We're box buddies!" he laughed.

Warren wouldn't have gone that far. "What's in it?"

"I don't know. Haven't opened it yet. How about yours?"

Warren said he was waiting for his box buddy to go first.

Telly could see that. "Sure you don't want a chip?"

Warren was sure. Maybe later.

Telly agreed completely. Later was what he was about to suggest himself. "The box came while I was talking with Ms. Henrietta. Man, she's a battle-ax, isn't she?"

Warren couldn't say. They had never met.

This amazed and delighted Telly. "Really? You didn't interview with her? Take any of her little employment tests like a lab rat?" Ms. Henrietta was famous for breeding small animals in her spare time, so the analogy was certainly an apt one.

Warren had done none of these things. He went straight to work for the mayor without the ax's approval.

Telly was astounded. "That's awesome. Just like Dave Winfield."

"The snooty guy from corporate?"

"That's Dave Wincher. I meant the Hall of Famer. Played outfield for San Diego, Minnesota, New York, Toronto and Cleveland," said the resident expert. He was forgetting the California Angels.

His best office bud nodded solemnly. It sounded like this Winfield guy spread himself a little thin in Warren's opinion (even by Kilobyte standards). After all, how many teams could one man play for at the same time? Warren would have thought two or three, at the most.

"And the amazing thing is," proceeded the baseball historian, "he never spent a day in the minor leagues. He went straight to the majors. Just like you."

Warren never would have thought of his position as the major leagues, but to someone of Telly's caliber, he supposed it must seem so. "Is that what you were discussing with Ms. Juanita? Dave Winfield and the majors?"

"Henrietta," Telly corrected. "And no. We were discussing you. Your professional background."

"Oh yes?" Warren never would have thought of his background as professional.

"The boss wanted it. Between you and me, I think you're getting a promotion."

It was about time, Warren figured.

Telly settled back in his chair. "The thing is, I've been thinking about your old job. What it takes to be a first-class bodyguard."

That made one of them, thought Warren.

"I guess when you stumble on an assassin, you have to get pretty rough with them. Use lethal force and all that sort of thing. There must be a lot of fatalities in that line?"

Warren agreed that there were, but not as Telly meant them.

The latter frowned. "I was wondering—I mean, it's not a big deal or anything—but maybe you could give me a few pointers sometime."

"Pointers?"

"On how to become a badass bodyguard. I thought I might draw on your experience. Don't get me wrong," he said, "business administration is awesome and everything, but I don't know that it's what I want to do with my life. It seems to me your old line, the personal-security line, might be more in my wheelhouse. Either that or vampire hunter."

Warren conceded that both had their attractions. It really depended on how much you liked to travel.

"So how about it?" Telly prompted. "Would you mind showing me the ropes?"

Warren sighed. Assuming he had nothing better to do, he would be glad to offer a few words of advice sometime—not now. Who knows, those few words might even save his life.

"And the life of a client," Telly remarked.

Warren said sure, why not? "Your phone is ringing."

Telly agreed that it was. He reached for the device and answered. "Hello? Hello? Nobody there." He pressed the receiver closer to his ear. "Wait, I think I hear something now. They keep going 'grrrrr.'"

"Grr?" asked Warren.

"*Grrrrr,*" said Telly, putting more emphasis on the *rrrrr.* "Now it sounds like *arrrrr.*"

"Arr?"

"*Arrrrr.*" He glanced at the caller ID. "Holy crap, it's the boss."

It took Warren a moment to realize that Telly's boss was also Warren's mayor. "The mayor is going *grrrrr?*" he clarified. "And *arrrrr?*"

Telly rattled his head yes. "He must be in trouble!"

Or imitating the mating call of a bobcat, Warren suggested.

"Come on!" Telly uttered, springing up from his chair.

Warren supposed they might as well take a look. In the meantime, he set his parcel down on Telly's desk next to its doppelgänger. It annoyed him that the kid hadn't opened his yet. Who waited this long to open a package? It was vexing.

Nonetheless, it was all handled now. Warren's conscience was clear. If the boxes turned out to contain something along the lines of explosive honeydew, it wouldn't harm Telly to have one more. He could start collecting them (for a short time, anyway).

"Place is totally deserted," panted the intern/collector, as he soared over desks and other office paraphernalia on his way down the hall.

Warren strolled behind at a more dignified pace, helping to lift the gazelle up off the floor at one point, following a miscue across the fax machine.

Telly thanked him. "Where is everybody?"

Warren had no idea. He figured Telly knew.

They reached the alcove outside the mayor's office. It, too, was deserted and desolate, with the exception of a small dribbling of blood along the carpet. The blood definitely brightened things up. Telly proceeded cautiously into their employer's lair.

Warren remained without, checking the status of his left cufflink. It seemed a little loose. Satisfied that it wasn't going anywhere, he followed the intern inside.

He couldn't say he liked what the mayor had done with the place since he last saw it. Chairs and tables were flipped over on their sides.

Scouting reports were strewn about. A remnant of past chaos hung in the air.

Telly was leaning over a particularly unkempt pile in the back. It was slumped on the floor alongside the mayor's giant mahogany desk. The wire of the phone projected up from the heap like a lightly tangled, intraoffice lifeline.

"It's the boss!" Telly exclaimed. "Holy crap! I think he's been murdered!"

Warren nodded a second time. In his experience, employers frequently were.

All of a sudden, Abbott let out a yelp, causing Telly to stumble back. He had stepped on his employer's hand.

"He's alive!" said the intern.

Warren agreed that this was, indeed, a special treat.

* *

Fifteen minutes later, the local authorities were still filing in and out of the office as Warren and Telly looked on—which is to say mostly Telly looked. Warren appeared more interested in his right cufflink. Taking after its rascally sibling, it had gone all wonky on his other sleeve.

In the midst of these compelling human dramas, a shrill voice cried out, "Where is my husband? I must see my husband!" Though clearly agitated, there was an odd boredom in its shrillness. Hence the peculiar vocal inflection of Mrs. Sheryl Abbott, jaded trophy wife.

Her attire suited the occasion perfectly, though some might have said it suited it a little prematurely. She wore a slinky black dress and black nylons, these blending nicely with her golden hair and sun-bronzed skin. She looked the perfect grieving widow, whether anyone had called for one or not. "I was told my husband had been shot!"

She was held briefly at the door by a middle-aged deputy with a large, playful mustache and a serious mouth. "Just a moment, ma'am."

She appreciated his tactfulness. "There isn't much blood, is there? I can't stand blood!"

Typically, as the deputy could have told her—having read several manuals on the subject—you were not going to have many gunshot wounds without a modicum of blood. This, however, was not your typical gunshot wound.

"Just a moment," he repeated. "Your husband is still speaking with the sheriff."

Mrs. Abbott stepped back. Her heavily made up eyes widened to the size of tar-edged Ping-Pong balls. "But shouldn't he be in the hospital? Or morgue?"

"Not necessary, ma'am," answered the deputy, with a cryptic twirl of his glistening mustache. He left it at that.

Mrs. Abbott hadn't gotten to where she was today by listening to men with pomade in their facial hair. She shoved by him and demanded, "What is going on here? Why won't anybody tell me what is going on? Where is my husband?"

She found the man of the hour sitting up on the sofa with a handful of trained medicos assembled around him. The assembly parted, and Mrs. Abbott began to see what the Mustache had meant by *not necessary*. On the pasty skin between her husband's open shirtfront there was a small, rectangular contusion—but no blood.

Mrs. Abbott took it like a real trooper. "Oh, Abby, weren't you shot?!" She sounded put out, but not unduly so. You have to take these things in stride.

Fred Abbott, or "Abby" as he was sometimes called, went harrumph. He was shot, shot like you wouldn't believe, but in a stunning turn of events befitting the best-written swashbucklers, he had been saved by the metal card case he kept tucked in the breast pocket of his jacket. He pointed to the tiny dented shield lying on a nearby table, all tagged and bagged and ready to be cataloged as evidence. If it hadn't been made of high-density titanium, and Abbott hadn't jammed it quite so full with his many, many business pursuits, he probably wouldn't be sitting here talking to them now.

"Talking" was a relative term. Since the arrival of the authorities, the mayor had waffled between shouting everyone from his presence and demanding more attention for his "wound."

"Oh, Abby!" sobbed Sheryl Abbott and flung herself on his chest.

"Argh!" cried Fred Abbott, and the spousal reunion was complete.

The sheriff still had a few questions. One might easily have been: *How did Mrs. Sheryl Abbott get into the building?* If a simple gold digger could breach their inner sanctum, then what was the point of posting guards at the exits?

But such was the burden borne by Sheriff Jenny Blake. When the lion's share of your men have their minds on other enterprises—such as the flamboyant gentleman standing behind her, shortly to be starring in a police-house rendition of *The Merchant of Venice*—you couldn't expect a person to accomplish a basic task like watching a door. It disturbed the artistic temperament.

Unlike everyone else in town, Jenny had no such aspirations herself. Somehow the Kilobytean life force that ran through her veins did not compel her to branch out. She did not multitask. She did not have multiple business pursuits, and other than its ability to deflect bullets, she had no use for a high-density case to carry her cards around in. She was simply a cop. That was all she ever tried to be.

Which was ironic, since her appearance betrayed that conviction totally. She did not look copish. Along with a doll-like countenance—large blue eyes, ingenuous in their gaze; prominent cheekbones, quite rosy—she had shoulder-length, strawberry-blond hair, which she refused to tie in a ponytail. There were no height requirements for law enforcement in the state, and this was just as well, because Jenny Blake was not tall. In fact, she was a few inches shorter than Mayor Abbott, which took some doing. The only thing about her that shouted "police officer" at all, other than her career stats, was her uniform—a spectacular beige—and even that came off as a lovingly tailored children's costume. She looked like a water pixie made up for a Halloween party.

"Perhaps you should start at the beginning," she told the mayor. His wife's histrionics had muddled his previous statement, and it was best to get these things straight while they were still fresh in the mind. "A man came into your office—?"

Abbott nodded rapidly. A man did. He crept in. "Slinked in" might be a better term. No, he couldn't describe him. Like all good politicians, Abbott seldom noticed a person's ethnicity. He was a man, that was all he could say, one of those courier fellows—meaning he had on a uniform from a courier company. No, Abbott couldn't remember which one. He had a gun. He fired it. It was at this point that Abbott threw a stuffed bunny at him. Yes, a bunny—a toy for the dog. It was the only thing he could think to do. He followed up the bunny with a bust of Henry Ford. (Both bunny and Ford lay on the table, tagged and bagged.) The bunny missed, but the bust hit home, bouncing off the man's head. This was between shots. The second shot struck the wall behind his desk; the first, as they already knew, struck Abbott in the chest—in the titanium.

Deputy 'Stache, arriving within earshot, winced. That must have smarted, he said. Right in the titanium. He whispered something to the sheriff, and then left her to her questions.

The mayor went back over the particulars of the brawl, leading up the perp's escape. Chairs were knocked aside. Tables upturned. The fight raged on. (Several minutes describing epic battle.) It reminded the sheriff of a reenactment of Hercules versus the Erymanthian boar, only more heroic. Finally, the mayor had come upon the Ford bust and let this fly, hitting his assailant and causing him to drop the gun. Disarmed and bleeding from the head, the man fled. And that brought them up to the present moment.

Or it nearly did. "You phoned for help after that?"

The mayor grunted. "I could hear people screaming and carrying on as the man came rushing out my door. The spectacle of him careering about covered in blood cleared out the whole floor, I'm told. Someone take a note that I'm counting that as a lunch break, and if they don't like it, let them speak to Ms. Henrietta about it."

Sheriff Blake did not take a note. "You phoned your intern?"

"Not at first. I phoned the guard Earl first. Useless blob. He didn't answer. I called my speechwriter, Kingsley, next, but he wasn't at his desk. He's never at his desk. Retired security expert, my foot! Finally, reluctantly, I tried my intern."

Telly smiled broadly. He was touched that the boss had thought of him.

"You should dock the other men's pay," Mrs. Abbott suggested, and her husband nodded appreciatively. Sometimes the little woman had very sensible ideas.

The sheriff was wrapping up. She did have one final question. "A man like you—"

"What do you mean a man like me?"

"An important man—"

"Ah yes."

"And one who must have many, many"—she paused—"*many* enemies…"

"What do you mean *many, many, many?*"

"Can you speculate who might be behind this?" asked Jenny Blake.
"Assuming he wasn't acting alone?"

The mayor was never short on speculation. He did wonder about
the sheriff's assumption, however. Why shouldn't the killer be acting
alone? A random nut, a loose cannon. What was wrong with that theory?

Before Sheriff Blake could answer what was wrong with it, one
of the medical staff applied balm to the mayor's wound, and Abbott
snarled at her. He snatched the jar from the woman and dabbed on
the balm himself. He hated balm.

The sheriff left him to his ablutions. She could get the rest of
his statement later on, preferably after the fumes of his ointment had
thinned out.

She spoke with Telly next. She was not relishing this portion of
the interview.

"You won't git nuthin' outta me, copper," he muttered, sitting back in the
mayor's chair with his feet up on the desk.

Jenny sighed—everyone else was doing it, why not her? "Dammit,
Telly, this is not a joke!"

Her witness eased up. "Sorry, sis, just trying to lighten the mood."

Since childhood, living without a mother to care for them and with
a father who cared too much for horse racing, her kid brother had
often tried to lighten the mood, usually to the same level of success.
"What do you want to know?" he asked.

She consulted her notebook. "Your official statement says you
'came into the office, and everything was all effed up.' Would you care
to elaborate on that?"

"Sure, sis. My buddy Warren and I got this call, or rather I did,
and it was the boss growling in my ear. We rushed to the office, and
everything was all effed up. By which I mean," he added hastily, "the
room was a mess, and the boss was sprawled out on the floor, groan-
ing. Or he groaned when I stepped on him anyway."

Jenny was not surprised by this. Her brother was the sort of guy
who would step on a mayor when he was down. "What about on the
way to the office? Did you see anything?"

"Just a trickle of blood in the alcove. More than a trickle, really. A dribble. Call it a *drickle*."

Jenny rolled her giant periwinkle eyes. "What about people? Did you see anyone?"

"Can't say that I did. I thought it was strange. Of course, it makes sense now. Everyone had run for it. I mean, my buddy Warren and I hadn't, but that's just how we roll."

His sister frowned. "You probably had those stupid headphones on and couldn't hear."

Telly agreed yes, there was also that. But mostly it was how he rolled.

"So you didn't actually see the perp?" she asked. She shook her head. "Earl says he seemed foreign to him, possibly Asian or Indian. Maybe Lithuanian. According to Earl, it's the sort of thing a Lithuanian would do. Did I mention that Earl's ex-wife is Lithuanian? The mayor, apparently, doesn't want to commit himself, out of concern for alienating voters of foreign birth. And you didn't see a thing!"

"Sorry, sis, can't say I saw something when I didn't. I never—holy crap, maybe I did."

"What do you mean?"

Telly leaned forward in the chair and ran his fingers through his ample mop. He picked up a stray cigar from his boss's private stash and crumpled it distractedly in his fingers. "I think I did see him. I did more than that. *I talked to him!*"

"When?"

"Half an hour ago. I had gone down to the third floor to file something for the battle-ax, and while I was there, I bumped into this guy outside the boss's office."

"What do you mean, the boss's office? We're in the boss's office now."

"Not that office, his other office. His third-floor office."

"The mayor has two offices?"

"Four, I think," said Telly, counting on one hand. "One for his mayoring, one for baseball, one for Abbott Enterprises—" He began to lose his place. "Anyway, he has three or four of them in the building. Usually, he's in the third-floor office on Fridays, but lately, by which I mean in the two weeks since I've been here, he's always in this office. I think he likes it best because it's near his press secretary for his mayoral duties and has a good view of the ball field for his baseball side. I don't know what he does when he's feeling *enterprising*—"

Jenny wasn't feeling very enterprising herself. She felt like she was ten years old again—only, sadly, the time had passed when a swat to the back of her brother's head could solve most any of her problems. "You bumped into a man?" she said.

"That's right. A courier. He was hanging outside the boss's office—his third-floor office. I told him he wasn't going to find the big man down here and explained about the boss's proclivities of late. The guy seemed confused, so I had to go over it a couple times."

And was it any wonder that the man became homicidal after that? Jenny mused. "So what you're saying is you directed the perp to the mayor's office?"

"He did what?!" roared Abbott, bounding up from the sofa.

Telly defended himself by retorting, in a straightforward and manly fashion, that the guy probably would have figured it out himself eventually.

The mayor snorted. "I'm surprised you didn't bring him to my door and offer to hold his hat while he polished his pistol!" He snorted again, and then his eyes widened farther as he observed the full extent of his intern's handiwork. "What the hell happened to my cigar?" he gurgled. He had seen carnage today, but not to this degree. "And what are you doing in my chair? Get up! UP!"

With the help of the balm applier, who was stronger than she looked, Telly's big sister helped to prevent a second attempted murder in the mayor's office that day. After a couple of false starts, they seated the mayor back on the sofa. He nestled in next to his wife (currently texting her hairdresser), and the sheriff continued.

"The important thing is, Telly, you saw the man. What did he look like?"

On this, Telly was still a little vague. He was a sort of a guy. Not too tall or too short. Like the mayor said, he had on a hat.

"Was your friend with you? Maybe he has a better memory for faces."

"Who—Warren? Nah, he wasn't there."

"Good-for-nothing bastard," said the mayor from the sofa. "Couldn't bodyguard his way out of a paper bag."

The sheriff wasn't sure what he meant by that. "I think I'd like to question this Warren myself," she said. She turned left, then right. "Where is he?"

That was the question. Once again, the ex-bodyguard, soon-to-be-ex-speechwriter had vanished.

"Sheriff?" asked another of her deputies, appearing at her side.

"What is it, Tony?"

"Did I hear you say you were looking for a Warren Kingsley?"

The sheriff was indeed. Did Tony have one on him?

"No, but thanks to a tip from him, I have something better." He waved his hand toward the entranceway, and a third deputy ushered in a harassed-looking man between thirty and forty years of age. "We caught the courier-assassin!"

The perp wasn't how she pictured him. He was slim and brown haired and fairly gentle in bearing. He was dressed in a sport jacket and jeans. "What makes you think this is the man?"

"Warren heard we were after a courier and gave us a spot-on description of this guy. We caught him trying to duck out the back exit."

"I wasn't ducking out of anywhere," the man protested. Jenny fancied she detected a slight English accent. "And for the last time, I'm not a courier!"

"Who's not a courier?" asked Warren Kingsley, reappearing in the doorway.

"I'm not!" said John Hathaway. "Dammit, Warren, what have you done?"

Had he done anything? Warren didn't think he had. He had been asked about a courier in the vicinity, so he had given them a courier.

"I'm not a courier, damn you! I told you that already!"

"Psst, sis," said Telly. "That's not the guy I talked to downstairs."

"Who the hell is that?" agreed the mayor.

The sheriff held up a hand to silence the rabble. "This is not the courier who shot at you, sir?"

"Of course it's not!"

"I repeat," said Hathaway, "I am not a courier. I'm—"

Sheriff Blake cut in before their guest could finish. "I'm sorry, Mr.—"

"Hathaway."

"I'm sorry, Mr. Hathaway, we've made a mistake. Let him go, Lance."

The third deputy, Lance, did so reluctantly. For the second time that day, John Hathaway left his friend Warren's presence shooting the other man a sour look.

Tony was also skeptical about their prisoner-release program. But she was the sheriff. "Should we let the guy from FedEx go too?" he asked. They were holding him downstairs.

Sheriff Blake would talk to him, but she didn't think FedEx was the guy, any more than this Hathaway person had been the guy. They were looking for a courier from an unknown company—that was how everyone described it. No one, not even her merry band of unreliable witnesses, would have called FedEx unknown.

It was at that point that Telly heard his sister say a bad word. The only thing she knew for certain was that her suspect was long gone by now.

* *

She was right. He was gone, though possibly not as long as she might have guessed.

About a mile and a half away, a not-so-short, not-so-tall man, who was not Lithuanian, moved about his local safe house. Plodded might be a better term. He went into the bathroom, switched on a light and examined the knot on his head. It wasn't bad. Just a tiny crack in his caramel-colored scalp, below the receding hairline. Nothing a little balm wouldn't fix.

He wagged his head as he applied it. This made the process a lot more difficult and the balm application all the more smudgy. He ceased wagging and reflected on himself, both literally and figuratively.

How could he have allowed this, this egregious error? He, the world's finest assassin. The assassin of assassins. The assassin you called when you were in a pinch.

He returned to the sitting room and, quite appropriately, sat.

If nothing else, he could be proud of his getaway. It was a masterful escape. Through the fourth-floor conference room and out onto the balcony. Over the rail, and in a mighty bound down to the third-floor balcony. From the third to the second, and from the second to the street below. It was more insect-like than anything human. The man prided himself on his athleticism. The athletics of an insect. No, a beast. The beast of assassins.

The beast winced. He had no business applauding himself this way. He had been hired for a job, a very simple job, and he had failed. Stupid, stupid failure! he said, slapping his forehead with his palm, then wishing he hadn't.

What were the odds of this happening, this foolishness in the office? A thousand to one? Perhaps more.

He vowed to make up for his mistake. He had been paid, and he would fulfill his contract. He was a killer, not an embezzler.

* *

In the alcove outside the mayor's office, things were wrapping up. Sheriff Blake had barely returned from questioning/releasing FedEx—he wasn't the guy—when a large, muscular hand fell on her shoulder.

"Sheriff, a moment, if you please."

It seemed she would be getting her Warren-time, after all. After the bogus lead he had given her men, she wasn't so sure she wanted it. "Yes, Mr. Kingsley?"

Normally, after an incident like this, Warren Kingsley would have spent some of his time canvassing the investigating officer's views on PR, seeing to what extent his name could be left out of the public press. Any assistance there could go a long way toward maintaining his image and helping to preserve future sales on those bodyguard memoirs he would someday write.

But since he wasn't the mayor's bodyguard, and therefore under no obligation to keep the old man safe, he could be much more selfless with his off-hours. His motives could be that much purer.

"I think you might want to see this," he said.

"Oh really?" A sheriff who's been given the runaround once isn't at her most hospitable. "And what do I need to see?"

He led her out of the alcove and down the hall a few yards. He pointed to a door. "That," he said in a muffled voice.

Without really meaning to, she matched his whisper. "What about it?"

"That door was open earlier."

"Was it?"

"It was. When your brother and I arrived, I stopped to adjust my cufflink. I stepped back out into the hall, because the light here is better. Do you know anything about cufflink science, Sheriff?"

"No."

"Well, these definitely seem to be off-kilter. They wiggle. I can't stand wiggling links. At any rate, that's when I noticed the door—while I was adjusting my person."

"Do you always notice doors?"

"Always," said Warren. Observing exits was part and parcel of becoming a bodyguard. Every good bodyguard knows the best escape routes to take. And your smarter client knows when to follow their bodyguard through those exits. "As you can see, the door is now closed."

The sheriff could see that.

"I assume one of your men did not close it?"

"Not that I know of."

"Then it stands to reason," concluded Warren, "that someone else did."

The sheriff could see merit in that theory. She stepped across and tried the handle.

"Locked," he said.

She could see that too. She banged her knuckles on the wood panel. It sounded like a woodpecker with a bone to pick. "Excuse me, is there anyone in there? Sheriff Blake here." As she said it, she undid the strap on her sidearm.

There was a sound of movement within. The door opened, revealing a severe-looking woman of between fifty and sixty, although many would have mistaken her for seventy. She was prim and formidable, and immediately her identity suggested itself to Warren.

The famous Ms. Juanita, he presumed.

It wasn't. It was the famous Ms. Henrietta, and she was very, very busy.

"We won't take long," the younger woman assured her and pushed past into the sanctuary of Human Resources. (Warren remained in the hall. He had yet to meet Ms. Henrietta formally and felt he was onto a good thing by continuing not to do so.) "Why did you lock that door?" the sheriff asked her.

Ms. Henrietta seated herself back at her desk. There was no muss or fuss in her office, and there was no muss or fuss about Ms. Henrietta. She was tight skinned and tight-lipped, and the sepia hair on her head was pulled back in a tight coiffure. A future generation, shown a picture of Henrietta Bragg, wouldn't be surprised to learn it was taken in '16. What would surprise them was it wasn't 1916.

"I closed the door because of the incessant hullabaloo," she replied sourly. Henrietta could not abide hullabaloos.

"That hullabaloo," explained the sheriff, "was my men and me searching for an assassin."

This was of no never mind to Ms. Henrietta. She could not abide assassins.

"We'll need to look around."

Henrietta said very well. She only asked that nothing be disturbed.

The sheriff would do her best. She called for her deputy Lance, who came in smiling all over his boyish face. At times, his enthusiasm reminded her of her brother Telly, without the hair. Lance had been bald since high school. "We found the gun," he announced proudly.

Ms. Henrietta sniffed.

So did Jenny Blake, in her official capacity. Sliding on a pair of latex gloves, she slipped the weapon from its bag and applied the nose test. "Recently fired."

Lance agreed it would be.

"Where'd you find it?"

"Under the mayor's desk. Along with a wad of spent dental floss"—he showed the floss—"this plastic clip thingy"—he exhibited the clip thingy—"and a bunch of dust bunnies." Dust bunnies not pictured.

Ms. Henrietta sniffed once more. Men were notoriously unkempt, especially in areas where they thought people were not likely to look.

"The gun must have slid under there during the struggle," the deputy theorized. "The desk is so huge who knew what was under it?"

The sheriff said who indeed. She removed the magazine. Forty caliber. "Plenty of ammo."

"Yup. Lucky the perp only got off two shots."

Jenny said yes. Lucky. She wrinkled her nose again, this time in thought. She had just realized something. There was a door behind them. She noticed it all on her own, without Warren Kingsley's assistance or anything. "Where does this lead?" she asked Henrietta Bragg.

The HR queen responded tersely, "That is the office belonging to Mr. Blue, Mayor Abbott's press secretary." She was also the former's assistant.

Sheriff Blake frowned. *Mr. Blue.* It sounded made up. "Is that his real name?"

"Of course. Why wouldn't it be?"

The sheriff couldn't think of a reason. "Has he come outside? Since the incident?"

He had not. Why would he? Henrietta naturally assumed everyone was as practical and uninterested in hullabaloos as she was.

The sheriff wasn't so certain. She marched across to the door and knocked pointedly. When no one answered, she gave Lance a look and proceeded inside.

**

"But I'm fine, my dear," said Mr. Frederick Abbott to Mrs. Sheryl Abbott.

The authorities had vacated his space, and the Abbotts were alone in his office now, just a husband and his "adoring" young wife. She could switch gears with the best of them.

For reasons known best to Fred Abbott and his balm applier, his arm was now in a sling. He hadn't been shot in the arm, nor was his shoulder all that sore, but the sling seemed to add a certain panache in the mayor's mind, and the applier of balm liked it because he couldn't wave his arm so much at her.

His wife barely noticed it. Her eyes were wide with concern. "But shouldn't you close up shop for today, Abby?"

"Nonsense!" he said. He was a busy, busy man, he reminded her. He had a town, a baseball team, a restaurant and several out-of-state B&Bs to run. "I can't afford to slack off for a simple gunshot wound."

"You're so brave!"

Abbott considered saying nonsense again, but instead substituted pish posh. "You'll understand this better when we've been married longer," he cooed, and no smarmy yes-man could have been quite as greasy as the mayor was now, "but the Abbotts don't quit. Not when their office has reopened and there is work to be done."

"It might not be reopened for long," said Sheriff Jenny Blake, appearing between them.

The mayor frowned. As one of two elected figures, he might not technically be her boss, but that did not prevent him from glaring at her as though he were. He protested this use of red tape, especially when he wasn't the one working the dispenser. "Nonsense, Sheriff. As I have told everyone, my wound is not severe."

The sheriff drew him aside, out of earshot of his wife. "I was not speaking of your injury, Mayor."

"What, then?"

"Your press secretary has been shot dead."

4 — CONFERENCE ROOM CONFIDENCES

"He was a good man," said Henrietta Bragg, staring down at the body of her employer, Daryl Blue. (The sheriff checked with the mayor, and that was his real name.)

The mayor, meanwhile, stood off to the side. There was a vague aloofness about his presence, a reluctance to get involved. Evidently, Frederick Abbott could not abide dead press secretaries.

Which was ironic, the sheriff thought, since it was the press secretary who had gotten the raw end of the deal. It would seem that the second bullet—the one that had missed Abbott a short time ago—had passed through their shared wall. It then went through Mr. Blue.

"The walls are so thin here," said the mayor, finally contributing something to the flow of conversation. "So very thin." It was one of those silly, pointless comments people make when they have nothing else to say.

The sheriff had been joined by deputies Lance and Albert (the 'Stache), and together they examined the scene. From the look of it, the bullet had entered the right side of Mr. Blue's skull. A thousand-to-one shot, one might have said. Maybe more. (Things at Abbott Enterprises weren't so lucky, after all, felt Jenny Blake.)

They examined the hole in the drywall next. It was larger than on the mayor's side—it would be—coming out through the plaster-board next to a mounted plasma TV. A couple of inches to the side and Panasonic would have taken the bullet for the unfortunate government employee.

Jenny swept around the rest of the walls, taking in the photos of the deceased on various hunting and fishing trips, a couple of pics of the Kilobyte K team, a few political snapshots and a stunning lack of any family or friends. Mr. Blue, it would seem, had been a bachelor and not much of a sentimentalist.

Albert picked up a smartphone from the floor. It was splattered with blood. "Looks like he was on a call when it happened."

The sheriff nodded and asked Lance to check the number.

"This is an outrageous tragedy," the mayor spoke up again. It would seem even more outrageous and tragic when he realized the person in charge of imparting this to the media was lying dead at his feet.

"What's going on, sis?" asked Telly, forcing his way into the office. Warren Kingsley followed, slightly less forcibly. Apparently, Deputy Tony was just as ineffectual at manning points of entry as his colleague Albert.

Jenny frowned at the unwelcome arrivals. "Not now, Telly."

"Holy crap! Is that a dead guy?"

"It's an official homicide investigation. You need to leave."

Telly stood firm. "What happened? Is the assassin still loose in the building?" He sounded more excited than concerned.

"May I speak with you a moment, Ms. Blake?" The mayor was at the sheriff's elbow. He motioned the officer over to the window, away from the body, and lowered his voice. "When you said the assassin might not be acting alone, what did you mean by that?"

The sheriff spoke softly as well. "We're pretty sure he had inside help."

"Why do you say that?"

"The gun. He couldn't have waltzed in here as he did without setting off the metal detectors in the lobby. The gun must have been planted in here ahead of time."

"The detectors are broken, Sheriff. Or so the guard Earl says."

"Only the small X-ray machine," inserted Telly, listening dutifully. "According to Earl, the walk-through detectors are A-okay."

The sheriff could only agree with her eavesdropping brother. The walk-through units were perfectly operational. She and her men had set them off when they arrived this morning. The way the lobby was set up, you could make it as far as the coffee stand and the Kilobyte K gift shop, but after that, no armed man was getting through without causing a major racket. You would have needed inside help.

She was still working through her theory on this. She would need to speak to Earl again, learn who had what access and when, and what the normal routine was for admitting people and packages to the building. One thing was for sure, whoever played the accomplice had plenty of bravado.

The mayor caressed his sagging jaw. He knew at least one person with bravado. "It's a lot to take on board," he said. "An inside job. I can hardly believe it." He ran his finger down the edge of the mounted television. Very dusty. "But what about packages?" he asked. "He was dressed as a courier. Couldn't he have hidden the weapon in a parcel?"

Warren Kingsley, the bravadoed star of Abbott's thoughts, peered up. A parcel. It was an interesting thought. He wouldn't have given the mayor credit for it.

The sheriff thought the package angle very unlikely. Earl had stated explicitly that the suspect had no parcels with him when he disappeared from the lobby, and if he had shipped a parcel here, how would he have gotten hold of it later? He would have had no way of knowing where it would wind up. No, it kept coming back to a two-person job.

She paused. A parcel. The man must have arrived with one; otherwise he would have appeared a very suspicious courier. She wondered what became of it.

Abbott shook his head. He still couldn't believe it. And now a case of attempted murder had become something much more serious. He placed his hands behind his back and assumed a more portentous air. He was in his element now, speaking slowly and pedantically, as all good politicians do. "You asked who I suspected might be behind this, Sheriff?"

"Yes?"

He took her further into his confidence, moving them into a distant corner of the dead man's office. Any farther and they would have toppled out the window together. "I do have a thought on that." He whispered something in her ear.

"Not Hank Busby!" said Telly, aghast.

His sister glared at him. She was not above using her nightstick.

She recognized the name, of course. Everyone knew Hank "the Base-Hitting Buzz Saw." If it hadn't been for a slightly more famous ball-playing Hank, Busby's name would have been synonymous with graceful, effortless hitting.

He had to be in his sixties now, Jenny figured, about the mayor's age. She was aware the two men had a history. "Isn't Mr. Busby running against you in the election?"

The mayor dipped his head. He was indeed. He and Busby did not care for each other. He repeated his opponent's recent remarks. When Abbott described the other's wish to see him, the mayor, dead on a slab, it pleased Telly to note that the boss used the word "lying" instead of "laying."

It was about all that pleased him. "You don't really think ol' Hank could have done this, do you, sis? Not Hittin' Hank."

The sheriff ignored him. "But would he have had access to the building?" she asked the mayor.

Henrietta Bragg injected her own two cents here. Mr. Busby worked for the team, she replied, the Kilobyte K's. He also had an office downstairs, on the third floor.

Sheriff Blake mulled over this new information. She turned back to the mayor. "I'm surprised you allowed him to continue working here—after the way he spoke to you."

The mayor sniffed. Firing Busby would have accomplished nothing. It would have only given the man ammunition in the upcoming election. Besides, he was an excellent scout.

"Is that what he is? A scout? Do independent teams have scouts?" she wondered.

Abbott said of course they have scouts! Hank Busby was one of the best. A good scout and a sawed-off bastard.

The sheriff raised a tiny, strawberry-colored brow. She knew that Busby was not a large man, for an athlete, but *sawed-off* was still a curious expression to use when you had Abbott's physical stature. "It sounds like there is more to this story than party politics?"

Abbott grimaced. "There is. The fact is—" He paused, clearing his throat. "The fact is, Busby and my wife know each other. She knew him first. I sometimes suspect..." He let the words trail off, speaking in his most muted voice yet.

Telly pounced on it. "You don't think he and Mrs. A—" He couldn't finish the thought. "Not the Buzz! He's old enough to be her grandfather!"

As a matter of record, Mr. A was old enough to be her grandfather as well. He did not point this out, however. Instead, he said, "Shove off, you insufferable twit! This does not concern you!"

Sheriff Blake concurred. "Go, Telly. It wouldn't be the first time I arrested a member of the family. Don't force my hand."

Telly did not force it. He said K, but his *K* lacked oomph and sincerity. It was a *K* of a very unhappy young intern.

As a devotee of the game, he had always looked up to Hank Busby. Not quite as much as he looked up to Warren Kingsley, perhaps, but not everyone cut the sort of figure Warren did. Hank was a local legend—and what's more, a local legend who used to hobnob with their father in the old days. Hearing him bashed this way, it made Telly sore. And he was not a man to take offense loosely.

He nearly collided with Mrs. Abbott on his way out. The cause! he growled. The reason for all this misery. Women! he sniffed to himself and was gone.

The woman in question took no notice of him. Sheryl hadn't gotten to where she was today by paying attention to the pained looks of callow young men with bad perm jobs.

"Abby, you never said where you were going. I've been looking everywhere for—"

The last part of this statement was either "you" or "a decent nail file," but she got neither out. Once again, Deputy Tony had not held his own. She sashayed past him into the late press secretary's office and froze dead on the threshold. The air had an eerie, earthy feel, she thought. She saw why. The desk, the lamp. THE BODY. Red splattered on everything. Dripping, oozing red—

"BL..." said Mrs. Sheryl Abbott concisely, and pitched forward in a faint. Tony, redeeming himself at last, caught her at the midpoint of her sway.

Sheriff Blake nodded with appreciation, both for her deputy's quick reflexes and the woman's honest show of emotion. It was good to know that the gold digger could demonstrate sincere feeling over something.

And it did seem sincere, Jenny thought. She was impressed.

* *

Around the corner, Telly continued his departure from the office, not impressed with anything. His giant clodhopper feet pounded the industrial-grade carpet in defiance (only Mayor Abbott's space was fitted with hardwood—another perk of his lumber business).

Telly would have liked to have given him a perk now—a big fat one. He tossed his shaggy locks in annoyance. The idea of railroading Hank Busby like that! It wasn't like the boss to be so narrow-minded. Then again, maybe it was like him. Telly contemplated this as he took a left through the kitchenette, a right through the copy room and another right into his personal cubby. Coming eye to eye with one of his miniature bobbleheads—a long-forgotten catcher with a sappy look on his grill—he snatched it from its shelf and flung it against the padded wall of his cubicle.

Unlike a bullet on drywall, however, the figurine did not penetrate. It bounced playfully off the fabric, ricocheted off the drop ceiling and struck Warren Kingsley in the back of the head.

"Ouch," said Warren Kingsley.

He spoke quietly. He had been sitting in Telly's chair with the tips of his fingers pressed together in thought. The action-packed catcher broke his concentration. It brought a new meaning to the term *battery mate*.

"Sorry, bro!" said Telly, not only aghast but now deeply chagrined. He picked up the bobblehead and replaced it on the shelf. He considered smoothing down Warren's hair in the process but thought better of it.

The ex-bodyguard attended to this himself. "I couldn't find your pita chips," he replied.

For the third time in as many minutes, Telly was appalled. "I finished them off while we were waiting for the police. Should I go buy another pack?" At his heart, he was a good host.

A second trip to the vending machine would not be necessary. Warren had already found a turkey sandwich in the intern's lunch bag. It could have used an aioli of some sort, he said, or possibly a tapenade, but it was acceptable. "You seem upset about something," he concluded. A good bodyguard notices these things.

Telly conceded the point. "Do you know who they think hired that assassin?"

"You?"

No. They did not suspect Telly of hiring the assassin. That was a good one! "They suspect Hank Busby. Ol' Buzz! Can you believe it?"

Warren could not, mostly because the name Hank Busby meant nothing to him. Nor did the moniker Buzz ring any bells. "Who's Hank Busby?" he asked. "Or 'Buzz,' as he is sometimes known?"

"You know him. The boss's opponent in the election."

Warren said ah. He did not concern himself with opponents. He only wrote the speeches.

"He used to be a ballplayer," Telly added.

Warren asked why shouldn't he be. It was a free country, with plenty of opportunities.

"He used to go through enemy pitching like a buzz saw," Telly explained, warming to his topic. "Think of a smaller, more compact Ty Cobb."

Warren would prefer to think of someone he had actually heard of.

"Hank had that kind of swing," said Telly. "Kind of like his namesake, Hank Aaron, only Hank, our Hank, is a white fella."

Warren wondered why this was relevant. Did white fellas hit differently than black fellas?

Telly didn't know how to answer this. "Anyway, he's running against the boss in the election."

"Hank Aaron?"

"Hank Busby."

Warren thought as much. Hank Aaron was too busy resting after hitting 755 career home runs. Only 113 behind Sadaharu Oh of the Yomiuri Giants.

Telly blinked at him. "You know about Sadaharu Oh?"

Warren said of course. He thought everyone knew Sadaharu. Also, Telly had a book of baseball trivia Warren had been perusing while he waited.

Telly marveled at Warren's powers of assimilation, then shook it off. What were they doing talking about Ohs and Cobbs? They were supposed to be talking about Hank Busbys.

"The guy they think hired the assassin?" asked Warren.

Telly said yes. Now they were getting it. "Can you believe it?"

There were a number of things Warren Kingsley could believe. Some of them would have shocked young Telly to the core. "You don't believe it?"

"That Hank hired an assassin?! Hank!"

Warren shrugged. If Ty Cobb could do it, then why not Hank Busby?

As far as Telly knew, Ty Cobb had never hired any assassins. Although, he had been an ornery one, they say. Who knew what he could have gotten up to in his spare time? "Not Hank, though. Hank's an old softy. He talks rough sometimes, but that's how these old dudes are. It was the way they were taught. It used to be a harsher game. If you showed up a pitcher in an at-bat, he would knock you down with a fastball the next time you came up. If you showed him up again, he would wait and knock you down with his car in the parking lot. It was just how the game was played in those days. It was how they rolled."

Literally, thought Warren. "So why have the powers that be fixated on this amiable old grouch?"

Telly scoffed. "Some guff about Hank messing around with the boss's wife. I don't believe that either. These old-school ballplayers have a code."

Warren could appreciate codes. He had some codes himself. Many of these would have also shocked Telly. "Have they worked out how the gun found its way into the building?"

"Nope. Jen thinks someone planted it here. The boss thinks the courier brought it in one of his packages. I don't know what to think."

Warren did, but that was not unusual. "I believe the mayor may be onto something," he said. "That's why I left—to consider these." He drew Telly's attention to the pair of mystery parcels on the intern's desktop.

Telly brightened. Now they were talking. "You think the assassin *did* smuggle his gun in this way?"

Warren shook his head. "Maybe not the gun, since these never left our possession. But something. There is only one way to find out." He drew Telly's attention to the boxes once more.

The youth took his meaning. "You're right; we need to open them. No," he said, holding up a hand, "I'll do it. No arguments."

Warren hadn't planned on offering any. "Of course, we could always wait for the bomb squad—I assume Kilo has a bomb squad? Or the sheriff. This is her case, after all."

Telly held up another hand. He would have stuck with the first, but he felt the gesture called for more emphasis. "If it blows up in any-one's face—I mean, really blows up—it should be my face, not Jen's. Call it part of my bodyguard training."

Warren would call it anything the guy liked. A person's last request should always be honored. He vacated the seat, and the brave young man took his place.

The trainee peered down at the return address. Funny, he hadn't noticed that before. "Just sing out if I do anything wrong," he said, prying up the tape.

Warren wasn't much of a singer. It was one of the few areas he did not excel at or even dabble in.

**

In the fourth-floor conference room, down the hall from Telly and Warren's escapades, Sheriff Jenny Blake and Deputy Lance Sten-gel gazed over the evidence from the investigation. It was spread out across the Olympic-sized conference table like a sheaf of freshly com-piled committee reports.

"I guess that's about all of it," said Deputy Lance, in preparation for packing up and returning to the station.

Sheriff Blake said she supposed so. "It was *almost* all of it," she muttered to herself. A somewhat more organic piece of evidence— the Mrs. Sheryl Abbott piece (or such was how Jenny Blake viewed her)—had been taken to the building nurse for care. There was nothing seriously wrong with her, just a fit of swooning at the sight of all the blood, but every precaution was still being taken.

It was funny—her husband had been shot not half an hour before, and he hardly required a bandage. Mrs. Abbott, on the other hand, has a fit of the vapors, and the machinery of the office grinds to a halt. The charming Mrs. A—Jenny was not a fan.

"You two know each other, don't you?" Lance asked, reading his superior's thoughts. "The wife?"

Jenny nodded. "Since we were girls." This explained the lack of acknowledgment when the two met this morning. Lance knew how that worked: he had a wife and five little daughters. He didn't pretend to understand the female mind. He was simply familiar with it.

"She was a drama queen, even in pigtails," Jenny went on. "A conniving little bitch, actually."

"As long as you haven't allowed your past to color the investigation."

No, the sheriff agreed. She would never allow that.

"Guess she married the old codger for his money?" asked Lance.

"What do you think?"

Lance said he thought she had married the old codger for his money.

The sheriff concurred. "And his power," she added, "and his notoriety." Sheryl had come from nothing and made a point of seeking out a rich and powerful man. That was her game plan all along. "She eventually got her wish," said Jenny. "And then she really hit the jackpot."

"Landing a mayor, you mean?"

"No, I mean she literally hit a jackpot. On their honeymoon, Mrs. Sheryl Abbott hit some casino lottery in the Caribbean, worth about a jillion bucks."

Lance smiled wryly. Some people couldn't catch a break. "Of course, having no taste or scruples and hitting a jillion-to-one shot—twice—doesn't make her an accessory to attempted murder," he pointed out.

No, Jenny conceded, it did not. She had often thought it would have made things simpler if it did. But her deputy was right. Sheryl being Sheryl didn't make her anything but a female anachronism and a very unpleasant young woman.

It wasn't like they didn't have other suspects to contend with, the sheriff realized, notably Mr. Hank Busby. Ol' Hank, another figure from Jenny's youth. She had Tony and Albert out locating him right now, "to assist them with their inquiries." That was how the official phrase went. An oldie but a goody.

She would worry about Hank Busby when he got here. For now, she peered down at the results of their makeshift scavenger hunt. Along with the more clinical items—shells and slugs and things of that ilk—there was a bust, a bunny, a weird-looking clasp and a gun. It sounded like the title of an absurdist thriller from the 1990s. *The Bust, the Bunny, the Clasp and the Gun.* "What's this plastic doodad doing here?" she asked her deputy, holding up the third item from the list.

Lance shrugged. He just thought he would add it to the pile. It was possible it had come off the perp.

Jenny didn't mind. As long as they left the dental floss out of it.

Lance was being unusually quiet. Call it the Kingsley effect. "I was just thinking," he said. "Now that we have a corpse and a bureaucratic whirlwind brewing, are we turning this investigation over to the state?"

They weren't, as of yet. The sheriff would keep them apprised of their progress, obviously, but for now it was Kilobyte's to solve. The mayor had seen to that. It was personal now, he insisted. Another overused phrase, but Sheriff Blake found herself agreeing with it.

Lance was still pondering. "Think the medical examiner will find anything unusual?" he asked.

Jenny didn't know. It all depended on their colleague's frame of mind. Having a coroner who also taught a community college course on popular conspiracy theory always made for a whimsical postmortem. And occasionally an effed-up one.

She held up the gun. "It *could* use a good polish," she whispered, sounding fairly whimsical herself.

"What?"

"Just something the mayor said earlier, when he was giving poor Telly a hard time. He said something about Telly standing by while the assassin polished his gun."

"He was probably kidding about that."

"He was, but maybe the perp should have taken his advice. Look at the thing; it's filthy."

Lance looked at it. He had seen cleaner pistols.

She turned and stared out the double doors. "Where's that lead?"

"Balcony, I guess."

He had guessed correctly. It did lead to a balcony. A large, empty one. A glimpse over the railing, and Jenny came back inside with a tiny frown.

Lance knew that look. He had seen it many times before, usually after the sheriff had successfully completed an especially difficult sudoku puzzle. "Think that's the way the perp escaped?"

She did. But that wasn't what interested her. "Telly said he met the assassin on the third floor. There are plant pots on the third-floor patio, a whole row of them, full of potting soil. What do you bet one of them has been growing SIG Sauers?"

Lance set down the evidence he had been examining and smiled. As always, the boss had a neat way of putting things.

* *

Telly set down the parcel he had been examining and frowned. "So that's that," he said. His face had not been blown off, which pleased Warren (his jacket was still slung over the young man's chair). "Did you see this?" Telly pointed to the return address.

Warren had. It struck him as strange.

That was how it struck Telly as well. Strange. "Three-K. Three is the third floor, this building's third floor. And you know what? I think I know what the *K* is."

"K," agreed Warren, following the intern out of his cubicle.

* *

Five minutes after her botanical epiphany, Sheriff Blake and her deputy arrived outside the third-floor conference room. It had taken roughly three and a half minutes to go down and lock up the evidence in the squad car, a minute plus change to head back up in the elevator and approximately thirty seconds in between to ask the security chief, Earl, to come by the precinct at his convenience for some follow-up questions.

They found the third floor mostly deserted now. A combination of liberal leave and spontaneous municipal holiday had sent the varied personnel in the building home for the day.

There were still a few stragglers here and there, people who were neither municipal in function nor inclined to leave, liberally or conservatively. None of them impeded the officers' progress to their destination, however. That impediment came inside.

"What the hell are you doing here?"

Like other questions before it, it was one that could have been posed by anyone in the room—Telly, Warren, Sheriff Blake or Deputy Lance—but it was the sheriff who ended up beating out her brother by a hair's breadth. Warren and Lance stood by as honorable mentions.

"We're here looking for clues," said Telly. "Why are you here?"

The sheriff glared. She was doing her job, she told him. She pushed past her sibling and went out onto the balcony.

The plant-pot verdict was in. From all appearances, the pistol used in the assault on Mayor Abbott had been hidden here first. The earth was clearly shoved aside where the gun had rested, and there was an even spraying of soil all around the pot, suggesting someone had been digging.

Telly was all about giving credit where it was due. "Nice job, Jen. When you said the gat was *planted*, you weren't kidding." He chuckled quietly over the remark. Wordplay never failed to amuse him.

The sheriff was less than enthralled with it. They had found the killer's hidey-hole, yes. Now they just needed the hidey-hole hider and the killer himself. "What were you doing down here?" she asked again.

Telly had nearly forgotten. "Just a coincidence, I guess. The packages Warren and I received this morning had this address on it. This room, as a matter of fact. Three-K—*K* for conference room."

Warren still couldn't fathom that logic. Why *K* for conference room? Was *Konference* some kind of weird Amish spelling? Perhaps it was Lithuanian.

Jenny shared his confusion. "What packages?"

Concisely, or as concisely as he could manage, Telly explained about the packages received by him and Warren today and their subsequent decision to crack the suckers open.

The sheriff, like Telly before her, was aghast. "You little moron!" she uttered, and the Jenny of old materialized briefly to administer a quick slap to the back of her brother's head. "What do you think you were doing, messing with that? Say nothing of what *could* have been inside those parcels; you tampered with evidence. What possessed you?"

Telly had no answer to that. "Are you upset, Jen? You seem upset."

Jen was upset. She took a deep breath and counted to five. "So what was inside them?" she asked. Her voice was calmer now.

Telly had that answer—in spades. "Nothing," he said. "They were empty." This was not counting some crumpled brown paper, he explained, and those little Styrofoam peanuts—he forgot what you called those.

The sheriff said you called them Styrofoam peanuts.

She might have guessed that the parcels would be empty. Why should there be anything inside them? They were merely the assailant's means into the lobby, plus a little extra insurance for getting Telly and Warren out of the way during the assault. (They each had to sign for their box.) "You still shouldn't have touched them," she scolded him.

Telly wasn't so sure. The box was addressed to him, after all. Why not open it? "Besides, you gotta quit acting like I'm a kid. We're not children anymore, sis."

"Sometimes I think you're going to be a child your whole life!"

"Is that some kind of gibe?" he asked, also defined on his Word-of-the-Day page as a *slur* or a *slight*, as well as a *jibe*.

"Of course it's a gibe! Only a child wouldn't know that. You act like a child, so people treat you like a child."

Telly didn't mind people treating him like a child. It saved a lot of tedious conversations about property taxes. Jenny, however, was a different story. "I opened the box to protect you," he said.

Now it was Sheriff Blake who had no answer. On her left, Deputy Lance edged quietly out of the line of fire. With five daughters and a wife, he had a natural aversion to family squabbles. As Warren Kingsley would recommend, the best thing you can do in these situations is steer clear and try to blend in. Lance was trying to blend in and look like an azalea plant. A large, bald one.

Warren, for his part, had taken an uncharacteristically proactive approach. He didn't involve himself in the Blake-family dispute— he was all about personal safety—but the dribbling of soil around the plant plot and along the patio had intrigued him. He thought he might investigate it. (It was either that or play with his cufflinks some more.)

He strolled idly across the tile to where a trail of earth led to a door, this apparently leading to a utility closet of some kind. It had been raining earlier, so the tracks must have been made recently.

He reached down and turned the doorknob, causing a body to topple out at his feet.

He hated when that happened.

* *

It would appear that the corpse had a name. Or a sort of a name anyway. D. Wincher. It was printed on the access card dangling from his hip.

And he wasn't technically a corpse. He was as alive as anybody else, assuming that anybody didn't get out much. He sprang to his feet and looked nervously around the party.

"What?" he wondered.

Nobody had said anything.

"No," he replied.

Nobody had asked anything.

Sheriff Blake decided to change all that. "Who are you, please?"

D. Wincher answered truthfully that he was D. Wincher—David Wincher, a short and pasty man utterly unremarkable in every way. He was clearly from corporate.

"I am from corporate," said Mr. Wincher.

Telly recognized him. "I know this guy. He's Dave Wincher from corporate." He held out his knuckles for the compulsory fist bump.

Mr. Wincher reciprocated with the greatest reluctance. He extended his fist, like some tentative animal accepting a treat, and knuckle met knuckle. The ritual was concluded.

"There you go, Dave," smiled Telly.

"David," Mr. Wincher insisted. "I am from corporate," he said a second time.

"Is it corporate's policy to lurk in closets?" asked Sheriff Blake.

Mr. Wincher resented the term *lurk*. "I may have slipped inside the utility closet, yes. But I was not lurking."

"What were you doing, then?"

Mr. Wincher sighed. He would not have been a true-blue citizen of Kilobyte if he hadn't. "I must admit I am guilty of a transgression, Sheriff. I have been violating our company's nonsmoking policy."

"You were having a cigarette?" asked Deputy Lance, putting the words in the vernacular of the common man.

Mr. Wincher bowed his head. "I stepped out here to indulge my habit, and that's when I heard the sound of approaching voices. I hid," he said, now shaking his head sadly.

"Why?" asked Warren Kingsley.

"I figured they would smell the smoke, and I would be unable to explain myself."

The sheriff stared him down. "You do realize this is a murder investigation, don't you?" Why did she have to keep explaining that to people?

"I do. I have been thoroughly informed by intraoffice gossip."

"Then I suggest you leave us to our investigating."

Mr. Wincher agreed wholeheartedly. "If you need to follow up with me, Sheriff, the name, again, is David Wincher."

"From corporate," agreed Sheriff Blake and held the door for him to leave.

Mr. Wincher went through it. And not a moment too soon. Already, his magnetic personality was beginning to have a most profound effect on the assembly.

"What a weirdo," said Lance.

The sheriff nodded in agreement. There was something not right about that guy. She could add him to the list.

"His smell was all wrong," said Telly.

Warren, Lance and Jenny slowly turned his way.

"Did you say his smell was all wrong?" asked the deputy.

"I did. You know I have a pretty good nose, right, Jen?"

Jen knew. She knew all too well.

"Well then, take it from me, the guy was full of crap when he said he was having a smoke. He wasn't smoking. I doubt he has ever smoked a cig in his life."

"Because his smell was wrong?"

"All wrong. If you smoke—especially if you cram yourself inside a confined space afterwards, you're going to smell smoky. Not Warren-aftershave smoky, but smoky."

The sheriff was inclined to agree. She would have preferred it if her brother sniffed people a little less, but you could not dispute his analysis. Anyone who has ever stood in an elevator with someone after their smoke break could attest to that.

"So if he wasn't smoking," she said, "what was he doing out here?"

That was the question.

* *

Later that evening, David Wincher (from corporate) sat in a small, unadorned apartment in the heart of the bustling Kilobyte downtown (it wasn't really bustling). He stared down at his kitchen table. On his kitchen table was a small, unadorned cell phone, and on that cell phone was its last dialed number.

That number belonged to the recently deceased press secretary, Mr. Daryl Blue.

Mr. Wincher had been gazing at it for a full fifteen minutes, and he would go on gazing at it for another fifteen. What to do now?

That was the real question.

5 — LOOSE LIPS

"So I tracked down that call," said Deputy Lance Stengel, coming into the Kilobyte Sheriff's Office the next morning and taking a seat at his desk.

Tony and Albert were already sitting at their desks on either side of him. (The one belonging to Albert was set at a forty-five degree angle, because he was an *artiste*.) Jenny Blake stood straight ahead of them, leaning on the lip of a counter they used for coffee, pastries and other treats.

Though she would have hated to admit it, she was not unlike Warren Kingsley when it came to shunning her private office. This was not because of its lack of a southern exposure or its chilliness in the afternoon, although it did possess those two shameful qualities, but because she preferred getting out and interacting with her men. She was a hands-on kind of girl.

Before Lance returned, they had been discussing the logistics of the case. The guard Earl had been by and filled them in on the protocol at the Abbott Building, along with his personal routine morning, day and evening.

Packages were to be delivered in the back, Earl had explained. He had made an exception yesterday and accepted the two parcels at the desk because the guy had talked a good game and it didn't seem like a huge deal at the time.

He was wrong about that, but how was Earl to know the man was an assassin? He didn't look like an assassin.

Normally, to get to the elevators, and by extension the rest of the building, Earl would have a newcomer sign in at the desk first. He would then meet the newcomer on the other side of the metal detectors to watch them pass through. He usually had an assistant, Larry, to help with this, but Larry had started his vacation Thursday. Bags were put through the X-ray machine, or would have been, if the X-ray machine had been working. In order to remedy this until the unit could be replaced, they had been examining people's belongings by hand. Before his vacation, Larry had done this with gusto, taking a perverse pleasure in ransacking bags, purses, briefcases and such. Earl, however, didn't like it.

Yesterday, he had barely looked through anything belonging to the regulars—the mayor's staff, team execs, people like that. Newbies still got their share of scrutiny, but the goods and chattels of several employees had passed through with hardly a poke. These employees included Daryl Blue; Henrietta Bragg; David Wincher; Jenny's brother, Telly; Warren Kingsley; and Hank Busby, the last of whom had come by early that day to drop off some scouting reports with the team secretary.

Earl couldn't remember who had bags with them, but suffice it to say those six could have slipped anything under his bulbous nose without him noticing. He was too kindly, Earl was; that had always been his problem (just ask the former Mrs. Earl).

After Earl had made his statement and gone, Jenny had phoned Ms. Bragg at her home. Henrietta confirmed that she had not left her desk yesterday morning, not even when the hubbub had started, and no one had gone into Mr. Blue's office or come out.

She was quite emphatic about that.

The sheriff learned that Mr. Abbott's personal assistant, usually on sentry outside the mayor's office, was also on vacation this week. This coincided with the assistant guard Larry's vacation, Jenny realized, but seeing as Larry was twenty-three and in a not-so-secret relationship with Kyle, the butcher's nephew, and Mildred was sixty-two and happily married, the sheriff decided to table any inquiry into the pair. Sometimes people just took vacations around the same time.

The final item of info they received that morning verified the perp's method of escape. A tanned and wizened man named Thomas came in to report that he had seen the getaway personally. Thomas had been part of the grounds crew at the ballpark for almost forty years now, and never in those forty years had he seen anything as remarkable as the death-defying departure at approximately ten fifteen yesterday morning. Over the railing and down the balconies the man had gone, one after the other. It was astounding to watch; much more exciting than the time the wind had gotten hold of the tarp in '96 and three of the crew had been carried over to the pit-beef stand. Or so said the witness Thomas.

It had been a morning full to the brim with dry, tedious information, and very little of it useful. By now, Sheriff Blake was ready for some progress in their investigation. She raised her eyebrows in silent anticipation of her deputy's announcement.

Unfortunately, she was destined to be disappointed again.

"Burner," he said simply. "One of those phones with prepaid minutes you buy in convenience stores."

Jenny knew what a burner phone was. "Any luck locating who bought it?"

Lance said they were working on it. The number had been tracked to a purchase at the market in town. He was waiting for the manager to get in, so they could kick around a few ideas.

Jenny would like to kick a few things, and not just ideas. Nothing seemed to be getting done here. Surely this wasn't how big-city investigators worked—or rather didn't work. Maybe she should have listened to the soft-spoken man on the phone this morning, calling from the state police. Turn it over to the experts, he had suggested. If it hadn't been for the mayor insisting they keep the matter "in the family," she wondered if she would have taken this advice. Given up, in other words. Maybe not—hopefully not—but you never knew what you were capable of until either you were capable of it or you weren't.

She stared off into the distance, wondering which she would be.

She reflected as she stared: Who would want to use a burner phone? Who used burners in the first place? she pondered. People who didn't want a record of their call; that was who. One such person had called Daryl Blue moments before he was shot. That person had been speaking with him when he was shot, and yet no one had come forward.

It was curious.

"Do we have the ballistics back yet?" she asked.

Tony and Albert shuffled meaningless papers around their desks, before Deputy Lance came to their rescue (again).

"I have it here. According to the tests, both the bullet that killed Daryl Blue and the one that plinked off the mayor came from the gun we have in evidence. No surprise there. But here's a really odd thing."

"Just one?" asked the sheriff.

"Looks like the gun jammed. After firing those first two shots, the next one got stuck. Some kind of flaw in the third bullet."

"The mayor is one lucky cuss," observed Albert, glancing up from his theater magazine.

"Or the perp is one unlucky one," suggested Jenny.

Once more, she found herself asking which one it was. Perhaps there was a third option no one had considered.

She stared off into the distance again, considering it.

* *

At his quaintly furnished cottage, about a ten-minute walk from the sheriff's office, Warren Kingsley was focused in on an item much closer in proximity. He was staring at his cinnamon rice toasties.

Call him crazy, but he could have sworn that he had left the box in the right-most corner of the cabinet yesterday. And yet, there the cereal was, a full three inches toward the left.

It was sinister.

Thus far in the investigation, a good deal could be said about Mayor Frederick Abbott's potential enemies and non-well-wishers. There was Hank Busby, the political opponent and possible rival in love. There was Mrs. Sheryl Abbott, a little too ready to embrace the idea of her husband's shooting death. Lastly, there were all the current and former business associates, current and former investors, and current and former Kilobyte K players who could conceivably have it in for a man of Abbott's stature.

But what of the enemies accumulated by a man of Warren Kingsley's stature? What could be said of them?

Simply this. Warren had his share.

At a glance, one could account for killers, assailants and other roughhousing individuals a personal-security expert might encounter in his day-to-day activities (not that Warren ever interfered much with these undertakings—live and let live; that was his motto). Nevertheless, there was at least one murderer brought to justice, thanks to Warren's somewhat offhanded efforts in Connecticut a few years back, and a handful of disgruntled associates who wouldn't mind a shot at him. Warren had not made many friends in his life. A bodyguard cannot please everyone all of the time, and Warren rarely pleased anyone.

And so, when a man in this position sees his cinnamon toasties out of whack, he examines the situation carefully.

Who moved the toasties? he asks himself. Why move them? With what insidious purpose would a person touch another man's toasties?

These questions and more passed through his mind that morning.

There were explanations, of course. The cottage he was renting had come fully furnished, with the use of a cleaning service twice a month, compliments of the management company, Homestead Inc. (a division of Abbott Enterprises). Perhaps one of those hardworking cleaners had messed with his muesli. But why mess? The cereal box was perfectly clean. There was no reason to mess with it.

Rather than risk poisoning himself—he had seen plenty of clients succumb to toxins, and it was never pleasant—he opted to have an egg instead. It was hard to mess with an egg.

He collected the necessary ingredients and began his preparations.

You wouldn't think it to look at him, but Warren was a wizard in the kitchen, and not just with an omelet pan. He had just poured his mixture into a little butter and herbs, and expertly flipped it with a flick of the wrist, when his cell phone rang.

He answered it with one hand while sliding a slice of whole-grain bread in the toaster with the other. (The bag appeared to have three twists in the cellophane closure instead of four, but he decided to chance it.) "Hello."

"*Is that Kingsley?*" Mayor Frederick Abbott did not make many calls himself and, as a result, had a tendency to be abrupt.

Warren Kingsley said it was he.

"Are you at home?"

Warren said he was at home.

"Well, I need you to be at my home. I need you to hold a press conference on my lawn in thirty minutes."

"On your lawn?"

"On my back lawn."

Warren supposed that if you were going to hold a press conference on a lawn, you might as well hold it on the back one. "Why can't your press secretary do it?"

"My press secretary is dead."

Warren said ah. He did recall something to that effect. He asked why he needed to do it, when there was a plethora of Tellys and Ms. Henriettas to be had—and at a reasonable price too.

"I'm asking you, that's why. You're my speechwriter, aren't you?"

Warren said he was. Why wouldn't he be?

"Then this is a natural extension of that. Put together a few words before you come."

Warren said he would put together a few. "Anything specific you want me to chat about?"

"Yes! Talk about the death of Daryl Blue. But not too much. Always leave them wanting more; that's the secret of any good press conference. Tell them the police are working diligently on it and expect to make an arrest shortly—"

"Do they expect to make an arrest shortly?"

"No. Say I'm too upset or I would have appeared myself."

"Are you too upset?"

The mayor said he was not. *"I'll see you in fifteen minutes,"* he remarked. There was a brief silence; then he concluded, *"I shall also be engaging you as my bodyguard. Bodyguard slash press secretary."*

"Bodyguard slash press secretary?"

"Bodyguard slash press secretary," said the mayor. *"And speechwriter. But mostly bodyguard."* The line went dead.

How fitting, thought the mostly bodyguard. Things usually did end up dead when people engaged him.

* *

"I'm just saying, it was more than flirting. The woman is man hungry."

Deputy Tony had made this definitive statement about Mrs. Sheryl Abbott while helping himself to a preluncheon apple fritter. The Sheryls of the world might be man hungry, but he was fritter hungry, always had been.

"I would never cheat on Cynthia, you understand"—Cynthia was Deputy Tony's girlfriend of three months, eight days—"but it wouldn't be for lack of offers," he said, dabbing apple fritter from his uniform.

"Offers from the First Lady of Kilobyte?" asked Lance.

"I'm just saying—"

"What *are* you saying?"

"That the woman is man hungry."

Lance shook his head. "She's like that with everyone—flirty—just ask the sheriff."

"This wasn't flirting, and the sheriff wouldn't notice, because she's a woman herself."

"Is she now?"

"She is. But not the Sheryl kind of woman. That kind eats you up with her eyes. If you wanna know the truth, it makes me uncomfortable." He gobbled up his snack with a relish that did not betray discomfort, at least not to Lance.

The voice of reason scoffed. "In case you're wondering, she flirted with me too."

"Oh yeah? Did she call you 'Handsome'?"

"Better. She called me 'Gely.' " He pronounced it with a hard *G*.

"What the hell is a *gely*?"

"An affectionate shortening of my last name. She does it with everyone."

"Not me. She calls me 'Handsome.' She and I have our own language, I guess."

"She never calls me anything good," sniffed Deputy Albert, peering up from his *Merchant of Venice*. He spoke dolefully. It would have been nice; that was all he was saying. Do mustachioed deputies not deserve the occasional flirt? he asked. If you snub them, do they not mope?

Lance could only deal with one delusional cohort at a time. "If she's man hungry for anyone, it's—"

"For who?" asked the sheriff, stepping out from her office. The one time she leaves these three knuckleheads alone to discuss a case, and she finds them nattering away like schoolgirls. "What are we talking about?"

Albert answered the question happily. With a quiet satisfaction, he repeated the substance of the conversation—who had called whom what and how this signified a man hungriness or a man not-so-hungriness. He was quite the mental stenographer, their Bert.

" 'Gely'?" she repeated.

"Short for *Stengel*," Lance explained. "You see, you take the *gel* at the end and—"

Jenny saw. You Sheryl-fied it. Very clever. "And you think she is the most man hungry for—whom did you say?"

Lance flushed. He had almost forgotten about the sheriff's past with the mayor's wife. She was no doubt sensitive about Sheryl's easy manner with men, considering the boss hadn't been in a relationship since that guy she was dating took the DA job up north.

For the sake of his career, not to mention his wife and five little daughters, Lance did not reply "Deputy Lance Stengel." Instead, he said, "Well, I mean—Hank Busby, I guess. That's what the mayor thinks."

It *was* what the mayor thought, the sheriff acknowledged. Whether it was what her deputy truly thought was another story. "And speaking of the Buzz Saw," she said, "you've rounded him up—where?" She peered around and observed no Buzz Saws in their midst.

Lance sprang into action. All the better to escape without any more discussion of Mrs. Sheryl Abbott. "On it, Chief. I'll swing by his place again on my way back from the market. The manager should be in by now, and we can try to get some answers on that cell phone."

"Thank you, Gely."

She paused. *Gely*. Of all the stupid truncations. Sheryl had always done that, from kindergarten on. Abby. Blakey. Chesty (for their first-grade teacher, Mrs. Winchester, who ironically was rather small in the breast department). And the halfwit was still doing it. It was obnoxious.

Jenny paused again, this time with a smile forming on her tiny lips. It wasn't obnoxious, she realized. It was perfect. Perfectly brilliant. "Wait a minute, Lance. You can skip the errands for now. If my hunch is correct, we won't need them. You're with me."

"Okay. Where we going?"

"The mayor's house."

Lance said okeydoke. "Why?"

"Because Sheryl Abbott called you 'Gely,' " said Jenny, grabbing her keys. "Come on, Tony, I might want you there too."

Tony said he'd be right with them, just as soon as he pocketed the rest of his bear claw. The three left to follow up on the sheriff's cryptic pronouncement.

And then there was Deputy Albert, all alone, reading his *Merchant*. No one ever asked him to follow up on any exciting hunches. It stung, that, but he was used to the slings and arrows of whatever it was from that other play that was not *The Merchant of Venice*.

Rather than go on moping, he did what he always did in these situations. He buried himself in the soothing words of the Immortal Bard.

The B and he—they understood each other.

* *

Across town, in the largest house in the county, Frederick Abbott— his brow drawn and his arm still in a sling—stared out from the large, arched window in his private library. It was about ten feet taller than he was.

His bodyguard/press secretary/speechwriter was at the railing of the patio, discussing the tragic death of Daryl Blue with various members of the press corps. A dozen reporters had joined the local media, coming in from such exotic and far-flung locales as Scranton, Pennsylvania. From the fact that none of them had knocked Kingsley aside and rushed the veranda, thirsting for scandal, Abbott could only presume the talk was going well.

It would have been agreeable if Jenny Blake had deigned to join them, he thought, but the sheriff was a woman, he realized, and, as a woman, prone to unpredictable behavior. At least he had Kingsley, he consoled himself, the presence of whom was nearly as good as the police. And what with all his hippy-dippy musings, somewhat like a woman too, decided the mayor.

It wasn't raining today. It was a clear morning, the temperature was mild and balmy, and the birds were chirping (or they would have chirped if Abbott allowed wildlife on the property).

His wife, Sheryl, was curled up on the velvet settee behind him with her golden retriever, Butterscotch (domesticated animals were acceptable, provided that they kept in line). The pup seemed in order this morning. He had a plush toy between his paws and was pleasantly attempting to tear out its insides. The novelty Abbott had purchased a couple days ago remained in evidence with the sheriff's department, but he was able to procure a replacement, care of his intern, Telly. Butterscotch didn't mind the last-minute substitution, so long as he could still ascertain the color of its stuffing.

Telly had stayed behind after his vital delivery, standing in the corner, fingering his employer's objets d'art. There was an atmosphere of quiet reflection in the room. Quiet reflection and the occasional thoughtful slobber from Butterscotch.

The publicity surrounding yesterday's incident had made working out of the mayor's office (all four of them) a virtual impossibility for Abbott. As Warren's sort-of British, sort-of American friend Hathaway might have said, the episode had caused quite a "brouhaha" in town. (Although Hathaway himself would have denied ever using such a word, since *brouhaha* was neither British nor American in origin. It was French.)

Generally speaking, men like Abbott didn't mind brouhahas, so long as they *broued* in the right spirit. He wasn't so sure that this one did. He might have thought after an attempt on his life a fellow would catapult ahead in the polls. Nothing doing. If anything, Abbott had catapulted backward. It was mystifying. The problem was all the sympathy was with Daryl Blue—which it naturally would be—but of the heroic efforts of the mayor, fighting off his would-be assassin with nothing but a bust, a bunny and the quintessential Fred Abbott tenacity, there was no talk whatsoever.

He wondered why he even bothered.

"What do I have to do?" muttered the politician aloud, unwittingly opening the conversation to the fiddly fingered young man in the back of the room.

"That's a tough one," Telly replied, stepping forward with a vase from one of the more ancient and fragile dynasties. He had read his boss's thoughts perfectly. "Do you want to know my opinion on winning the hearts and minds of the populace?"

Before Abbott could reply that he would like few things less, Telly carried on. "I have come to an epiphany about it."

"You've finished that report on office inventory?" his host prompted him.

"Not at all," said Telly. That wasn't the epiphany. "The epiphany is this: no one really likes you."

From the direction of the settee, Abbott could have sworn he heard a chortle. It could have been Butterscotch swallowing a mouthful of stuffing the wrong way, but it sounded like a chortle.

"If you want a chance at reelection," Telly proceeded, "you're going to have to exhibit more humanity. I know that's difficult for you—humanity—but you have to try. And in trying, it doesn't matter what you say with your words; your body language has to say it for you. That's what Warren says anyhow. He's big on body language, Warren is."

The mayor shimmied. His body language communicated volumes, none of which befitted the dignity of his elected office.

"People can sense when you're uncomfortable," Telly pointed out, "when you don't like something. Yeah, like that. Your body language has to convince them that you aren't and that you do. Or that's what Warren believes."

"He does, does he?"

Telly agreed that he did, and as if on cue, the laconic lecturer came in from his talk. "Well, that's done," he said.

Abbott glared at him. "You're looking pretty pleased with yourself. I'm guessing it went well?"

"Well enough," said Warren. "They didn't lift me up and carry me around the lawn or anything, but they were a spindly bunch, so I didn't think to ask."

"You explained the matter concisely?"

"Concise enough. They seemed satisfied."

"*Satisfied?*" The notion of media satisfaction was alien territory for the Mayor of Kilobyte. "Didn't they insist on pelting you with questions, even after you had stated everything six times and in six different ways?"

"Not that I noticed. We finished up, they nodded, and that was that. It took a little longer than expected because we stopped to shoot the breeze after that. You know how it is."

Fred Abbott did not. Never in his life could he remember shooting the breeze with any reporters. He wouldn't have minded shooting a few of the reporters themselves, but never the breeze. "Well, don't get used to it," he snapped. "As soon as I find a replacement press secretary, you're out, you understand—out."

"Understood," said Warren. He was out.

"In fact, you can go back to being my speechwriter right now. And bodyguard."

Warren understood that as well. He wasn't sure when he'd consented to do any security consulting for the mayor, but he didn't anticipate it would affect his schedule much.

It seldom did.

"Actually," he smiled, "one of the reporters suggested a fourth profession. I mentioned public speaking wasn't my normal gig, and a reporter said she wouldn't have thunk it and suggested I go pro. Hit the circuit for myself, in other words. It's a thought," mused the speechwriter-slash-bodyguard-slash-temporary-press-secretary-slash-possible-pro-talker. "Lot of money in that."

Abbott's expression underwent a complete transformation. He gaped, dumbfounded. "They said you should become a public speaker?"

"Or something."

"But you're my press secretary!" Abbott lamented.

Warren was well aware of the fact. The mayor's *temporary* press secretary. It said so on the hastily scrawled placard outside.

At this juncture in the proceedings, Sheryl Abbott stood to take her dog for a walk. She rarely walked Butterscotch herself—that was what servants were for—but she had become weary of all this talk of work and professions, and needed to stretch her legs.

As she passed, she made a point of looking straight through Warren without blinking. Warren, meanwhile, made a point of staring straight ahead and not giving a damn. It was how they had always acknowledged each other. (Butterscotch, unaccustomed to any existing traditions, merely sniffed the man's kneecap and trotted on.)

His owner slammed the door on her way out, bringing Abbott around with a jerk. He hadn't liked the look his wife and temporary press secretary had exchanged, not liked it one ounce. It smacked of passion. In the minds of men like Fred Abbott, there was only one type of passion in the world, and it was indistinguishable from hate.

He renewed his glare in Warren's direction.

Telly noticed it first. Showing more perception than his sister would have given him credit for, he said to Warren, "It looks like you had them eating out of your hands, bro. During the press conference, I mean."

Warren turned and looked at him. He supposed there was a suggestion of nibbling, yes.

"What's your secret? I was telling the boss that it's all in the body language, but I bet there's more to it than that."

Warren supposed there was a little more. You have to start by showing them who's boss, he explained. Not the Abbott type of boss, he clarified, but *boss* boss.

Telly nodded. *Boss* boss. He never thought of that.

"It's easy enough after you establish that," said Warren. He turned back toward Abbott, oblivious to the annoyance in the man's eyes. In the minds of men like Warren, annoyance was indistinguishable from admiration. "As I told you before, Mayor, people talk too much. And politicians and the media talk more than anyone else. Too many people saying too many things about nothing at all. That's politicians and the media. So I turned the tables on their expectations and did the exact opposite. And that's the secret."

Abbott continued to glare.

"That's the secret," Warren repeated, uncertain if the mayor had heard him or not. Older gentlemen frequently did not. "Letting people talk themselves out," he stated clearly, "while you keep quiet about what you're thinking. From the unexpressed thought comes power," said Warren Kingsley.

Abbott blinked at him. He had already gotten his fill of this yesterday. It made him long for getting shot at. "From the unexpressed thought—"

"Comes power. Correct, Mayor. When I went out there to speak, I said very little. The media asked their questions, and I said even less. Eventually, they fell under the spell of my reticence and stopped asking."

"The spell of your reticence?"

"The spell of my reticence. The next time you have to appear in public, try saying nothing, and see if you don't become a better, finer person for your silence."

The mayor scowled. He had no desire to become a better, finer person. "Get out!" he shouted.

Warren was not surprised by this outburst. Older gents frequently had them. "We can discuss it later," he agreed. "And by discuss, I mean communicate not so much through the spoken word, but—"

"Leave!" said Abbott.

Warren left—or he would have, had he not run into Sheriff Jenny Blake at the library door.

Initially taken aback by the wall of pressed Armani in her path, the officer imparted her message, and the wall turned to the room and relayed it.

"The sheriff is here," he announced.

Abbott could see that on his own. He had no wish to speak to her.

She had no desire to speak with him either. "She's here for your wife," said Warren, and happily took his departure.

* *

The sheriff had gone to find Sheryl on the grounds. Abbott and Telly remained in the library, frowning at each other.

"What do you think my sis wants with your wife, boss?"

Abbott was wondering that himself. He declined to answer, but he was wondering it.

Telly tactfully changed the subject for a second time. "So how's the little woman holding up?" he asked. "It was hard getting a read on her earlier, what with her dog making all those slavering noises."

Abbott said she was doing fine. And she was not his *little woman*.

Telly thought her small enough in some areas, not so small in others. "That's good. That she's fine, I mean. Because I thought it strange that she didn't seem all that upset about you getting shot yesterday."

"Well, it isn't," said Abbott. "Not strange in the slightest."

"Because she's fine?"

"Very fine."

Telly was glad. "And I wouldn't worry yourself about the look she gave Warren just now. I'm sure lots of married women ogle men's press secretaries like that. It was nothing."

"I wasn't worried," said the mayor.

"That's good. That you weren't worried," Telly explained.

Abbott's glare continued to bore through the shut library door. "If you must know," he said, with all the conceit he could muster, "she's busy planning a romantic getaway to Acapulco as we speak."

"With you?"

"Of course with me!"

"Cool," said Telly. "I mean, I'm glad." He picked up a nutcracker from his boss's coffee table and frowned at it. "Can I have this?"

"No." With his good arm, Abbott wrenched the nutcracker free from the intern's grip. "Don't you have some place you ought to be?"

Telly shook his head. He never had any place he ought to be.

"Well, go there anyway," Abbott told him. "Go work on those inventory reports. I left them in the guest room in the back of the house. They need updating in the database."

Telly laid another *K* on the man. He was nothing if not cooperative.

* *

"You're looking good, Sheriff," said Sheryl Abbott, sitting on a hickory bench on the back lawn, watching Butterscotch dash to and fro. "Very smart."

Sheriff Blake made no reply to this comment. In a shocking second parallel to Warren Kingsley and his proclivities, she was letting her quarry *talk herself out*.

"You really must introduce Abby to your tailor," said Sheryl, looking her childhood playmate up and down with a scornful smile. It only took a microsecond. "Great cut on that uniform. Very butch."

Sheriff Blake acknowledged the insult with a smile. Keep going, she thought; they'd get there eventually.

Sheryl was becoming bored with this conversation. Strange, since normally she adored the sound of her own voice. She peered off into the distance, past the sprinting form of Butterscotch, now chivvying a reporter with a Fred Abbott–like tenacity, and up at the sheriff's parked squad car. The figures of two able deputies were set against the horizon, gazing down at them from the ridge.

"I see you've brought your men with you. I trust they're not here to assist you in an official capacity?"

"Any reason why they should?" asked the sheriff.

Sheryl ignored the question. It would have only led to a productive discussion. "It must be nice having command over the male sex for a change," she said. "You never were very successful there, were you? Not with the boys at school—not ever, really. You must have taken after your mother in that way. I always thought it fortuitous that she ran off with my father. Otherwise, she might have drowned you and your brother in the river, rather than spend another minute in that house with her husband. So sad, a failed marriage, isn't it?"

Jenny smiled. "*Fortunate* not *fortuitous*," she replied. Telly was not the only Blake who enjoyed word power. "Common enough mistake," she said, fixing her ex-schoolmate in a disarming gaze.

Sheryl ignored that too. "And then there was Hank Busby," she continued. "I always wondered about him and your mother—before she left, of course. I wondered about him and *my* mother too, now that I mention it. He was quite a rogue in his day. I understand you still haven't located him?"

"We're working on it."

Sheryl sneaked another peek at the men in blue, or more precisely, the men in beige. "You know you can't shield suspects, don't you, Sheriff? I understand he was like a surrogate parent to you at times, but it won't look good, you protecting him like this. You haven't developed a crush on him yourself, have you? I understand that's common enough," she remarked. When Sheryl Abbott said "common," she meant it in every sense of the word.

The sheriff had been called worse. "The consensus is you're the one with the crush on Hank Busby, Sheryl. Or something more than a crush."

Sheryl laughed. "What, me and Buzzy? No, Sheriff, you got that one wrong. I don't know who's been spreading these rumors, but they're ridiculous. One dilapidated lover is enough for this girl."

"I seem to recall you used to go in for the athletic type."

"Only the ones without walkers, dear."

The sheriff nodded. Hank did have some mileage on him, she supposed. Perhaps too much for a Sheryl plaything. "You would want a younger model. Someone like Daryl Blue."

Sheryl did her best to recover from an inadvertent flinch. "Daryl?" She laughed again, but not as emphatically. "That's a hoot. What put *that* idea in your head?"

"Various things," said the officer.

She didn't bother to explain that Sheryl's penchant for nicknames had started her along that train of thought. Abby, Gely, Buzzy. A long time ago, before the two girls realized how much they loathed each other, there had even been a period when Sheryl referred to Jenny as "Blakey."

Not anymore. Now that nomenclature was reserved solely for cherished associates. And those who did more than "associate" with her.

"Feeling better after your episode?" Jenny asked. "We were all concerned about you, you know."

Sheryl stared at her, wondering what was going through the sheriff's pretty little head.

"You certainly got to the scene quickly yesterday," the latter congratulated her. "After the attempt on your husband's life, I mean. I assume you were in town when you heard?"

"That's right."

"Ironic, since you were no doubt coming to meet up with, well—" She let the name hang in the air.

Sheryl took a swat at it. "You don't seriously think I was having an affair with—"

"Daryl Blue? I do. I'm curious—what was your pet name for him? Something adorable, I'm sure."

That had been Jenny's epiphany this morning: Sheryl's reaction to seeing the deceased. It had never felt right, that swoon. It wasn't that it was too exaggerated. If anything, it was a tad restrained, given the facts. Then there was the stammered word before the swoon. "Bl…" Not short for "Blood," as one might expect, but rather "Blue" or "Bluey" or some Sheryl-modified monstrosity. It was the sputtered wail of a woman confronted with the body of her dead lover.

"That's why you bought a burner phone, I guess? So you and he could speak without your husband getting wise? So sad when a man pores over his wife's phone records, isn't it?"

Sheryl was steaming. Butterscotch had returned to relate the successful vanquishing of the *Scranton Star* correspondent, but for all his triumphant barks, he might have been speaking sotto voce.

"I suppose you realize you can assist us," said the sheriff. "If you were on the phone with Daryl when he was shot, you can help us piece things together. I'm not entirely satisfied that we know all there is to know. If you cooperate and tell us—what the hell are you grinning about?"

Sheryl Abbott's face had cleared. When she spoke, it was with a complete openness, which the sheriff wasn't so sure she liked. "I used to call him 'My Little Blue Boy,' " she said dreamily. "After the Gainsborough painting. Daryl looked like the boy in the picture. After a while that seemed kind of queer, though, so I started calling him 'Bluebeard,' because of the goatee he was growing out. I'm not sure which nickname I preferred."

Jenny shivered. All she knew was both names gave her the creeps. "I'd have thought you would have gone with the rhyme. 'Daryl and Sheryl.' "

"Oo, I like that even better," squealed the female half. "Nice one, Blakey."

"So you two were having an affair, then?"

Sheryl did not reply. "He was wasted in my husband's office, you know, absolutely wasted. He could have been a Hall of Famer if he hadn't blown out his arm."

The sheriff was distressed to hear this. "You were having an affair?" she asked again.

Sheryl peered up at her. She batted her eyelashes prettily. "Who was, darling?"

She knew damn well who! "You and Daryl Blue, your little Bluebird or whatever."

"Oh him. He was a dear boy, yes. And we certainly *could* have been an item. Shame you have no proof of it."

"I have the phone," said the sheriff. Or at least a record of a call from that phone.

Sheryl batted her lashes some more, not so prettily. "But that's how I *knew*, darling. When you talked about me calling Daryl yesterday. That's how I knew you didn't know anything."

Now the sheriff was certain she didn't like this.

"Funny story about that phone," Sheryl declared, leaning back on the bench and tickling Butterscotch's tail. "You're right that it had been mine at one point—nice detective work there, by the way, or a damn good guess anyway—but I never actually *purchased* the thing. I was at some boring foundation meeting recently, sitting next to old Mrs. Klondike and wishing I had brought a bludgeon with me—for either her or me—and she was rambling on about her niece, Samantha, and how Sammy was going off to college and how her mother was concerned because she wasn't the most responsible girl with the utility bills. And that's when she showed me the prepaid cell phone she had bought—Mrs. Klondike did. She lugged it out right there at the board meeting. Well, I don't know what you would have done in my place, but to me my next move was obvious. When the old biddy wasn't looking, I swiped it. I thought it would be an ideal way for me to communicate with—well, you know who. Impossible to prove, of course, and I'll deny everything if you bring it up again. But that's what I did."

"Why are you telling me this?" asked Jenny. It must have been the strangest confession she had ever heard.

"Because that's the best part. I don't have it anymore. I must have dropped it at the hairdresser or somewhere, or some naughty board member got the same impulse I did and snatched it, because I haven't seen it for days. I don't know who called Daryl on it yesterday, but it wasn't me. So I guess you won't be getting any assistance from me, after all. Too bad. And when we were getting along so well too."

**

From his desk in the guest room, Telly looked up to see his sister storm across the back lawn, get in her squad car and drive off (braking briefly to allow Tony and Lance to hop in). She hadn't looked pleased. Telly wondered what was bugging her.

It certainly wasn't filling out an office inventory report: a boring list of boring products and boring product serial numbers for boring old insurance. That was all Telly.

He leaned back from the computer screen and took a rest. He didn't object to doing a smidgeon of work now and then—he would have been a pretty rotten intern if he did—but even good interns need a break. It had been a full twenty minutes, after all.

He was curious what was bothering Jen. He hadn't seen her that annoyed for a while, not since the sheriff's department had to release a traveling pickpocket because Albert forgot to read him his rights. Telly wondered if it was something like that.

The god of happenstance, disinclined to answer his thoughts directly, arranged the next best thing. A phone was what bothered his sister, and a phone was what rang right now.

Telly nearly fell out of his chair, hearing it. The ringer was set to the fullest volume, and it sounded like a trumpet blast to the back of the head. He pulled himself up and peered across at the unit.

Young men of Telly's generation did not have much experience with landlines. There were phones at work, of course, but they were direct lines, more or less like a landlocked cell phone—not the open-circuit model of these antiques. The idea that someone else could have answered the call and was even now engaged in a conversation never occurred to him. He reached for the handset and placed it to his ear.

A well-trained intern would have said, "Mayor Abbott's residence," or, at a minimum, "Hello." A conscientious one would have hung up as soon as he heard voices on the other end. Telly Blake did none of these things. He sat eavesdropping, with his mouth hanging open.

From the kitchen extension, Warren Kingsley had picked up the call (between bites of sandwich), and what Telly heard being said to him was appalling.

6 — PIPE DOWN

That evening, Warren went to bed with a lot on his mind.

For the first hour, he lay on top of the sheets, staring up at the ceiling. He wasn't normally this restless. Most nights, the span from ten to eight was his time to shine, the period when he truly surpassed himself. Warren was an excellent sleeper. At Sir Roger Banbury's estate in Maine, he used to sleep like a drugged wildebeest. That is, he did until—

But there was no reason to dwell on that.

He had been okay in Kilobyte at first, but lately his customary ten hours had eluded him. He was lucky if he got eight or nine now. Between the Daryl Blue incident and all his new responsibilities—not to mention disturbing phone calls at lunchtime and someone moving his cereal boxes around in the kitchen—it was a wonder he could sleep at all.

Of course, he wasn't sleeping at all. He was lying there, staring up at the ceiling.

Funny things, ceilings. They didn't serve much of a purpose, he realized, other than as ceilings. Walls, on the other hand, were multi-taskers. They divided up the room and provided a backdrop for art-work and doodads and things. Not ceilings. They were just ceilings.

Not that different from roofs, when you thought about it, but in a way, he observed, totally different from them. You could stand on a roof. Warren couldn't think of a good reason why you would want to, but you could if you liked.

Warren had climbed up on a roof twice in his life—one of those times, climbed, fought and fallen—and it was not a practice he would like to repeat.

He rolled over on his side and tried staring out the window. Funny things, windows.

He wondered if that text message he sent went through okay. He hadn't gotten a reply on it yet, and it had been well over ten hours.

In the distance, some creature of the night bayed. Then another one howled. Then about sixteen bayed and howled together. Warren lived next door to Henrietta Bragg's animal farm. A horde of dogs and cats and other zoological extracts the woman housed in that old barn of hers (which probably wasn't zoned for it). Warren wondered how many she had. About a jillion, he estimated.

He would very much like to know how he was supposed to sleep with all this screeching and caterwauling going on. Not that he was sleeping. But if he had been sleeping, there would be no way he could have slept now, if that made any sense. It made sense to Warren.

He rolled over on his other side and picked up his watch from the nightstand. 10:47. Only an hour and thirteen minutes until midnight. This lunacy must end, he decided. He propped himself up against the headboard as another series of growls and gurgles made itself heard. He wondered if that meat ax he saw earlier was still in the kitchen drawer.

He climbed out of bed to check.

* *

Henrietta Bragg lay awake in her bed. It was a small bed, ideally suited to her thin, solitary frame. She hadn't thought about the solitary part for quite some time. She wondered when she last had. She couldn't remember, which was odd, because Henrietta Bragg had an excellent memory. It was of no consequence. Some things were best left forgotten.

She stared up through the skylight. You could see all the stars in the sky tonight. Well, not all of them perhaps, but a good deal of them. Stars beaming down on Kilobyte.

That Blake girl was a rising star, Henrietta thought. She wondered if she felt alone. She no doubt did, in the company of all those men all the time. Her subordinates. It had to be tough on her, that.

Henrietta remembered that young man the sheriff had been seeing. A district attorney, he had become. There hadn't been anyone since. She wondered if Jenny felt alone in that way too. If she did, she most certainly thought about it, Henrietta decided, and could remember thinking about it too!

Such a nice girl. Perhaps she preferred being alone, as Henrietta did. Did Henrietta prefer it? She really didn't know anymore.

She remembered little Jenny growing up, her and that brother of hers. And those parents. They were quite a pair, those two! Some people should never have children. People who shouldn't always seem to wind up with them, though. It was the way of things.

It was probably good that the mayor hadn't had any. Now, there was another duo—he and that awful new wife of his! Abominable woman! How Daryl Blue could have allowed himself to be led around like that. Quite like a little puppy dog he had been.

And now—

Henrietta froze. Something had disturbed her concentration. The disturbance was the sound of silence. A sudden hush had fallen on her bedroom, and she didn't like it. On the topic of little puppy dogs, hers weren't barking. It was curious.

It was more than curious. It was alarming.

She climbed out of bed and opened the drawer of her antique sideboard. Warren Kingsley might have his meat cleaver, but Henrietta Bragg had a more subtle method for dealing with disturbances in the night. She reached for her Glock 9mm. She cocked the slide, threw on her heaviest bathrobe and went outside.

**

Down the road, Telly burst into the sheriff's office like a man pursued by the Hound of the Baskervilles. Or, short of that, one of Henrietta Bragg's beasts of the night. In reality, he wasn't being pursued by any of them. He was simply anxious to see the sheriff.

"Is my sister here?" he asked Albert, who seemingly hadn't moved from his desk since breakfast time.

The deputy pointed toward the back, where Jenny emerged, hot and flushed, struggling with a six-gallon water jug. "Telly?"

"Jen. I've been looking for you all day."

Telly had been by the station no less than eight times that afternoon. Every time, he had been received by Albert—in that exact position—and every time Telly had decided against confiding in the deputy. What he had to say was for the sheriff and the sheriff alone.

"Where have you been?" he demanded.

Jenny replied that, along with her normal duties, she had been up at Hank Busby's place. She declined to mention that Sheryl's reproaches had anything to do with that. Like her brother earlier, she had come up empty in her search. As soon as she conquered this water bottle, she would probably need to call in some kind of warrant for the Buzz Saw.

But first things first. "What are you all worked up about?" she asked.

Telly took her aside, pausing to help her with the water jug. Spilling about half on the floor, he got it poised on the opening eventually and proceeded with his reasons. "I'm all worked up about Warren Kingsley," he said.

"Oh?" Jenny was becoming more than a little concerned with Telly's recent obsession. He really needed to meet a nice girl. "What has Warren been doing now?" she asked cautiously. "Or not been doing," she added, as was far more likely with Warren.

"It's not what he's been doing," said Telly. "It's what's being done to him. Or might be done to him, if you want to get technical about it."

"What are you talking about?"

"I'm talking about the call he got this morning. At the boss's house."

"And?"

"And I happened to overhear it. Did you know that you can hear a conversation if you pick up a landline in the middle of a call?"

"Of course. Everyone knows that."

"I didn't. But that's neither here nor there," said Telly, who didn't believe everyone knew it at all. If you grew up with a father who barred a phone in the house, on the grounds that it would only provide a conduit for bill collectors, telemarketers and your estranged wife, why would you? (Why did Jen, for that matter? She had grown up in that house too. But that was neither here nor there.) "Anyway, I heard this call Warren got, and it shocked me."

"Well, take a couple of deep breaths, and tell me about it. And watch where you're walking while you do it. You're tracking water all over the place."

Telly watched where he was walking. "Like I said," he went on, "Warren picked up this call at the mayor's house. I came in on it about ten seconds after that."

"How'd Warren know the call was for him?"

"Probably didn't," said Telly fairly. "But it was. The guy knew all about him. He said, *I saw you.*"

"Saw Warren doing what?"

"That's what Warren said. The guy replied, *You know what! That little routine of yours on the balcony.* Remember, Warren gave his speech at the boss's house this morning. Stood at the railing out back and gave his speech like an old-timey president making a whistle-stop tour."

Jenny was amazed her brother knew what a whistle-stop tour was. That, but not how telephones worked. It was weird. But then again, so was Telly. "Actually, it's more of a veranda or patio he was on," she said.

"Whichever. Maybe the guy said patio. Anyway, Warren said, *Oh that.* It was nothing, he remarked, just something he threw together on the spur of the moment. Then he asked the guy how he looked out there. Was his hair okay? The guy snorted at this—or it sounded like a snort. Could have been a sneeze. Then he said, with a sneer— it sounded like a sneer—a person could get himself in a lot of trouble, doing what he did. Then he said he would be in touch and hung up, cutting Warren off as he asked, *Trouble how?*"

Jenny was impressed. "Why am I only hearing about this now?"

"I told you, I came looking for you about fifty times today. I also called your cell about a million times."

Jenny remembered ignoring those calls. It had probably been closer to a hundred thousand than a million. "You could have told Albert."

"Could I?"

Jenny peered across at her deputy. His magazine was resting precariously on his chest as his mustache drooped in sleep. "Perhaps not," she agreed. She took a sip from her newly filled water cooler. It hit the spot. "Evidently, someone doesn't like the idea of Warren taking over as the mayor's press secretary."

"Seems like it."

"But why would anyone care?" she wondered. "Unless," she said, taking another swig from the cooler. She was hitting it hard now. "Unless, the mayor was never the real target. Daryl Blue was the target—or the person in Daryl's position was."

"But how could the mayor not be the target?" asked Telly. "He was shot at."

"And was supposed to die, yes," said Jenny impatiently, addressing this side issue. "But what if that second shot, the one through the wall, was all a ruse?"

"How do you mean?"

"I mean, what if the assassin had already taken care of Daryl Blue? What if he had a double assignment, the mayor *and* the press secretary? He shoots Daryl, making it look like an accident; then he takes care of the mayor, shooting through the wall to cover the first murder."

"But wouldn't there be an extra bullet?"

"What?"

"If you're right, there would be a third bullet, wouldn't there? One bullet for the mayor, one for Daryl Blue and one for the wall?"

Jenny frowned. She hated when her brother was right. And he was right. Only two of the bullets had been fired. After that, according to Lance, the gun had jammed.

She said a bad word again. She was saying and thinking a lot of bad words lately.

"Besides," said Telly, "Ms. Henrietta claims no one went through her office. Unless someone scaled the building and came in through

Daryl Blue's window, he had to pass her. She'd mention an assassin, wouldn't she?"

"Would she?" asked the sheriff.

Telly was a little surprised by his sister's tone. "Don't you like Ms. Henrietta?"

"I don't know."

Telly wasn't sure he did himself. But that didn't make her a liar. "Why are you so fixated on Daryl's death?"

Jenny didn't know this any more than she knew if she liked Ms. Henrietta. Something didn't seem right with the setup, that was all. It was just a gut feeling.

Telly couldn't speak to that. His gut never told him anything, except when to eat. "But why should the guy threaten Warren?"

The sheriff could think of a lot of reasons, but nothing specific to their case. "If someone doesn't want Warren talking," she speculated, "it means he may say something dangerous, something the killer—the person who hired the assassin—doesn't want said. Let's say there was some secret this person didn't want known. If the hit on the mayor had gone properly, this secret, or whatever it is, would remain buried. But now the mayor is alive, and he's got a new press secretary, and something one of them—" She shook her head. She just couldn't see it. "What did Warren say at the conference—do you know?"

"No idea. All I know is he killed it. Sorry, poor choice of words. You know what I mean."

Jenny knew. "Perhaps I need to talk to your buddy Warren again. I notice he didn't say anything to me about this."

"I was just going over to see him," said Telly. "I didn't get a chance to talk to him before he left. Then I had a bunch of inventory reports to finish," added the intern sourly.

"Did you tell the mayor about the call?"

"I mentioned it. Don't think he was listening. Kept muttering something about his wife and Warren and someone called Othello being misunderstood. Who's Desdemona?"

Like the mayor, Jenny Blake wasn't listening. She answered, absently, that it sounded like the name of the woman who had taken over the hostess job at the local diner.

"I'd love to know where that call came in from..." she said.

"I might be able to help with that," Telly told her. He reached in his pocket and pulled out his phone. "I jotted down the number."

Jenny stared at him. "How——?"

"It was right there on the caller ID on the desk unit. I put it in my notepad. Here it is. You can run it through your database, if you like."

She had no need to run it through her database. She recognized it immediately. "It's the missing cell phone. The number that called Daryl Blue this morning."

Telly was impressed. "So the man who told Warren to back off also called Daryl Blue just before he was shot? Wow, maybe you're right. Maybe there is more to this than meets the eye."

There certainly seemed to be to Jenny Blake. "Maybe Daryl was in on it. Maybe——" She stomped her foot. Nothing made any sense. "If only we could trace who made those calls! Damn burner phones!"

Telly remarked that he might be able to help there too. He was all about deferred reveals this evening. "I recognized the voice. Or I think I did. It sounded like David Wincher. You know, the guy from corporate we ran into outside the conference room?"

The sheriff's thoughts swirled around her chaotically. Wincher—— *from corporate*—another person she didn't feel right about. *Wincher. Bragg. Sheryl.* There were so many loose cannons on this case. "Let me get this straight. David Wincher called and threatened——"

The voice of Deputy Albert broke in on their conversation. "Sorry to interrupt, Sheriff, but Tony's on the line. He's all gingered up about something."

"Gingered up about what?" asked the sheriff. She was trying to think here.

The deputy yawned into his sleeve. "Apparently, he's arrested someone at the bus station. Foreign-looking fellow. He came along quietly, but Tony doesn't like the look of the guy. Seems like a crafty sort."

"A foreign-looking fellow," repeated Jenny thoughtfully.

"And crafty," yawned Albert.

"The wayward assassin," muttered Telly on the back end.

The pieces were all snapping into place.

** **

The air felt cool and crisp on Henrietta Bragg's ankles. She could see the stars even better now. Fifty-four hundred of them, she estimated, not a star more.

She tramped across the turf in her slippers and found the padlock on her barn hanging on its latch. This was getting more ominous all the time.

She opened the door and reached for the light switch.

The light was already on. Her eyes were immediately drawn to the middle of the floor—Henrietta called it a floor, though technically it was the same earth from outside. In the middle of this earth floor knelt her new tenant neighbor, Kingsley. In his pajamas.

Surrounding him were her babies. Dogs, cats, ferrets—you name it, they were there, staring up at the interloper with awe and understanding. Even the smaller animals, in their crates, peered up over the edge, trying to get a glimpse of their fascinating guest.

Henrietta was shocked. For women like Sheryl Abbott, dogs and the like were ornaments, toys to distract her from her dull and jaded life. For Henrietta Bragg, they were her children. Children she kept in her barn. "What the…"

Fortunately for Henrietta, she had not come into her barn gun-a-blazing—you learned the proper way to handle a firearm at an early age in Kilobyte—and also fortunate for her, she managed to curb the word that now trembled on her lips. Let that last one sail, and it would have shot her ladylike reputation to hell like so many 9mms.

"What in Heaven's name are you doing, Mr. Kingsley?"

Warren Kingsley stood. He had been engaged in a kind of inter-species repartee with a small mixed-breed terrier named Cookie, and it took him a moment to drag himself away.

"I thought they might be hungry," he explained, "so I decided to bring over some chopped meat. As it happens, I have the chopper, but no meat to chop with it. So I came over myself, and it turns out they weren't hungry—they just wanted to talk."

Henrietta blinked at her new neighbor. She wondered if he was quite well. "You came over to talk to my animals?"

Warren said sure. They had a lot to get off their chests.

"How did you get in here?" she demanded.

Warren was tempted to reply "a trusting collie with long paws," but decided against it. The time for witty repartee had clearly passed. "I picked the lock," he replied simply. He was good at picking locks, having examined the technique of many a hitman over the years.

Henrietta took a moment to frown disapprovingly. Then she turned and shut the barn door. Already two of her Siamese were eyeing the open air with their customary guile. "I must admit," she said, "I have not seen them this calm for ages."

"There was nothing much to it," Warren stated, his standard reply for describing anything that came to him naturally (and inexplicably). "Animals just like to make noise," he said. "They bark and bark, and then they bark some more. They don't have many unexpressed thoughts, animals. The secret is to take it all in and let them talk themselves out. After that, you can just give them *the look*." He gave Henrietta Bragg *the look*. "You have to show them who's boss," he explained. Had Telly Blake been present, the intern might have remarked that he had heard something to this effect before.

Henrietta said she would have to remember this advice. "I apologize if they woke you."

"I wasn't really sleeping. I haven't slept much these last couple nights."

Henrietta admitted that she had not slept much herself. "It's not often that we have a killer on the loose," she confessed.

It was not so much the loose killer that bothered Warren. An assassin was simply a tool, he argued, and tools eventually get put in their place. It was the men who used these tools you had to watch out for. They call you up at lunchtime and speak a lot of rubbish at you.

"I beg your pardon?"

"The hitman-hirer called me," said Warren. He thought he had made that clear.

"But what—what did he say?"

"Oh, he just threatened me. Said he didn't much care for my speech from the mayor's balcony this morning, which went rather well, incidentally. It got me to thinking that I might have a future in that line."

Ms. Henrietta said she would make a note of it in his employee file. "You were saying something about the man who hired the hitman…"

"Oh yeah, him. He was pretty brusque. Implied that if I didn't step down as press secretary, I'd wind up like Daryl Blue. Things like that."

"This is extraordinary," said Ms. Henrietta. "Are you the mayor's press secretary?" she wondered, after a moment's pause. "No one informed me."

Warren agreed that no one had informed him either. He picked up a kitten, currently sharpening its claws on his pajama leg, and gave it *the look*.

"So you have assumed that role?" asked Ms. Henrietta.

She was still concerned about the assassin in town, but sometimes it's hard to take the human-resources manager out of the troubled constituent.

"It depends who you ask," answered Warren, "and when you ask it."

Henrietta Bragg could well understand this, having worked among politicians for the better part of thirty years. "But why would anyone object to you acting for Mr. Abbott in this capacity?"

"There you have me. But it won't be for long. I have other fish to fry," said Warren Kingsley, who typically had plenty of fillets in the batter.

Henrietta's mind was boggling. "You are certain the man who called you is the same man who hired the assassin? You are sure it was a man?"

"It sounded like a man," Warren replied. Actually, it sounded like a man he had met recently. He couldn't place where. "Is it important that he's not a man?" he asked.

Henrietta said no—it wasn't that. "You should really speak to the sheriff about this," she concluded.

The thought had not occurred to Warren. Having worked so long in the private sector of personal security, he never considered involving official channels. So much red tape. "I suppose I could run it by her," he said. He returned the kitten to the turf and glanced at his watch. "She's probably gone to bed by now, wouldn't you say?"

Ms. Henrietta would not. If she were any judge, the sheriff was out scouring the township as they spoke. As far as Henrietta Bragg was concerned, the Kilobyte police never slept.

"I'll leave her to her scouring, then," Warren remarked, yawning. "My stuff can wait until morning."

Henrietta gave him another disapproving frown. "You mustn't be so glib about this *tool*, as you call him, Mr. Kingsley. I believe he is a greater adversary than you give him credit for."

"Oh yes?" asked Warren glibly. "You act like you know him?"

Henrietta looked around. A cage of brown rabbits flared their nostrils in her direction, lending their support. She thought about the description of the assailant yesterday, how he had vanished from the scene, and that (coupled with the supportive bunny noses) decided her.

"I believe I might," she said.

"No kidding?"

Henrietta Bragg never kidded about knowing assassins. "They had a name for him around here once," she declared, in a far-off voice.

Warren was glad. Having a name as a hitman was essential—especially when you got around to sending your bill. "What was his name?"

"It was more of a pseudonym, really."

"What was his pseudonym?"

"Soparla."

Warren was impressed. "Like the deep-fried pastry?"

"Not *sopapilla*, Mr. Kingsley. Soparla. It means *the reptile*."

"Italian?"

"Romanian."

That was Warren's next guess. "Why Romanian?"

"No one knows for sure. There have always been Romanian families in Kilobyte; the Soparla handle almost certainly originated with them."

"Makes sense."

"He was a force of nature, people used to say, cold blooded and impossible to pin down. Some claimed he was not entirely human. He was part beast."

It seemed to Warren that, with a nickname like that, he was more likely part Bulgarian, but he didn't like to argue. "When was this?"

"About ten years ago. During Mayor Crenshaw's term. Several members of his staff met with unfortunate accidents. Corruption was rampant at the time, and many people looked on these 'accidents' as a sort of housecleaning. One staff member was found with his skull crushed, as though by a giant prehistoric monster."

Warren agreed that was, indeed, an unfortunate accident to happen.

"The authorities explained it away on the pretense of a construction crane coming loose, but most of the locals didn't buy it. After that, the mayor stepped down," explained Henrietta blandly.

With his staff all smushed, Warren could see no other option. The mayor angle struck him as significant, though. Two staffs targeted in one decade. Every politician had demons, he supposed, and apparently in Kilobyte they had giant lizard demons.

"I wouldn't have expected you to subscribe to such tall tales," he said, peering across at the eminently pragmatic HR madam. "Vengeful lizard-men and all that."

Normally she would not have. If she hadn't witnessed Soparla with her own eyes, that is.

"No joke?" asked Warren.

Ms. Henrietta never joked about witnessing legends. "And he was not a lizard-man. His so-called transmogrification was simply part of a foolish myth. The man himself exists, however. I saw him fleeing the scene after one of the 'accidents.' I am not the only one to have seen him. Just ask Hank Busby."

Before Warren could ask—or would have asked, had Buzz been there to answer—another sound crept in on their conversation.

A click of the latch, and they were alone no longer. (If you can ever be truly alone with two dozen small animals dashing in circles and sniffing each other.)

They were joined by an ethereal young woman in a white nightshirt and bunny slippers. If this was the kind of creature that lurked in the Kilobyte night, Warren was all for it.

"Pardon, Ms. Henrietta, are you in there?" she asked.

Ms. Henrietta said she was in there, and the young woman came fully inside the barn.

"Aha, Mr. Kingsley, you are here too?"

Warren Kingsley found it difficult to speak. He waved a ferret at the newcomer in a friendly manner and said nothing.

She turned to her other neighbor. "I am not disturbing anything, am I?"

Henrietta Bragg said of course she wasn't disturbing anything. "What are you doing out this late, Maria?"

Maria Stengel hesitated to answer. She had medium-length brown hair, the color of a freshly laid hen's egg—or so the poetically inclined Warren would have described it. She had bright blue eyes, a mischievous mouth and high cheekbones. She had little need for makeup and seldom wore any, day or night. "I am sorry, but I seem to have misplaced two of my girls."

"Misplaced two of your girls!" Once again, Ms. Henrietta was shocked.

"I am sure it is nothing. They often sneak out on balmy nights to play with the animals."

"They often…" Henrietta's astonishment had reached new heights.

"You have not seen them?"

Henrietta Bragg's next response—a cold and emphatic *certainly not*—was usurped by a crash in the back of the barn.

A moment later, a small, blonde, sprite-like child, in one-piece purple PJs, emerged from behind a pile of crates. She had a tiny, round face, intense, beady features, and a well-worn teddy bear in her right hand. In tow was a smaller, slightly blonder child of almost identical aspect. It was as if she were being tailed by a perfectly shrunken, mirror image of herself.

Observing the packed house, Gladys—for it was Warren's little friend and popular critic who now crossed the stage—played to her audience. "Grr!" she said, scrunching up her face and hands in a convincing imitation of a tiny lizard-girl.

"Grr," spoke up her sister Millie. (Despite frequent script readthroughs, she somehow managed to come in late on her cue.)

"Over here, now!" said their mother, and over they came.

Warren saw Maria had given them a variation of *the look*. She did it well.

"I'm sorry you were troubled," she said to Henrietta, who sniffed haughtily. (The latter did not care for biped children.) "What do you think you were doing?" Maria asked the older of the two girls. "How did you get inside here?"

Gladys stepped out of character long enough to explain that they had climbed in under a loose plank in the back of the barn. It was a very tiny opening, she explained, but they were very tiny animals and very fierce too. "Grr!" said the duo, in stereo.

"You need to say you are sorry for disturbing Ms. Henrietta."

"Grr!" said the girls to Ms. Henrietta.

Ms. Henrietta snorted.

"I'm the Soparla!" Gladys announced to her mother. "Grr! Grr!" she said, crawling around on all fours, pushing her bear's face into the dust. She had one good tagline, and she intended to get all she could out of it. "Grr, I'm the Soparla," she said again. "Grr! I eat bugs! Grr!" (Asked about this later on, Gladys admitted to adlibbing the bug line. She came up with it off the cuff and simply went with it.)

Millie did not participate in a supporting role this time. Goggling intently, she clutched at her mother's leg and watched, as one in the presence of a master of her craft.

Maria appeared more astonished than her daughter. *"Soparla,"* she whispered meaningfully.

It seemed to Warren that her pronunciation was more spot-on than Ms. Henrietta's had been. There was a rolling of the *r* and a pleasing ethnicity he had not heard before. Warren had a good ear for accents and generally assumed most came from Bulgaria.

Maria's did not. Although the average man on the street would have guessed Italian or Spanish—or, if not so average, Bulgarian— Maria, in fact, hailed from Romania, born and bred. Warren might have found this suggestive, had he known.

"You look like you've seen a ghost," he said, finally finding some words.

Maria turned, startled. "No. No, I am fine." She was herself again. "Do I understand correctly that you were once a bodyguard, Mr. Kingsley?"

Warren sniffed modestly. Bodyguard, orator, pet whisperer. He liked to dabble.

Maria beamed at him. "With Lance working so much, it's a relief having such a capable man living next door."

Warren made another vague gesture. For a client like Maria, he said, he could even see taking a bullet. Provided that it was a small caliber and didn't graze anything too vital.

Maria knew how to respond to levity—even when the person delivering that levity wasn't trying to be funny. She smiled warmly and tapped his arm in a swift, generous motion. It made Warren feel warm and brave.

"Can we get you a cup of cocoa?" he asked. He was sure Ms. Henrietta could put something on.

With a melancholy smile and a tiny tilt of the head, Maria was forced to decline. Lance would be home soon, she said, and she should really be getting her girls back to bed.

"Sorry you were troubled," she told Henrietta.

"You already said that," the other woman sneered. Gracious to the last, that was Ms. Henrietta Bragg.

Maria said it once more anyway, smiled absently and went to leave. She nearly collided with her husband on her way out. "Lance!"

The deputy's name was nearly drowned out by the squealing of his girls, flinging themselves into his arms. Lifting them off the ground, he kissed them both and gave everyone else a bright smile. He wasn't sure why they were all out in Henrietta Bragg's barn, but he didn't feel it was any of his business to ask.

"You okay?" he asked his wife. "You said something about Gladys on the phone…"

Maria was quick to respond that everything was fine now. Just high-spiritedness.

Lance said good, good. He turned to Warren. "Oh, hey there, buddy. Didn't see you there. How's it hangin'?"

Warren assured him that it was hangin' fine and reciprocated with a kindly inquiry of his own.

Lance answered that it was hangin' good, good. "Oh, you might be interested in this," he said. "I just got a call from the station. We've nabbed the mayor's would-be assassin."

Warren nodded dully. His world was cold and empty now, and he had little interest in would-be assassins, however nabbed they might be.

"They got him?" asked Maria.

"That's what the sheriff said. Unfortunately, that means I gotta run back out again."

"But you just arrived home!"

"I know, I know, but they need me."

"Squeak! I'm a monkey!" said Gladys, crawling up on her father's shaved head. She was still working through the character and had yet to explore all its nuances.

"I shouldn't be too long," the climbing post told his wife. He turned to his daughters wriggling about in his grip. "Say good night to Warren and Ms. Henrietta, girls."

The girls said good night to Warren Kingsley and Ms. Henrietta. Gladys even went so far as to poke her sister in the leg and say, "That's my friend Warren. He doesn't have a wife."

Millie gasped in horror.

The Stengels departed soon after, monkeys in hand, leaving Henrietta to bring down the curtain on their conference with one final snort. "Fancy that! Misplacing your own children!"

Warren Kingsley wasn't listening. He was thinking about monkeys, the one representative from the animal kingdom lacking in Ms. Henrietta's barn.

"And blaming it on high-spiritedness," sniffed the other. "It wasn't like that in my day. That Maria woman has no clue."

Warren couldn't agree more. "She's lovely, isn't she?" he replied, and left to salvage the last few of his nine hours.

On his way across the lawn, he seemed to recall the deputy-husband, Lance, saying something about assassins arrested. That was one thing off Warren's mind anyway.

7 — SPEAK UP

"**H**ello? Mr. Kingsley? Are you there?"

Mr. Kingsley was there, in spirit if not in mind. His cell phone was pressed gently against his right ear. The rest of him lay sprawled out across his economically sized mattress.

It was 6:35 a.m., hardly six hours and change since his adventures of the night before.

Despite his disturbing lack of sleep, he still had his wits about him. They were primed and ready to go.

"I never asked for the papaya," he said. "Take it away, and bring me a grapefruit juice. Two straws."

"Mr. Kingsley, this is Sheriff Blake, calling from the station. Did I wake you?"

"Too much pith," he muttered. "I won't drink it. Give it to the liz-ard-man. He'll drink anything."

"Mr. Kingsley, this is Jenny Blake. Please wake up. It's important."

Warren woke up. He scratched his head with his cell and said, "I'm awake. What can I do for you, Sheriff?"

"Sorry to disturb you on a Sunday, sir, but I need you down here ASAP."

Warren mused on the term ASAP. It was a funny term. It stood for *As Soon As Possible*, which sounded nice and congenial, but it was never spoken congenially. It was a demand.

"ASAP," he said pleasantly. "ASAP. ASAP." The letters trailed off in a congenial undertone.

The sheriff tried another tack. *"The suspect is finally talking."*

"People love to talk," agreed Warren. "What has he been saying?"

"He wants to see you. He won't say anything more until you come down here."

"Makes sense."

"So you'll come?"

"Where?"

"Down to the station."

"Why?"

"The assassin, Mr. Kingsley! The man we've been looking for. We have him in custody, and he's insisting on speaking with you."

Warren said ah. He seemed to recall hearing something about an arrest last night. A cocker spaniel or someone had told him. And he was not surprised about the call for a personal appearance. All the best assassins wanted a piece of Warren Kingsley.

"I can be there in fifteen," he said, rising from between the sheets in spectacular fashion. "Have you seen my pajama bottoms?" he asked vaguely.

Jenny Blake hung up before the conversation could become any more intimate.

* *

Returning her phone to her belt, Jenny watched as Deputy Tony leaned back in his chair and recounted his astounding detective work from the night before. It was the fourth time he had recounted it since hauling in his suspect, and the third time he had blocked access to the coffee service as he did so.

"I don't know what it was," he remarked, chewing on a toothpick from the local diner, "but I didn't like the look of him. Didn't like the look of him one iota. Caught him asking about a ticket out of town. *Out of town*," he repeated. He made this pronouncement with a sense of sinister accusation.

The sheriff nodded and snatched a cup from behind him. There was always a brief window as he emphasized the phrase *out of town*—a slight tilt forward. Jenny capitalized on it. Having poured herself out what passed for coffee, she took the steaming mug away from the mounting narrative. She needed a little alone-time.

She spent this time walking up and down the storage room, up and down the cell block, out the back door, and up and down the back alley. Having said hello to Kyle, the butcher's nephew, out emptying the garbage, she returned to the office. She paused outside the primary holding cell, the only one currently occupied.

Through the bars, she gazed in at their prisoner, lying peacefully on a plank bed.

She wasn't entirely satisfied with the man Tony had apprehended. It wouldn't be going too far to say that she was feeling some apprehension about that apprehension.

He was an urbane individual, certainly of foreign aspect. That aspect was not exactly a crime, but it was worth noting. He more or less fit the "description" given by the mayor—or *not given*, if you wanted to get technical about it. Age, fifty to fifty-five. Not tall, solidly built. Black hair, graying. Thin, black mustache, also graying. Olive hue to his skin. He was well dressed for his trip.

"You searched him?" she asked Tony. She had returned to the desk area now.

Tony had searched him.

"*And* acquainted him with his rights?"

Tony had acquainted him.

The sheriff said good. They didn't want any more eff-ups there; that much was for sure.

Tony had been correct about one thing. The man had come along quietly. Too quietly, in Jenny's opinion. He was gracious, respectful. He reminded her of an instructor at the academy, the man everyone had called "Pop." And yet that didn't encourage her any. Somehow, her prisoner's ready acquiescence to lie in a cell and wait for Warren Kingsley perturbed her. His calm exterior seemed to suggest that shortly none of this would matter.

"I'm here," said the emissary in question, arriving in the middle of her reflections.

He would have been here sooner, he explained, but he had discovered a peach pit in his garbage can this morning, and that had given him pause. Warren didn't eat peaches. A nectarine, perhaps, but never peaches. He didn't care for the skins.

The sheriff said good. About his arriving. Not the part about the peach skins. "I appreciate you coming in."

"It's not a problem, Sheriff. Even though I did have to forgo break-fast to get here so quickly."

"I'm sorry, sir."

"It's no big deal. You wouldn't happen to have any breakfast on you, would you, Sheriff?"

The sheriff did not. Albert, perking up in response to a subject he was well versed in, recommended the diner next door. Best Spanish omelet in the county. Tony seconded his recommendation and sug-gested the bear claws.

The sheriff brought the subject back around to Warren's visit. She nodded toward the holding cell and said, "I'm guessing you two will be wanting some *privacy?*" She leaned on the word *privacy* as much as her deputy had leaned on his *out of town.*

"That should not be necessary," said the man in the cage, now standing at the bars.

Warren concurred. He turned and fixed the officer in a harsh stare, one part bewilderment, the rest censure. From the iciness of its consistency, you would have thought she had been trying to foist papaya on him again, wrapped in the hides of a hundred slain peach skins.

"What have you done?" he asked.

Jenny was nonplussed. Done? Had she done anything?

"You've arrested Mahrute!"

It was not a name she had come across before. Perhaps it was Lithuanian.

"Borodin Mahrute," said Warren Kingsley. "The world-famous bodyguard."

**

"Let me get this straight," said Sheriff Jenny Blake. "This man works with you?"

They were sitting around a large, butcher-block table in the back room of the police station, the area primarily used for lunch and car-ryout dinners—but also useful for clearing up police errors and curb-ing false-arrest inquiries.

"We have in the past," Warren explained. "I texted him yester-day."

"He's your backup, then?"

"Something like that."

The sheriff nodded. For once, Warren had done something that made sense.

Again, she offered her apologies for the misunderstanding. She would have insisted on Tony offering his, only she had already sent him out on indefinite traffic duty.

Mahrute continued to embody graciousness itself. There was no inconvenience, he said. The misapprehension (in both senses of the word) had simply spared him the need to find a hotel room last night. And he should have known better than to inquire about departing buses in the presence of the deputy. Mahrute had only just arrived, but it was always helpful to know the schedule when it came time to leave again. Like Mary Poppins, Borodin Mahrute never stayed in one place long.

Jenny could see the solid little man as a badass Poppins. "Well, I'm still very chagrined about the whole thing."

"You should not be, Sheriff. It was a mistake that could happen to anyone."

The sheriff agreed with him. With deputies like hers, it could. "Can I give either of you a lift somewhere?"

Both men declined her offer. They hadn't eaten any breakfast yet, and they had a lot of catching up to do. "We figured we'd try the diner," said Warren. He had heard good things.

Jenny congratulated them on their choice. "I notice you don't have any luggage with you, Mr. Mahrute?"

The condensed bodyguard bowed his head. "I always overnight my belongings to myself whenever I'm traveling. It saves the hassle of transporting these things myself."

Jenny frowned. "That might be a problem," she said. Ever since her deputies had grilled the delivery drivers at the Abbott Building, the major carriers had canceled their regular routes in Kilobyte. "They'll come off their high horse eventually, I'm sure, but that won't help you any today."

"It's not a problem," said the 6'4" Warren, with an airy wave. He had become the gracious one now. "I'll loan you some of my duds. They're Armani mostly. You'll love them."

Mahrute gave an uncertain nod, and the three returned to the main office.

"There you are at last!" snapped Frederick Abbott. "I've been waiting for you for hours!"

The deputies might have contradicted the mayor on this point, but they had already had enough of the man's venom for one morning. Dissatisfied with their assistance, he had done everything short of knocking their heads together in frustration. And this was only because one of his arms was in a sling.

The sheriff took charge. "Can I help you with something, Mayor?"

"I was talking to him," snarled the tycoon, and pointed.

"Warren?"

"Warren Freakin' Kingsley," said Mayor Abbott.

Warren didn't mind being addressed as this. His middle name was, in truth, Horatio, so *Freakin'* was actually an improvement. "You wanted me?"

"I wanted you last night," growled the mayor.

The eyebrows of Deputy Albert and Deputy Lance arched on their respective foreheads. Albert, in particular, had suspected something of this sort from the old cuss for some time. With a wife like his, Abbott was obviously trying to overcompensate for something.

The mayor elaborated on his statement, which may have been taken out of context. Politicians like himself were forever being taken out of context. "I saw a figure on my property last night," he clarified to the sheriff.

"A figure?"

"A skulking figure, up to no good. My wife's dog chased it off."

"Was it reptilian?" asked Warren.

"Was it—what?" asked the mayor.

"Reptilian? Lizard-like?"

"Soparlo," whispered Albert, who had heard of the legend a long time back, long before he could grow a fanciful mustache.

"I thought it was 'Soparla,' " said Lance.

"*Soparlo*," argued Albert. He knew about these things. Or thought he did.

The mayor carried on without responding to the Kilobyte Kops. "I've hired you as my bodyguard, have I not?" he asked Warren.

"Technically not," said the untechnical bodyguard.

"I—well, that was my intention," uttered the mayor. Politicians like him were forever having their intentions misunderstood. "You've dedicated your life to preserving and protecting the lives of others, have you not?"

Mahrute could easily have fielded this question. The answer was "Not." He resisted fielding it, however, and the mayor swept on with his tirade.

"And yet, you were nowhere to be found when I needed you the most!" He shot the deputy with the greasy mustache a hard look. "Of course, none of that matters now," he remarked, his tone abruptly lightening. Someone poetically inclined—someone like Warren Kingsley—might have said a rainbow had formed above the storm-ravaged horizon of Mayor Abbott's rhetoric. Warren did not say this, but he could have.

The mayor continued. There was a certain complacency to his voice now. "I understand the sheriff's office has arrested the culprit. It's about time, Ms. Blake, about time."

Ms. Blake would beg to differ. "I'm afraid it isn't," she said. "We arrested the wrong man."

The mayor stared at her. The rainbow toppled over with a clang. "The wrong—you mean, the culprit is still at large? How disconcerting. This changes everything."

The sheriff could sympathize. "We can increase police protection for you, if you like?"

Abbott shook off her proposal with a hasty sneer. He didn't need to look over at Lance and Albert again to know that he didn't want any of that. "I'll hire my own protection, thank you very much."

The sheriff was happy to conform. "And on that note," she said, "Mr. Kingsley has brought in some additional help. This is Mahrute. I understand he is one of the best bodyguards in the country."

Warren awoke from his daydream. He had been trying to decide if he should order a Spanish omelet at the diner or a bear claw. He had heard good things about the bear claws. "One of the best bodyguards in *the world*," he said stiffly. "You don't find many better bodyguards than Borodin Mahrute."

Jenny accepted the correction. "One of the best in *the world*, then. Perhaps between him and Warren, Mayor, you should be able to ride out this storm—"

Warren gave her another of his censorious stares. "What are you doing, Sheriff?"

Doing? Was she doing anything? "I was only—"

"You were proffering my protection. Never volunteer another man's muscle," he said. "I brought in Mahrute for myself."

"For...*yourself?*"

"Of course. Why do you think I texted him?"

"I thought—" The sheriff didn't know what she thought. "When you said you worked together in the past..."

With regard to this question, Mahrute did feel he could field it. "I have provided personal protection for Mr. Kingsley from time to time," explained the bodyguard's bodyguard.

The sheriff faced the speaker. Personal protection *for* Mr. Kingsley. "Was this before he became a bodyguard himself?"

"No," said Mahrute simply, and quietly disappeared through the main exit. He had perimeters to secure.

The sheriff gaped at the shut door. So did the mayor. They gaped at it together.

"What are we talking about?" Abbott lamented. "Have I got a bonus bodyguard or haven't I?"

The sheriff wasn't so sure he had a single bodyguard. "Sorry, Mayor, I—misspoke."

Abbott could not abide this. One should never misspeak. It came from talking too much in the first place. Everyone talked too much. "What are we going to do now?" he asked.

Warren didn't know about the mayor, but he and Mahrute were going to try a Spanish omelet and maybe a bear claw for dessert.

As he opened the door to seek out these comestibles, Sheryl Abbott came sailing through it. She was accustomed to doors being held for her. "I need police protection," she said. "Someone is after me. I need protection, and I'm willing to pay for it." Sometimes she was very much like her husband.

And much like her husband, she was destined to be disappointed. The only bodyguards in town were on their way to try a Spanish omelet.

And possibly a bear claw.

* *

David Wincher sat in his tiny apartment and stared.

He was staring at a small cell phone. A burner phone, they were sometimes called. He was fairly certain that was the term. He had been staring at it for hours.

He wondered why he had ever started this. An ego trip? David Wincher seldom took trips, of the ego variety or any other kind. Corporate never sent you anywhere. Why, then? Why couldn't he have just left well enough alone?

He picked up the phone—why not; it was what started this mess—and dialed a number.

It was about time he put an end to things.

* *

The sheriff gazed across at her new station guest. The two women were back at the butcher-block table in the storage room, but this time, unless Jenny was off base, she had the upper hand. "What's all this about protection, Sheryl?"

Mrs. Abbott sighed. They were alone. The mayor had been asked to give them a moment.

Always the adoring husband, he had tried his best to placate Sheryl first. "If this is about the figure we saw on our property last night," he said, "I can assure you—"

It wasn't about the figure. It was just girl talk, she explained, and the mayor had nodded his ready assent. He understood the need for a female to commune with other females. You don't have half a dozen wives without picking up some insights.

And so here they were. Two girls—not really talking.

"Are you ready to discuss Daryl Blue?" the sheriff began.

Sheryl scowled. Not everything was about Daryl, she grumbled.

"What, then?"

"It's about—Javy Clark. That's when it really started anyway."

Jenny wasn't certain what she'd expected from this sit-down, but this wasn't it. She threw her mind back. Javy Clark. Javy Clark. "You mean, the ballplayer?"

Sheryl nodded.

Jenny remembered him now. Javy, the local hero. Appeared in town one afternoon and immediately took the Kilobyte K's by storm. Hardly on the team a week before he was picked up by a major league club. Left for fame and fortune, only to vanish a few weeks into the season. No one had seen him since. Pressure got to be too much for him. That was the popular opinion.

"What does Javier Clark have to do with anything?" the sheriff asked.

"I—knew him. Before he joined the K's. We were—well—sort of *buddies*."

Jenny Blake bet they were. Sheryl Abbott was buddies with all the handsome young men in town. Buddies with every inch of them. "So you knew him? So what?"

"He was—one of them."

"One of who?"

"You wouldn't understand."

Sheryl was correct. She didn't understand. Mostly because the woman hadn't told her a damn thing. "If you know something, Sheryl…"

Sheryl knew more than Jenny could ever imagine. She shook her head dolefully. She was running the full gamut of petulant facial gestures. "He didn't just *run off*, you know. Clarkie didn't."

"No?"

"No. They—took him."

"Who took him, Sheryl? Took him how?"

Sheryl ran her heavily polished fingers along the butcher block. "There's this group—only, they're not really a group. They're more of a, well—society." She paused. "They're highly skilled. Highly secretive. Out of Europe or somewhere. If you want things—*done*—"

"Yes?"

Sheryl had ceased communing. In her mind, she was replaying a tête-à-tête from the evening before. The tête-à-tête that had brought her to the station this morning in such a frenzy.

"You've been very naughty, haven't you, luv?" the despicable little man had said to her, in that cloying drawl of his. *"Very naughty indeed."* Oh, how she hated seeing him again! The Society's tiny enforcer.

It was all her fault. She had started this. If only she had left well enough alone—

In a flash, she lifted from her reverie. All at once, she seemed to realize who she was talking to and who she had almost confided in.

"Sheryl?" asked the sheriff. But the mayor's wife had clammed up.

"Excuse me for interrupting," interrupted Deputy Lance.

The sheriff took him aside. She wasn't annoyed. The Lance-Albert-Tony trio wouldn't be her deputies if one of them didn't interfere in an essential meeting at some point. "What is it, Lance?"

"The mayor wanted his wife to know he's walking over to his office."

"Excellent." She would let the missus know.

"Also, I just took a—call—"

Jenny was getting a little tired of everyone speaking in dashes. "Yes?"

"It's from David Wincher."

The sheriff had not forgotten about David Wincher. In fact, they had been trying to get in touch with the corporate dynamo since Telly's tip last night. For a small town, it was getting increasingly difficult to track anyone down. "Tell him I want to talk to him."

"He already hung up."

"Awesome."

"Before he did, he asked us to come by his place later. He has some information for us and—"

"Yes?"

"He wants to make a sort of confession."

The sheriff was dumbfounded. Two sort-of confessions in one hour. Before now, she wouldn't have known what a sort-of confession was. Now she knew all too well.

She turned to see how Sheryl Abbott, the first almost-confessor, had taken this, but Sheryl hadn't taken it in the slightest.

Sheryl Abbott had vanished. Just like her "buddy" Javier Clark.

8 — TALK SOFTLY

When a town has a futuristic name like *Kilobyte*, one expects to find a certain amount of space-age innovation at work. A dash of high tech. Warren Kingsley had expected these things. And so far, he had been disappointed.

There were no automated sidewalks and no flying automobiles. There was not a single android manservant. He was beginning to think that the place had a lot of nerve calling itself Kilobyte. The name was wasted on it.

That all changed when he and Mahrute arrived at the town diner. The Kilobyte Diner was innovative. The lines of its decor were sharp and clean. There was a good deal of metal around the room (mostly brushed titanium, like Fred Abbott's business-card case), plastic dividers (made to look like carbon fiber) and floors fashioned from reclaimed wood—because reclaimed wood was so much better for the environment than standard wood (and because Abbott's former timber firm couldn't provide enough new hardwood at a decent wholesale price). Its edgy style was not the only thing that helped transform the Kilobyte Diner into a sci-fi utopia. It had *tech-nol-o-gy*.

One such component Warren and Mahrute experienced immediately after taking their seats. A small, carbon fiber–esque box, which took most major credit cards, greeted them as they sat. It welcomed them to the Kilobyte Diner, a division of Frederick Abbott Enterprises and the newly formed conglomerate Ab-Eat-Co, and went on to ask if they wished to hear a '50s rock song, have their fortunes told or order an appetizer. Warren and Mahrute wished for none of these things, so the box suggested they tap the button on its main screen and a server would be right with them. Warren tapped, and a heavyset woman in faux silver foil was right with them, a short eight and a half minutes later.

"Welcome to the Kilobyte Diner," she sighed. "What can I get ya?"

Warren was more interested in the method of her manifestation than any food she might bring. "I haven't come across anything like this before," he said, pointing at the box.

"No?"

"No. How does it work? Is there an elaborate wall of buzzers and light-emitting diodes in the back, signaling you to the table—*Downton Abbey* meets *Buck Rogers*—or do you have some kind of implant, one that administers a slight electrical shock when you're needed?"

The waitress stared at him. "Do you see that red bulb there on top of the machine?" she asked. Warren saw the red bulb. "When you press that button, the bulb turns on. I see the bulb, and I come over."

Warren was blown away by its simplicity. What would these innovators think of next?

"Now what will you have?" she asked him again.

But her customer was too busy marveling at scientific breakthroughs in the restaurant industry to choose a meal. He sent her away with another of his airy waves and peered down at the menu in his other hand, specifically the section entitled, "Breakfast Meats (pick only one, please)."

After a couple of minutes, he set this tablet precursor aside and addressed the associate at the table not made of fake carbon fiber. "Good of you to come, Mahrute."

"My pleasure."

"Although, you could answer a guy's text, you know. I lay awake all night last night, wondering if I was going to be stood up or not. Perhaps you're the one who needs an implant."

Mahrute was distressed to hear this. "I'm sorry for the inconvenience. Shortly after I received your text, I was liberated of my satphone."

"Oh yeah? Who liberated you of it?"

"Several drug runners operating in the village I had pledged to protect."

Warren nodded. So he was protecting whole villages now? Same old Mahrute.

"Get it all worked out?"

"I believe so."

"Excellent." Warren paused, frowning. "I assume this village had a pay phone," he said, as their waitress returned with another purposeful stare.

Warren placed an order for turkey sausage and turkey bacon to go with his Spanish omelet (it was only one "building block" of meat), and the silver server flounced off again. "You're probably wondering why I sent for you?" he asked Mahrute.

Mahrute did confess to a certain curiosity.

"I mean, I've been working pretty well on my own, you know," said the processed-turkey lover.

"I am sure of it. How is Sir Roger, if I may ask?"

As far as Warren was concerned, Mahrute mayn't. He did not wish to discuss previous clients, the most previous one especially. He had come to Kilobyte to forget.

"This has nothing to do with my last job," he said.

"No. No, of course not."

"I am no longer in Sir Roger Banbury's employ."

Mahrute had assumed as much. "He is well? Sir Roger?"

Warren replied that this had nothing to do with Sir Roger's wellness. Sir Roger was in the past, and they had other flounders to sauté now. "We have things to go over, Mahrute, and not much time to go over them. How much do you know about Romanian lizard-men?"

"Pardon?"

"But I'm jumping too far ahead. Or rather too far back, since the reptile-man technically appeared on the scene before I arrived. How about this? I'll tell you what I know."

Mahrute could think of nothing better.

Without further ado, Warren related the facts of the attempt on the mayor's life, the death of Daryl Blue, the call Warren received yesterday morning and finally Henrietta Bragg's campfire fables from the night before. He was remarkably detailed and thorough in his recounting, if not a tad unorthodox. Warren had better-than-average powers of observation and a good memory (when he chose). Some great thinkers have what is known as a "mind palace." Warren Kingsley had a mind funhouse.

"And so that brings us to the Soparla," he said. "Our opponent in this death match. We've had a few doozies in our time, haven't we, Mahrute?"

Mahrute agreed that there had been a few, yes. "I'm not certain how well I can protect against a *lizard beast*, though," he said, with some hesitation.

Warren scowled at him. "Don't be stupid, Mahrute. There is no lizard beast."

"No?"

"No," said Warren. He was fairly certain there wasn't. "That's just a local Romanian legend, such as you'll get in any small provincial town—with Romanians in it. No, Soparla is a myth. What is not a myth is the would-be assassin. We have a killer at large. And someone is guiding that killer. That's why I called you in. Kilobyte needs you. When little Gladys Stengel goes to bed at night, I want her dreams to be free of murderers roaming the Kilobytean countryside. And the same goes for her mother—who is a peach, by the way. Have I told you about Maria Stengel, Mahrute, my peachy neighbor?"

Oddly enough, in the twenty minutes since their reunion began, Warren had not told Mahrute about Maria.

He told him now. He discussed Maria, her loveliness and her little daughter's capacity for wounding aging bachelors who have not yet chosen to settle down.

"They were both out and about last night," he wrapped up, having emphasized Maria's penchant for touching your arm when she spoke and Warren's wholehearted approval of this gesture. (Maria's husband, Lance, was mentioned in passing, but without the same enthusiasm.) "When the name Soparla came up, you should have seen the look of horror on Maria's face. I think she's pretty worked up about this business. The whole town is. That's where we come in."

Mahrute understood. And he approved. In the past, Warren might have requested Mahrute's services for a more singular reason. The Warren Kingsley he had known then had changed. Warren was concerned not just for himself now, but the whole town. Give him a few years, and he would be defending villages against legions of drug traffickers without a second thought.

On the other hand, Mahrute tried not to dwell too much on the Stengel-family aspect of Warren's newfound nobility. If he were to dive down the rabbit hole of the younger man's psyche, he would have concluded that tiny Gladys's comments about marriage had touched a nerve in his associate's subconscious. A four-year-old mentality would seem about right for that. Which was not to say Mr. Kingsley was incapable of more complex thought. Mahrute had frequently been amazed by some intellectual one eighty from the man. (As for Gladys's mother, Maria, "the toucher," all Mahrute could think was, it wouldn't be the first time Warren had fallen for a woman who was already attached.)

"I'm delighted to be of service," he said. "You can rest assured that I will do everything in my power to keep the town safe."

Warren looked perplexed. "The town? I don't follow you, Mahrute."

"You…you wish to guard the town from this assassin, do you not? Perhaps bring in more men, set up a buffer against the menace?"

Warren appeared blank.

"Maria Stengel and little Gladys…" Mahrute prompted.

"Oh, that," said Warren, finally catching the gist. He shook his head. "Little Gladys can take care of herself. She has four sisters, not to mention a policeman father. No, she's fine. When I said the town needs you, I meant it needs you to look after me."

Now it was Mahrute who did not follow. "Look after *you?*"

"Look after me, Mahrute. As my bodyguard. Nothing has changed there. You heard what I said about the threatening phone call. Somebody has it in for me. If I continue on this path, they will do something about it. You're here to make sure they don't."

"And the town?"

Mahrute half expected Warren to reply the hell with the town.

Instead, his response was even more baffling. "That's my job," he replied. "Or it will be, if all goes according to plan. Didn't I mention my plan? Ah. Well, I probably should have led with that. I'm thinking of running for mayor, Mahrute. Lord knows Abbott isn't up to it. When I was delivering that speech for him yesterday, it dawned on me that I could go into this line myself. For myself. And that's what

I intend to do, assuming the town bylaws allow for it. So that's that. I'm running for mayor, and you're here to protect that position. Mayors need protection."

A man in Borodin Mahrute's line of work is not easily flummoxed, especially a man who has had the character-building experience of working with Warren Kingsley in that line. But this announcement flummoxed him. It was all he could do to eat a portion of his egg-white frittata when it arrived—and when their bill followed, pay it.

* *

Unaware of the political machinations going on in her backyard— and how these machinations might someday lead to her addressing Warren Kingsley as "Mayor of Kilobyte"—Sheriff Blake and her deputy Lance turned the corner at Chesterfield and Sixth, only to pause in their stride as they approached Fifth Avenue.

A crowd had begun to form in the alley alongside David Wincher's apartment building. Jenny wondered if it could have anything to do with the call they'd received. She didn't think so. Wincher's call had caused a stir at the station, it was true, but surely that wouldn't have reached the public's ears this quickly. It had to be something else.

"There's Tony," Lance pointed. "Maybe he knows something."

The sheriff nodded him over and asked. "What's going on, Deputy?"

Tony's plain-to-average handsomeness was clearly ruffled by the commotion. Too many brouhahas in Kilobyte, that was his opinion, or would have been if he used words like *brouhaha*.

"I don't know, Sheriff. Apparently, someone spotted something in the alley. A mob began to gather, and now we have half the town here. I've been trying to get some answers, but no dice. Looks like the desk attendant from the building is playing crowd control—they say he used to be a nightclub bouncer. I haven't been able to break through to ask him what's going on."

Jenny knew her duty. She turned to plunge into the throng, first sending Tony and Lance up to Wincher's apartment. She didn't want this hullabaloo spooking their corporate confessor before he could speak.

The elevator was out of order, so the deputies took to the stairs.

"Wincher called us?" asked Tony, as they rounded level one.

"Yup," said Lance. "Apparently, he's ready to spill the beans."

"You're kidding. I miss everything."

"Not everything. You had your big bad arrest yesterday. That was all you."

"Don't remind me," said Tony, pausing for a rest after the third flight.

There was an informal rivalry between the two men, and neither could stand one getting a leg up on the other. Lance had always been more athletic than Tony—Tony could accept that—but dwelling on last night's false arrest, that wasn't cool.

"I made a mistake, okay? Don't rub it in."

Lance didn't mean to bring up a sore subject. "Say, how was traffic duty?" he asked cheerfully.

"Shut up," said Tony, bounding up the stairs past him. He exited onto the fourth floor.

They found the door of David Wincher's apartment slightly ajar. Despite constant instances of this sort of thing in film and television, neither deputy seemed perturbed. They proceeded inside and called out their invisible host's name.

Receiving no reply, they shook their heads, glanced around the room and sighed (Tony sighed; Lance whistled). "Must have stepped out," said Lance.

"Or he's in the bathroom," suggested Tony. "I guess we wait." They continued their conversation. "I wonder if this Wincher knows something about the attempt on the mayor."

"Maybe corporate can point us in the direction of Soparla," chuckled Lance.

Tony looked confused by the reference.

His friend quickly brought him up to speed on the local mythology resurgence. Tony sighed again and said he missed everything (again). "So Warren Kingsley was talking about this?"

"Not directly. He made some quip about the mayor being stalked at his house, and Bert butted in and said it was Soparla. Only he pronounced it *Soparlo*."

Tony shook his head and said Albert was a dunce. Lance didn't argue. No matter how many legs up they might get on each other, they could always agree on the dunderheadedness of their mustached coworker.

"I'm not saying I believe in these superstitions myself," Lance qualified.

Tony didn't believe in them either. A creaking noise broke the silence, and he jumped a foot in place. "Of course, theoretically speaking, it could explain how the guy shinnied down the Abbott Building so easily."

"Are lizard-men known for shinnying?" asked Lance.

"They're bound to," argued Tony. "But whether he's supernatural or not, this guy is out there somewhere, and I wonder if the mayor has taken the necessary precautions."

"How do you mean?"

"Think about it. The assassin has to be steaming. Professional pride and all that. He'll be bringing everything he's got now. One part-time bodyguard might not be enough."

Lance supposed Tony had a point. "Abbott *did* bash him with a bust," he said. That would wound the feelings of any sensitive hitman.

"Bust?" asked Tony.

"The Henry Ford."

"Oh right." Tony remembered it now. He was the one who had tagged and bagged it. "Henry Ford? Is that like Indiana Jones?"

Lance rubbed his shaved head. No, he said, it was not like Indiana Jones.

Tony didn't see why not. "You realize 'Indiana' wasn't his real name, right?"

Lance stared and rubbed while Tony continued to explain. "It was 'Henry.' Remember, in the third movie Sean Connery was Henry Sr., so that would make Indy Henry Jr."

"So what?"

"So, *Henry* plus *Ford*, makes *Henry Ford*."

Lance made a gesture of exasperation. "You're mixing together 'Harrison Ford' and 'Henry Jones,' dumbass!"

"Henry Jones *Jr.*," Tony corrected. He brooded on the name. "You know they were going to call it *Indiana Smith* originally? Don't think I would have cared for that."

Lance wouldn't have cared for it either, no more than he cared for *Indiana Ford and the Last Five Minutes*. He would never get them back again. "Anyway, just so you know, Henry Ford was a famous industrialist."

"Oh yeah?" Tony agreed that you learned something new every day. "Was this before or after he went into acting?"

Lance's response—whatever this might have been—never got off the factory floor. Another noise from the back of the apartment, more of a squeak than a creak, brought him around with a start. "Mr. Wincher? Is that you?" Still no answer. He gave Tony a look, and the other man nodded in comprehension as they moved off to investigate.

They arrived at a bedroom off the living room. There was nothing special to see, but even still, both men drew their guns.

"Lance, Tony, where the hell are you?" It was the voice of the sheriff, calling to them from the front door.

They rejoined her in the living room. "Wincher isn't here, Sheriff," said Lance, reholstering his gun. "Have you seen him?"

As a matter of fact, the sheriff had. "He's down on the pavement," she muttered.

"Down on the pavement?" It was Tony who asked this, and for once, it was not a stupid question. "What's he doing down on the pavement?"

"Not a whole helluva lot," said Jenny. "It looks like he fell off the balcony. Or jumped. Or he was *shoved*. That's what the nosy crowd was gathered around. His body."

Made sense to Tony. If he were a nosy crowd, he probably would have gathered around it too.

* *

"Hey, bud, how you doin'?"

The voice of Telly Blake arrested Warren Kingsley as he departed the Kilobyte Diner with Mahrute. It was the second unjust arrest Warren had seen that day.

"I've been looking everywhere for you," said the intern, joining them in their constitutional. "You don't want to go that way," he said.

"Chesterfield is mobbed. Some kind of accident. Come this way. I'll show you a shortcut."

Warren and Mahrute reluctantly followed.

"Who's your friend?" asked Telly.

Warren made the introductions. "Borodin Mahrute, Telly...*Something.*"

Telly Blake said it was a pleasure. Mahrute assured him that sentiment was all Mahrute's.

" 'Mahrute,' " repeated Telly. "Cool name. Wait." He paused along his shortcut. "That sounds kind of foreign. You're not the assassin, are you?"

Mahrute said he was not the assassin.

"That's too bad." Telly was hoping somebody would be.

"He's my bodyguard," said Warren, his words naked and unashamed.

Telly didn't appear taken aback in the slightest. "The bodyguard's bodyguard. Cool. Hey, you know what? As part of my training, I could guard Mahrute, and then I would be the bodyguard's bodyguard's bodyguard. How cool is that?"

"Training?" Mahrute asked Warren, and the latter said, "Long story."

They turned onto Third Avenue, where Telly had parked his truck. "Say, guess what?" he asked.

Neither Warren nor Mahrute had any inclination to guess.

"I think I may have tracked down Hank Busby."

Neither Warren nor Mahrute had any inclination to care.

Telly looked discouraged. He thought bodyguards were all about leaving no stone unturned. Or was that geologists? "Don't you get it? We could question him before my sister gets there. Get the real skinny on the investigation. She's off somewhere sheriffing right now, so we would have Hank all to ourselves."

"And why would we want him?" asked Warren.

Telly frowned. "I know—I don't think he has anything to do with the murder either. Not old Hank. But he might have some useful information for our investigation. We should talk with him."

"Yes, but why?"

Mahrute cleared his throat. "Perhaps he has a point. Unless I have misinterpreted the campaign posters displayed around town, Mr.

Busby would be—*ahem*—one of your opponents in the upcoming election. Perhaps it would benefit us to check out the competition."

Warren considered this. "Size him up, you mean?"

"Indeed."

Now this was an idea Warren could get on board with.

"Opponent?" asked Telly. "Election?"

"Long story," said Mahrute, and Telly nodded shrewdly. He knew all about long stories.

"This is my ride," he announced. "Pile in."

**

The desk attendant from David Wincher's apartment building, who, along with being an ex-nightclub employee, had also once worked as a physical therapist and chiropractor, had done all he could do.

"He's had it," said the bouncer MD, and cleared the way for the deputies. Sheriff Blake was a few feet away, questioning possible witnesses to the fall.

Lance, always upbeat, said the guy didn't look all that bad for a four-story plummet. Tony, reserving judgment, couldn't really say. He hadn't seen Wincher before he landed.

Like their predecessor, they tried to do what they could.

"So, what happened there, fella?" asked Tony brightly.

His colleague nudged him. This wasn't a fender-bender, so he shouldn't talk like it was. Perhaps the other man's future did lie in traffic duty. Lance assumed a more solemn tone. "Can you speak, Mr. Wincher?"

Mr. Wincher could speak. Barely. *"Bal-con-y,"* he quavered.

Lance nodded. "Yes, you've had a nasty fall off your balcony. Help is on the way. Maybe you can tell us what happened? Did anyone push you?"

"Or were you just depressed?" interposed Tony. Lance gave him another elbow.

"Bal-con-y," insisted David Wincher. "Saw...on...balcony."

"Who was on the balcony with you?" asked Lance.

"And did he seem *shovey* to you?" wondered Tony.

"Knew..." said Wincher. He shook his head, adjusting his verbal tense. "Should have known better..." He settled back against the pavement in a pool of blood.

"He's done," said Tony. "I guess we'll never know what he knew. These corporate types—you never can get a straight answer from them."

Just as he said this, the corporate type sprang to life again.

He was determined to unburden himself. As Warren liked to say, people love to talk, even with their dying breath. He seized the deputies by both shirts, which was too bad, because blood doesn't come out of beige. He spoke almost clearly now. "Do you know," he whispered, "what you do all day...when you're from corporate?"

Lance and Tony shook their heads.

"Me neither," said David Wincher.

And then he was dead. Really.

9 — And Carry a Large Bat

A short distance away, a man prowled the rooftops of Kilobyte. He was a nervous and frustrated man, as only a proud assassin with not one but *two* failed hits under his belt could be. He had a knot on his head—in the imprint of Henry Ford, not Indiana Jones—as well as a wonky knee, courtesy of Sheryl Abbott's dog, Butterscotch. (Going over the mayor's fence in haste, his foot had landed funny on a rock coming down, and that had produced the aforementioned wonkiness. It's always the little things that do you in.)

It was the man's own fault. He never should have tried to assail his target another time without first scouting the terrain. You must always scout. Fail to do so, and you only end up coming face-to-face with angry dogs. The man with the knot and the knee did not care for dogs.

There might be some in Kilobyte who believed him to be Soparla, the ruthless lizard, but that didn't make him any friend of the animal kingdom. This was especially true when that canine representative was endeavoring to chew him in some private area, and chew him good.

Shivering as he thought of this, the man gazed down from his rooftop perch. He had a bead on his prey now. Ten minutes before, the mayor had departed the sheriff's department and proceeded to walk down Chesterfield toward his office. The man on the roof had tracked him with a reptilian determination. He was using the scope on his rifle, which not many reptiles do, but the determination was still reptilian. He was also eating his second peach of the morning, which one might suppose some reptiles eat, but not as much as they eat bugs. (The man did not care for bugs any more than he did dogs.)

He was waiting to make his move. Chesterfield and Sixth. That was the perfect spot.

He peered through the scope again and gasped. The mayor had never made it to Sixth Avenue. He had been engulfed by a large, disorderly mob. The man knew nothing about this mob, and he didn't like it. He could never pick out his target from this multitude. Not with any precision, and the man now choking on his peach was all about precision. He had been hired for one hit, not several. He was strongly opposed to giving freebies.

With a final dejected cough, he began packing up his rifle and scope.

He would have to resort to Plan D now. The man did not care for Plan D. It did have one thing going for it: he had scouted it.

But it was not precise.

* *

"You're probably wondering how I found Hank," said Telly, as he, Warren and Mahrute raced along the country road toward their destination.

In fact, Warren and Mahrute were not wondering this. They were far more concerned with the intern's driving and not sailing out of his pickup truck on one of his sharper turns. (Mahrute was particularly mindful of this, having drawn the cargo area for the journey.)

"Not many people know this," Telly proceeded. "But Hank loves to hunt. When not scouting ball clubs or running for mayor against the boss, he's happiest at his hunting cabin. I know where that cabin is. Not many people do," he said, bookending his remarks neatly.

Warren gave a distracted nod from the passenger seat. "Relative of yours?" he asked.

"Not technically," said Telly, shouting to be heard over the bumps and rumbles of their route. "He knew my mother, and when she took off with Sheryl Abbott's father, Hank looked in on us every once in a while. My father didn't seem to mind, seeing that he was hardly ever home himself. I guess you could call Hank an honorary uncle."

"Isn't that what the mayor is?" Warren asked. "An uncle?"

"The boss? Nah, we're not technically related either. My Aunt Clarisse is the boss's sister. She married my mother's brother, so that would make the boss, well, nothing really."

This disappointed Warren. He was planning on using Telly's family genes in his campaign speech against Fred Abbott. "But you *are* related to your sister?" he said.

Telly agreed he was. She was his sister. "Anyway, I think you'll like Hank. He's a little odd, and takes some getting used to, but he's a good egg all in all—and was an even better ballplayer. He looks a bit like Gene Hackman in the face. The actor, not the novelist."

Warren had stopped listening after they had settled whose sister was whose, so the image of Hank Busby remained unspoiled in his mind, much like the forest now engulfing the road remained unspoiled by developers.

In the last five minutes, the woodland had become increasingly thick around them, compelling Telly to slow it down under eighty for the final leg of their expedition. "I think we're almost there," he said. "Hey, that might be him now."

A figure, short and slightly hunched over, like an aging orangutan, peered out from the clearing. He had a face like the actor Gene Hackman (not to be confused with the novelist Gene Hackman, who looked remarkably like the actor), and wore a plain gray cap, not promoting any professional franchise. He had just finished chopping firewood alongside a quaint log cabin.

"That's Hank alright," said Telly, applying the brakes. "Ready to meet the best doubles hitter in the history of Kilobyte?"

Warren was as ready as he would ever be. He hoped it wouldn't be a long meeting. If they were going to announce his candidacy this afternoon, they didn't have all day.

**

Telly took care of the introductions this time. "Warren, Mahrute—Hank Busby. Hank, this is Warren Kingsley and Mahrute, um, Mahrute."

The three men shook hands. A wry smile creased the hitting legend's already-crinkled features. "Nice, firm grip you got there. I respect a man with a good handshake."

"Thanks," replied Warren.

"I was talking to Mahrute Mahrute," said Hank, and the smaller man acknowledged the compliment with another of his trademark bows. He still had a layer of road dust to brush off himself. He attended to this now. "I bet you handle yourself pretty well at the plate," added the ex-ballplayer. "Am I right?"

Mahrute confessed that he had played a little cricket in his time, but never baseball. He had always wanted to learn the differences.

"Well, today's the day," said the Buzz Saw. "Got a batting cage all set up by the lake. Come on. We'll see what you're made of, Mahrute." He strode off with his long, beefy arm hooked around the bodyguard, leaving Telly and Warren to exchange a puzzled look.

Apparently, they were going to see what Mahrute was made of.

It turned out he was made of something pretty special. He hit nine out of the thirty-one balls Hank's pitching machine threw at him, a .290 average, three of these going into the lake for extra bases.

"Is that good for the environment?" wondered Telly, peering out after the third ball went *splook*.

Hank Busby said never mind the environment. The fish enjoyed fielding balls—gave them something to gnaw on. "What about you, young Telly? You ready for your turn?"

Telly, like Warren earlier, was as ready as he would ever be.

Hank studied his form. "I haven't seen you or your sister for a while. Did you stick with the game after I went away?"

"A little in junior high school."

"Were you any good?"

"I once knocked myself unconscious going after a ball."

"No shame in that."

"It was in the bus on the way to the game," Telly explained. "One of the kids was playing keep-away with it, so I tried to snag it and bonked my head on the passenger window. You can still see the scar."

Hank was sorry he asked. "That's all in the past. You won't be doing any of that here."

"No?" The younger man sounded disappointed.

"You just need to remember what I used to tell you about the secret of hitting."

"Don't drop my shoulder, don't grip the bat too hard——"

"Forget all that. The secret is, see the ball, hit the ball."

"That's it?"

"That's it. Just remove all thoughts from your mind."

"K," agreed the intern. That last part shouldn't be too hard.

He stepped to the plate. After the first six balls whooshed by the batter in a flurry of humiliation, Hank adjusted the setting on the machine. This helped, allowing Telly to clip the eighth pitch and send the bat twirling over Warren's head into the lake. Hank watched as it, too, went *splook*.

"That should keep the fishes busy," suggested Warren, and Hank frowned at him.

"Well, I guess that about does it," said the old man. He adjusted the machine back to its fastest setting—the setting *he* personally used. "I'd offer you a turn, big fella, but I only have the one other bat, and it's probably a little heavy for you—forty-two ounces, the weight I used to use when I played."

Warren understood and picked up the bat to weigh it. Felt more like forty-one to him.

As the other three began to walk away, they heard the thump of a crushed ball echoing out across the lake.

They turned in time to see it sailing over the pine trees into the next county.

"You hit that?" squawked Hank.

Warren nodded idly. The other man was right. Just remove all thoughts from your mind. It worked every time.

* *

Hank Busby had warmed to Warren Kingsley. He reminded Hank of a ballplayer he knew once. Javier Clark. Javy had no training or background either. But, man, could the kid rake.

Warren observed the number of deciduous trees sprinkled about the property and nodded. The cabin holder certainly could have used his services come autumn. "What happened to him?"

"He crapped out, that's what," answered Telly, strolling a few feet ahead of them.

Hank grimaced. "You young bucks always make assumptions about things, and you have no idea, no idea whatsoever."

"So did he crap out or didn't he?" asked Warren.

"He disappeared," said Telly. "You have to understand, it's rare for a guy to go from an independent ball club, like the K's, straight to the majors. But Javy did it. He got picked up by a big club, and wouldn't you know it, a few weeks into the season—in the middle of a game, no less—he just took off. No one has seen him since."

Mahrute offered his own refined take on the incident: "I assume the pressure to perform can be quite overwhelming for some athletes."

"It can be," Hank conceded. They had arrived at his back porch. He wound his way up the steps, pausing to gaze out over the water. "But that's not what happened with Javy. It was—complicated. You follow me?"

Warren didn't, really. He asked complicated how? But Hank didn't answer. He appeared to have entered a kind of trance. Presently, he shook out of it. "It's like you said, Mr. Mahrute, sometimes the pressure gets to be too much. And then some people just have bad luck. Take Daryl Blue. He was pretty good, Daryl was. As a pitcher, I mean. Not Javy-Clark-good, you follow me, but good. Then he blew out his arm, and that was that."

This was the first Warren had heard of Blue's ball-playing days. He'd have thought the bad luck Hank mentioned was accidentally getting shot through a wall. But mucking up his pitching career must have annoyed him as well. "Blue blew out his arm?"

"Blue blew it, alright. Then he had to settle for that stinking office job. No wonder he spent so much time at that place up the road, just like Javy before him. It becomes a sort of second home for some guys, ex-ballplayers especially. It gives a guy a place to go. The Colony—what a name, what a name."

"What are we talking about?" asked Warren. This was the first he had heard of any colonies.

Once more, Hank had left them for some distant reminiscence. "It's not important," he said, dragging himself back to Earth again. He faced his guests. "I've heard tell that your sister's gunning for me, little Telly. I suppose you're here to bring me in on her behalf?"

Little Telly wouldn't have put it quite like that. "She's been looking to speak to you, that's all. She has this crazy idea that you might have it in for the mayor."

"I do have it in for the mayor!" Hank retorted. "That's why I'm going to kick his ass in the election."

Mahrute glanced at Warren, who didn't appear worried. Dark horses never are.

"Don't take this the wrong way," proceeded Telly—there was no good way to ask this—"but you didn't hire any assassins to take him out, did you, Hank?"

"Hire an assassin?" The candidate laughed. "I do my own heavy lifting, kid; you know that."

Telly was glad. "Then you should go talk to her—to Jen. She'd be delighted to see you."

"Would she?" Hank wasn't so sure about delighted. "I guess I shouldn't leave her hanging, though. Should I come with you or drive in my own vehicle?"

Telly wasn't sure either would be necessary. "Looks like her deputy found you first." He pointed to a car rolling down the country road.

"Is that Tony or Lance?" asked Hank. He had trouble keeping the two straight.

It was Tony. And not just Tony. Tony and girlfriend Cynthia.

After the disquieting scene with David Wincher in town, the deputy had stopped off at Cynthia's house for one of his spare uniform shirts. (Some guys just don't know how to lie there and die without getting blood all over official personnel.)

It was at Cynthia's that Tony had gotten a tip from a neighbor that Hank Busby had been spotted at his old hunting cabin up the road. With Cynthia, Cousin Bart, Uncle Neal and a tree trimmer all pulling in after Tony, there wasn't time for them to juggle cars around in Cynthia's driveway, so they had taken Cynthia's station wagon.

So explains the arrival of Deputy Tony in a nonregulation vehicle.

Just to round out the lack of protocol, it was Cynthia at the wheel (at Cynthia's insistence), a detail that brought a sniffle of disgust from Hank. "It's appalling how men these days have women driving them about."

Telly was shocked by this unenlightened view. "Kind of sexist, isn't that?"

"How can it be?" asked Hank Busby. He was criticizing the man, not the woman. "I don't approve of women driving men. It's not masculine. There are only three reasons why a man should ever be a passenger in a car with a woman driver: he's teaching her to drive, he's been shot, or his car has broken down and he needs a ride—and only then if his home is more than a day's walk away and he's been shot."

From the look of Cynthia and her wagon, Warren wasn't so sure that two out of three of those conditions wouldn't apply by the end of the afternoon.

"Well, I guess we'll leave you to it," he told the chauvinist legend, satisfied that he had learned all he needed to learn about the other half of his mayoral competition. "See you on Election Day, Hank."

They left the Buzz Saw with a brow twisted very much in the mold of Cynthia's. Cynthia's brow was twisted because she had missed lunch and her boyfriend was Deputy Tony. Hank's was a more inquisitive contortion. He was wondering what the big feller had meant by that Election-Day crack.

* *

Telly was pensive on the drive home. In a show of well-received benevolence, he had allowed Mahrute to drive his pickup truck, while he, Telly, took the cargo bed. (He figured this substitution would be okay with Hank Busby. It wasn't like Mahrute was a chick or anything.)

In many ways, the get-together with his honorary uncle had not been entirely satisfactory for the symbolic nephew. The man hadn't asked about Telly at all—his hopes, his dreams, how his asthma had improved since they last saw each other. Nothing. Just a lukewarm inquiry about him, Telly, playing baseball. What did it matter if he played any stupid baseball? Telly was sick of baseball. Actually, he wasn't—he couldn't get enough of it—but he was sick of something. He couldn't put his finger on what.

He knew what he had to do. He, Telly Blake, would have to solve this crime. Track down the assassin. Wow the town with his bravery and acumen. That would teach them. He wasn't sure who "them" was exactly, but whoever they were, they, the "them," would be impressed.

The wind blew through his raven locks. He hadn't remembered Hank being so sexist—sexist and old fogyish. They were in the twenty-first century, after all. Women could vote and drive cars and everything. They weren't simple sex objects any longer. They—

The amazing modern male froze in his meditation. His thoughts and the passing landscape had converged in a crescendo of opportunity. "Hey, Mahrute! Hold up! Hold up!" He reached around and tapped the driver on the shoulder.

Mahrute braked the truck, and Telly hopped out of the back.

There had been a moment there when the intern's forearm, appearing through the driver's window, had nearly caused Mahrute to take hold of it and shatter the bone with a simple twist of the wrist. Luckily, he overrode these instincts at the last millisecond, and no harm was done.

"You could have snapped it off at the stem, as far as I'm concerned," said Warren, correctly reading the other man's reflexes.

Together, they peered out the passenger window and saw a plain white building with a plain yellow sign in bright neon. It read "The Nudist Colony" and was shaped like a woman's well-curved ankle. Another part of the sign, announcing show times and holiday hours, was shaped like a woman's well-curved something else.

"It's a strip club," said Telly. "This must be the place Hank meant, Daryl Blue's home away from home. There might be a clue in there." He gazed across at the golden sign meeting his eye, calling to him, beckoning even. It was beckoning because there might be important information to be found inside and women weren't sex objects. "You're welcome to join me in my investigations, but if not, that's cool. I'll just say this—if I'm not out in an hour and a half, three hours at the most, come in after me."

In order to emphasize this last part, he stepped up and poked his head earnestly through Warren's window. Not one to let an opportunity grow stale, he dashed off again before Warren could say anything in response; also before the bodyguard could reach up and snap that head off at the stem.

10 — REVEALING REMARKS

Warren and Mahrute—who had, in fact, joined Telly in his investigations—returned home to Warren's cottage at ten thirty that evening, having parted ways with the intern at his place up the road. The last mentioned had satisfied his analytical curiosity at the Nudist Colony, and then some.

With plenty to think about and review, the bodyguards had walked the final half mile in no time, conversing on various topics. They discussed aspects of the mysteries surrounding the town of Kilobyte, aspects of Warren's plan to run that town as a firm-though-benevolent monarch and aspects of a performer known as "Kiki," whose work at the Colony was putting her through a double major of sociology and party planning at the local university.

The first person they encountered on their arrival home was Warren's neighbor Henrietta Bragg, with whom there could be no starker contrast to the recent Kiki. "Out kind of late, aren't you?" she asked. She had been puttering around her back acre with a bullmastiff named Captain Drayton, whose night-owl habits were more generally well established.

Warren supposed he was a tad late. Normally, he was in bed thirty minutes before now.

He never did get to announce his prospective candidacy that afternoon. There was no doubt about it: Kilobyte was becoming a corrupting influence on him. Perhaps his administration could address this after he took office (and found a position for Kiki, whom he was certain would make a dynamic press secretary/county treasurer—assuming they could work these new responsibilities into her schedule at the Colony).

"Who's your buddy?" asked Henrietta.

Warren introduced Borodin Mahrute.

"Is he your, uh, 'gentleman friend'?"

Warren replied tartly that he was nothing of the sort. Mahrute was a gentleman, and he was a friend. That was all. He wondered where people got these ideas!

He went on to clarify that, outside their friendship, Mahrute was the man who looked after his, Warren's, body—and if that didn't set the record straight on who was straight, Warren didn't know what would.

Fortunately for all concerned, Henrietta was no longer listening. It was a habit she had picked up from Warren.

She was especially delighted to learn that Mahrute "did not swing that way," as the young people liked to call it. Gazing brightly at the handsome new stranger with the David Niven mustache, she offered to get the men a snack before bed. It was good for the digestion, she said, a light snack. Perhaps some brownies or a brandy Alexander.

The suggestion seemed somewhat out of character to Warren—Henrietta had never offered to bring him any desserts or alcohol before then—but it was the cheery smile, more than anything, that struck him as off-kilter. He assumed she must have turned her ankle walking the Captain, or perhaps had a touch of the gout.

"I'll be right back," she declared.

Before Warren could reply that he seldom drank, and even more seldom partook of confections like brownies—unless they were infused with caramel and served with freshly brewed coffee—she had bolted.

He sighed and sat down on the porch step. Mahrute took the swinging bench behind him.

Captain Drayton, abruptly abandoned by his master, came up and placed his head in Warren's lap.

"Is that what it is?" the animal linguist wondered. Captain Drayton gave a clipped, military woof in response. That was what it was.

Now Warren understood. He peered up at the Henrietta Bragg's farmhouse and frowned at the bright tune drifting out from the kitchen window. Evidently it was summer, not springtime, when a middle-aged woman's fancy might turn to love.

* *

For the most part, conversation over booze and brownies remained light and impersonal, the way Warren liked it. At one point, the small talk did work its way around to Warren's arrival in Kilobyte a couple months ago and how he had managed to pick such a quaint, out-of-the-way locale to reside in. Surely, he was more of a big-city man, Henrietta assumed. Mahrute was also curious about this.

"That was our friend Blake," explained Warren, still seated on the porch step.

"Blake?" Mahrute inquired. "As in Mr. Harvard Blake?"

"That's right. Harvey Blake. He's the one who put me onto this town and its quaintness. I bumped into him a while back, and he mentioned that when you're feeling worn out and in need of some battery recharging, Kilobyte is the place. Apparently, he's got some relatives here."

"I assume that would be Mr. Telly and his sister, the sheriff," said Mahrute. "Their last name, I understand, is Blake."

Warren had never noticed. "Anyway, other than the murder and the violence and all the political turmoil, Harvey was right. This place is very relaxing. I have to remember to thank him for the recommendation. He's a good friend."

Mahrute was in complete agreement with this. Mr. Blake had stated his admiration for Warren several times at his wedding last month.

"Wedding?" Warren did not recall hearing anything about a wedding.

"A lot of people come here to rest," agreed Henrietta, seizing her reentry point to the discussion. "Sometimes I wonder if that isn't their undoing," she added grimly.

"Why is that?" asked Mahrute.

Henrietta was thinking about Mr. Blue. He had settled in town after his baseball career had gone *phut*, looking for the easy life, and he had received a bullet in the head for his trouble.

"But surely that was an unfortunate accident—"

Henrietta wasn't so sure it was. She wasn't sure what had happened. "I can't help thinking that he got himself involved in something he shouldn't have. Vigorous men like him, bored with a 'normal life,' often do."

Mahrute repeated his last comment. If it had been an accident—

"But was it?" insisted Ms. Henrietta. "I know, I'm not making sense. I don't know how it could have been anything but what it appeared to be, but it just seems like there was something sinister swirling around Mr. Blue. It was all that woman's fault—I know it was."

"Woman?"

"Sheryl Abbott, the mayor's wife. Oh, I'm not gossiping here," she said, gossiping. "It's well known how she gets on with the men in town. She and Daryl were quite the couple for a while there. Sheryl has never been what you would call discreet. And I'll tell you something else; she is not a good influence for a young man—for a man of any age. She knows some very odd people, some very off-putting people."

Mahrute nodded solemnly. It was the second such mention of "very odd people" they had heard that evening. The first had been at the Nudist Colony.

"And then there is poor Mr. Wincher," continued Henrietta.

Mahrute had not heard anything about poor Mr. Wincher.

"Mr. Wincher from corporate. He was killed today. Jumped out a window, they say, or off a roof; I haven't heard all the particulars. They're calling it a possible suicide, but I don't believe it. Why would someone with a nice middle-management position commit suicide?"

Mahrute could think of several reasons, but in this instance, he tended to agree with her. It was too coincidental. Two deaths in so many days. "You think these 'very odd people' had something to do with the 'accidents'?"

"Them—or *something*," she muttered. She whispered the word *Soparla*, the strangest something of all.

A heavy silence hung over the trio and their brandy snifters after that. Even the crickets seemed to have quieted down out of respect for the Beast of Kilobyte.

A few moments later, Warren weighed in again. "I definitely never received any wedding invitation," he said emphatically.

Mahrute answered in his most kindly vein, "Perhaps Mr. Blake felt a little"—what was a nice way of putting this?—"*concerned* about your high regard for his future wife."

"Who—Loren Hamilton?" Warren frowned. He did not have any undue regard for Harvey Blake's Loren. As soon as he saw those two had something special, he backed off. "I don't pursue other men's women," he concluded matter-of-factly.

As he spoke these words, the bedroom light of the farmhouse on the other side of their cottages switched off. Their neighbor Maria— that would be "Mrs. Maria Stengel," wife of Deputy Lance Stengel— had gone to bed for the evening and would not, it seemed, be taking one of her midnight strolls. There was nothing keeping Warren up now.

"Well, I guess I'm off to bed now too," he said. He stood up and stretched. It was late, and he needed his beauty sleep.

"Too?" asked Henrietta Bragg.

"I'm off to bed," said Warren, with a hasty squint.

Henrietta's expression remained light and uncharacteristically cheerful. "Such a nice, virtuous young fellow, our Mr. Kingsley. Early to bed, and early to rise." She applauded this behavior wholeheartedly.

Warren shrugged. He supposed this virtue came naturally to him. "Besides," he pointed out, "I could use a shower to wash off all the stripper grease I got on me tonight. Stuff really sticks to you."

**

After his rinse, Warren found Captain Drayton lying faithfully at the end of his bed. He supposed it didn't matter. Even in the summer months, you could use something to keep your feet warm on chilly nights.

He climbed between the sheets and lay pondering the ceiling again. It seemed to Warren he was doing a lot of ceiling pondering these days. He wondered what he found so fascinating about it.

They had learned a lot today, he realized, and yet, in a way, they hadn't learned anything at all. He supposed that's what made it a mystery. Warren wasn't sure he liked mysteries—no more than he liked threatening anonymous phone calls and unexplained items in his trash. He was a humble public-servant wannabe, and he liked his reality quiet and uncomplicated.

He peered up from his pillow. Captain Drayton mirrored the gesture.

They had heard a noise. Warren was always hearing noises, even before he started finding peach pits and things in his garbage. If he didn't know better, he would have thought he wasn't alone in this house.

Perhaps he had never been alone here…

Shaking his head and putting the sound down to Mahrute and Henrietta whooping it up on the front porch—either that, or a squirrel running wild in the attic—he laid his head back on the pillow (Captain Drayton laid his on the comforter), and they continuing their pondering.

Warren thought about the mysteries in town; Captain D about the briny, briny sea and the many gulls he had chased there.

It wasn't in Warren's nature to ponder the inexplicable very long. Unsolved mysteries were fine by him.

He began thinking about his campaign. He wondered if it was difficult being a mayor. It didn't seem very difficult. He had seen many people far stupider than him do it. Why not him? It seemed to him he had just the right amount of stupid to get the job done.

He heard the noise again.

Captain Drayton also heard it. Not content to lie there idly, he galloped from the room, perhaps to go to battle stations (or possibly not).

It was clear to Warren that it was not Mahrute or any attic squirrel keeping him awake. The noise he had heard this time was nearby, a sort of creaking sound. Mahrute would never come into Warren's bedroom and creak at him. Nor, for that matter, would a squirrel. Not a squirrel who knew what was good for him.

Warren lifted his face from his pillowcase one more time, coming face-to-face with a small-boned man sitting on the end of his bed. It was a handy spot now that Captain Drayton had vacated it.

He looked a bit like a squirrel, this small-boned man, if squirrels wore vermillion running suits and had faces like degenerate weasels.

"Evening, moonbeam. I didn't wake you, did I?" He spoke in a gruff yet fluid accent—sandpaper meets maple syrup. Warren couldn't quite place it. It sounded a little cockney in parts, a little Australian in others. Warren wasn't altogether certain it wasn't Bulgarian/Lithuanian.

He answered honestly that his visitor had not woken him. He was not asleep. "Who were you again?"

"Name's Basil," said Basil. "And you're Warren Kingsley," he added helpfully.

Warren nodded. All correct so far. "And why are you here?"

Basil leaned forward. He tapped the bodyguard on the chest. "Nice jammies, chum."

"Thanks." If Basil liked them so much, he could tell him where he purchased them. Actually, he couldn't, since Warren hadn't technically bought them himself. He had taken possession of this spare pair from a client who *no longer needed them*, but he was fairly certain he could steer Basil toward the correct manufacturer. They probably even had children's sizes.

Basil was not interested in pajamas. "I'm here, since you ask, to have a word wiff you, oh large silken one."

"Oh yes? What about?"

"About you sticking your nose in where it don't belong."

The large silken one considered the claim. It didn't seem to him that he had done any nose sticking lately. Or ever, really. His motto was stay out of things and blend in. When had he ever stuck in his nose?

"I know about your visit to the Colony this evening," said Basil.

Warren nodded again. He had this guy all taped out now. He was a pimp. A little cockney pimp, out for a midnight jog. He looked the part, what with his nylon running suit and his face—assuming pimps also had heads too small for their bodies and the bone structure of underweight hummingbirds.

"I think I understand," said Warren.

It was beginning to make sense to him. Basil had seen Mahrute, Telly and himself interacting with the young ladies at the club tonight and, totally misinterpreting their visit, had come to arrange for future business. Warren assumed that was how pimps worked: always upselling. It was admirable in its way. Showed initiative and a go-getter spirit. But Warren was forced to disappoint him.

"I'm sorry," he said, "but it's no deal."

"No deal?"

No deal, Warren was afraid.

There hadn't been much of a crowd at the club that evening, it being a Sunday, but what few performers they had on staff were not Warren's cup of tea (excluding Kiki, that is, although he had it on good authority that she had recently begun seeing her sociology professor).

"I'm not interested in dating any of your girls, Basil. Don't get me wrong. They were very fine young women. Nicely made-up and flexible, but I'll shortly be an old geezer of forty, and I like my women a little more demure now, and less tattooed. Perhaps you should check with my friend Telly Blake, of the Connecticut Blakes. He seemed more open to trying new things."

Basil took Warren's objections on board with a nod of his tiny weasel head. He had an objection of his own to air: "I'm not here to talk about girls, am I, mate?"

Warren really couldn't say. It seemed to him that Basil *was* here to talk about girls. If not girls, then what?

"You spoke to a Hank Busby today, didn't ya? This Hank—he talks too much."

"Everybody does," agreed Warren.

"And after talking to Hank, you paid a visit to the Colony club. You went there looking for information on a certain Javier Clark."

Warren wasn't so sure that they had gone there for that. If they had, they had grossly overpaid on the cover charge.

Javy Clark. The name seemed familiar to Warren. *Javy Clark. Javy Clark.* He had it pegged now: Hank Busby had mentioned someone called Javy Clark. The ballplayer who had made it to the major leagues, only to vanish in a puff of self-doubt the first month of the season. "Oh, that Javy. People say I remind them of him, you know."

"You're no Javy Clark," said Basil—a little cruelly, thought Warren. He hoped they wouldn't be this cruel at the debate tomorrow.

Basil went on disapprovingly, "His disappearance and everyfing to do wiff it is none of your business. He was one of us, Javy was, and what happened to him, that's Society business, got it?"

Warren would hate to interfere in society business. That really would come under the heading of sticking one's nose in. "When you say society," he asked, "what society are we talking about?"

Basil glared. "You know, chum."

His chum really didn't. He didn't think he did anyway. He tossed his mind back a moment and thought.

He did recall something about "a society" discussed tonight, now that Basil mentioned it—a society made up of "very strange people."

Warren reviewed the minutes of the meeting in his head. A waitress at the club had said something about this society—a *secret society*, in fact. With so many servers moving to and fro pushing drinks on you—drinks Warren didn't want but somehow ended up paying for, or Mahrute ended up paying for—Warren hadn't caught all of the conversation, but he had gotten the gist of it. He seemed to remember this waitress—tall, slinky and blonde, nice navel—sharing certain theories with Mahrute, theories that speculated that everything going on in Kilobyte right now was related, somehow, to this organization, based out of the Nudist Colony, which she believed was secretly aliens from another world or possibly vampires. Perhaps that was the society Basil was talking about.

"Was it supposed to be a secret?" Warren wondered.

He had no wish to get their source in trouble. She seemed like a good gal, if not a little loquacious (people love to talk about aliens and vampires).

Basil was growing impatient. He cast a glance over his shoulder and addressed an incorporeal companion behind him. "We got a real wise guy here, hafn't we?"

The ether did not reply, so Warren had no way of knowing how wise he actually was (according to disembodied public opinion).

He tried a little diplomacy. It was good practice for the job. "I mean, it's nothing to me if you guys want to throw your weight around. That's what secret societies are there for, right? So what are you fellas? Mafia?" Maybe that was why Basil resented Warren's impersonation of a wise guy.

Basil said not Mafia, no.

"South American drug runners?" asked Warren.

Basil sighed.

Warren didn't want to be an alarmist, but it didn't seem like his diplomacy was making the grade. When he became mayor, he would have to hire some people for that.

The other man stood. He scowled. "You don't know anything, do ya?"

Warren had never suggested that he did.

Basil shook his head. He took out a pack of cigarettes, scowled again and lit one.

Now it was Warren's turn to scowl. Interfering with a man's beauty sleep was one thing, but stinking up his bed chamber with some infernal smog stick was something altogether different. It was entirely unacceptable. Paraphrasing another great politician, well respected in his time, there were some things up with which Warren would not put.

During his smoke break, Basil had taken to strolling idly around the room, fingering knickknacks and generally fiddling about. On his third fiddle and his fifth puff, he opened Warren's closet door, perhaps looking for more PJs. That's when Warren made his move.

He climbed out from the covers, glided silently across the floorboards and shoved the little smudge pot into the closet. He then slammed the door and propped his weight up against it.

That was that solved.

He peered around. He could hear that creaking sound again. Captain Drayton? It didn't sound like Drayton.

Warren needed to think here. Echoing Frederick Abbott's words from earlier that day, where was his bodyguard when he needed him?

* *

His bodyguard, Mahrute, to answer that question, was exactly where Warren had left him: still chatting with Henrietta Bragg on the porch swing. (If there ever was a time that Warren felt people talked too much, that time would be now.)

They were discussing their mutual likes and dislikes. Mahrute thought highly of Warren's neighbor. Possibly not as highly as she appeared to think of him, but she seemed a fine woman. Formidable exterior, but of solid stock and no doubt possessed of a kindly heart.

Having discovered that they both liked classical music, films of the 1940s and semiautomatic weapons over revolvers, they moved on to infamous dictators in history, notorious gangsters from the past and present, and people who don't take their grocery carts back up to the storefront when they have finished with them—all of whom fell under the banner of their mutual disapprobation.

"Your friend Warren is a funny cuss," said Henrietta abruptly. It was difficult to say which class of prominent figures made her think of him: the infamous or the notorious.

Mahrute agreed that they made few cusses funnier.

"How long have you two worked together, if you don't mind me asking?"

Mahrute didn't mind. It had been several years now.

"Did you meet him over there in England? You are English, aren't you?"

Mahrute was English enough to be getting on with. He had actually traveled extensively when he was a child—too much, really—so much so that his exact place of birth remained a mystery to him, even to this day.

And no, he had not met Warren overseas. Except for the occasional car or train ride, Warren Kingsley did not travel. He certainly did not fly.

Henrietta nodded her head and tossed the newly arrived Captain Drayton a piece of jerky. The old salt appeared agitated about something, but his master was too caught up in entertaining her guest to notice.

She continued her appraisal of Warren Kingsley, psychological superspecimen. "He seems like he has a touch of the man-child in him, that one. You must have your hands full, looking after him."

Mahrute spread these hands in a gesture of uncertainty. "He is a complicated individual," he equivocated.

"He seems downright simple, if you ask me."

"He does make that impression, certainly. On first blush, he appears aloof, careless even. He doesn't seem concerned about anything or anyone. But as you get to know him better, and realize what he is capable of, you find that he actually cares far less about things than even that. It is this all-consuming indifference, this appearance of a man—or man-child, if you wish to call him that—out of sync with the world around him that actually endears him to me."

"It sounds like he relies on you pretty heavily?"

"I've never truly determined if he does. Warren Kingsley is a surprisingly capable man when he wants to be. He has excelled at virtually everything he has ever tried."

Henrietta found this hard to believe. But if Mr. Mahrute said it, it must be so.

"The two notable exceptions," the latter continued, "are his personal relationships and his bodyguarding." At bodyguarding, Warren Kingsley most certainly did not excel. "With most everything else, however, he appears to possess an instant and unearthly knack."

He refrained from mentioning the unearthly one's upcoming attempt to govern Kilobyte. Mahrute had come to enjoy his time with Henrietta and did not wish to poison the evening. "The key is he has to come at a task obliquely."

"How do you mean?"

"He cannot be *assigned* a chore. He has to spring out on a task from the shadows, surprising the undertaking—and himself—with his sheer talent."

It sounded a little like a surprise party for your aptitude, if you asked Henrietta Bragg.

Mahrute supposed it did. He paused. He had heard a disturbance in the house behind him: possibly someone springing out of the shadows at his or her aptitude.

"Squirrels in the attic," explained Henrietta, and Mahrute nodded. "Do you think you and your friend will figure out what's going on in Kilobyte?" she asked. "It seems like you both have taken some interest in our little town."

Mahrute had taken an interest, and he would do everything in his power to bring matters in town to a satisfactory conclusion. The citizens of Kilobyte—some citizens more than others—deserved it.

As for Mr. Kingsley, that all depended on how much the mystery imposed itself on him, and how much he felt put upon by it.

There was a lull now, and Mahrute took this time to reach down and pet Captain Drayton. He considered his next words carefully. He usually did. "I've heard something of this local legend of yours," he said.

"You're speaking of Soparla?" asked Henrietta. She was not ashamed of their legends.

"Yes, Soparla. You do not—" How could he put this? "Surely, you do not believe in an avenging Fury—a beast—seeking retribution from wrongdoers in Kilobyte?"

Henrietta hesitated with her answer, partly because she wished to appear wholly sane and rational in front of her new friend, but also because a great, bone-rattling growl, echoing out over the darkened hillside, had belayed her response.

All in, it sounded like a wolverine locked in mortal combat with another wolverine—this death match officiated by an especially irascible wombat.

At the start of the yowl, Captain Drayton had perked up at Mahrute's side, as though wondering if he should damn the torpedoes and investigate. But as the snarl drifted past and lingered awhile, he bowed his head slightly, entertaining other options.

"More squirrels?" asked Mahrute.

Henrietta shook her head and said no.

"Not squirrels," she said. She then mouthed a name—Romanian in origin—but made certain Mr. Mahrute didn't see her doing it.

* *

Inside, Warren had heard the growl too. Normally, he would have suspected one of Henrietta's wild things, but it hadn't sounded like it had come from the barn. He turned to the closet door, which had ceased rumbling with Basil's banging, and asked, "Did you just grr-rrr?"

The closet door made no reply.

It didn't matter. Warren didn't think he had grrrrred. "You better not be smoking in there," he said. That was the closet where he kept his Armani (another "gift" from his conveniently built former client).

Propping a chair under the doorknob, he went over and sat on the bed. It was a very tall bed, and his feet dangled slightly off the plush area rug surrounding him. It made Warren feel slightly ridiculous.

He supposed he should go fetch Mahrute now. He didn't like leaving Basil alone, though. His visitor was small, but he was scrappy. Scrappy guys can be a real pain, he realized, especially when they have their own personal fire-starter kits and several yards of worsted wool, which may or may not have been flammable.

There was nothing else for it. Mahrute would know what to do next. That was what Warren was paying him for.

Touching down on the plush area rug again, he suddenly found this rug ensconced around him and his old friend, the ceiling, beaming down at him with sympathy and understanding. In a word, Basil, inexplicably free, had sneaked up from behind and knocked Warren's legs out from under him.

"Ouch," said the householder. He was beginning to dislike Basil. "How'd you get out? Are you some kind of conjurer?"

The possible conjurer did not reply at first. He blew a few smoke rings and said, "Get up."

Warren attempted to stand again, but Basil knocked him back to the rug with another sharp kick to the ankle. Warren glared. He thought the man wanted him up. Some guys just can't make up their minds.

Slowly, he rose—making it last this time—and from there he assessed the situation.

"You wanna make a run at me?" taunted the scrappy one.

What Warren wanted was to knock the man's head off with Hank Busby's forty-two-ounce bat, but he would settle for a run right now. He made a grab for the menace and somehow wound up on the other side of the nightstand.

In a word, he had missed.

"You really are a slippery little leprechaun, aren't you?" asked Warren. Had Henrietta Bragg been present, she might have called him a slippery little cuss, but these things are a matter of style and upbringing.

"Slippery enough," said Basil. "Is that all you got?"

It was not. Warren took another stab at him. He landed in the same heap by the wardrobe.

"Tell you what," offered Basil. "I'll tie one hand behind my back. Got a fancy sash to go with those silken jammies of yours?"

Warren wasn't sure. He had simply collected the sleepwear and the Armani. He hadn't checked for any robes or sashes.

He made another lunge.

"Getting closer," said Basil.

Warren frowned. He would need to go about this smarter. Standing once more, he strolled gradually around the area rug, in a slightly counterclockwise motion. Then all at once, he charged his target. Basil slipped the tackle, and all at once Warren charged through the drywall of his bedroom.

Construction methods in Kilobyte not being what they might have been, he smashed straight through and landed in a dusty mess on the other side.

He was in his sitting room now.

Warren had never really determined why he had a sitting room, and what he was supposed to do with it now that he had it, but this wasn't the time for cracking architectural enigmas. He leaned up and coughed.

Basil stepped through the breach and nodded appreciatively. "Nice work, mate. I love what you've done with the place. Really opens up the room."

Warren brushed off the broken pieces of Sheetrock and propped himself up on the stubby remains of a wholly inadequate two-by-four. He coughed again.

Basil was wagging his head. "Now, see, this is not what I would call hospitality. I was all set to let bygones be bygones and leave you be, but then you had to go and antagonize me. It wasn't hospitable locking me in a cupboard, now was it? Why'd you want to go and do that? It pissed me off, didn't it?"

Warren supposed it did. He never claimed to be a good host. "I'd like to know how you got out, though."

"Perhaps I'll explain it to you on your birfday," said the escapee, and punctuated the promise with an early gift: a kick to Warren's jaw. He went to the well a second time, but Warren managed to catch the tiny foot mid windup. He flung the punter back.

"Nice one, chum," said Basil, on his feet again.

Warren was on his feet too and took a swing at Basil's cherry-colored face. Not surprisingly, he failed to connect and, in so failing, toppled through the sitting room doorway and out into the living room.

He got up again, only to be kicked in the stomach by the ever-present Basil. He stumbled backward, careering into the kitchenette and taking half the contents of the countertop with him. He really wished he had that meat cleaver he was looking for earlier. It would come in very handy right now.

Basil stepped up. He had a knife himself. Not quite a cleaver, but effective enough for its purpose. "Now then," he said, "let's see what color you chaps are on the inside."

His physiology lesson would have to wait.

"Excuse me, sir," said Borodin Mahrute, and with one swift motion knocked the blade from Basil's grip.

Basil quickly clenched his empty palm in protest and took a jab at Mahrute, but Mahrute repelled that too, and there the matter stood.

Warren also stood. He dusted himself off and watched the resulting tussle. It was about time, he muttered.

Basil and Mahrute came into the skirmish at roughly the same height, but Basil maintained his advantage in the early rounds. They fought their way through the living room, busting up what parts their host had not succeeded in breaking himself. This included two end tables, four lamps, a leather ottoman and a print of a Victorian man and woman at the seashore, which Warren had always liked. After the broken print, the combatants paused. It could be Mahrute's imagination, but he couldn't seem to get a hand on the man.

"You'll pardon this inartistic method," he said, breathing a little heavily, "but I believe this activity has outlasted its charm." He reached down and produced a small pistol (semiautomatic) from his ankle holster. It was such an obvious hiding place he was amazed the sheriff and her deputies hadn't spotted it. "Stay where you are, please."

Basil did not stay where he was. He moved in a blur across the room and commandeered the gun. In next to no time, he had it pointed at Mahrute's head.

"Nice piece, old bean. Let's see what color *your* insides are, then."

Sadly, it was not in the offing for Basil to see the inside of anything human that evening.

Warren was back in the mix. (Some things just have to be done yourself.)

He had learned from his earlier mistakes. He needed to go about this obliquely. You weren't going to beat Warren Kingsley at the oblique.

"The Great One," Wayne Gretzky, had once described the best way to track a puck on the ice as going not where the puck *had been*, but where it was *going to be*. Warren, like the Great Wayne, went to where Basil was *going to be*. As the gunman turned to avoid Warren's approach, the part-time bodyguard made a move entirely contrary to his own instincts. He swung for the space on Basil's left, and upon contact, knocked the sassy little hockey puck halfway across the room.

It took Basil a little longer to recover than before. A snappy comeback was not immediately forthcoming.

He got up, caught his breath and said, "Nice job. And here I was finking all along you were some ordinary Opie."

"Opie who?" wondered Warren. He wasn't aware of any cockney slang having to do with the name Opie.

Mahrute had retrieved the fallen firearm. "Hold it right there, sir."

Basil did not hold it right there. He snapped his fingers, and a hulking accomplice hove up beside him. Warren found himself wondering if he was the kind of guy who might go grrrrr in the night.

Where he had been keeping himself all this time was another mystery to Warren. Perhaps, like Mahrute, he had spent some of that time chatting with new friends on the front porch.

He was roughly 6'10", Warren estimated, roughly fifty inches across the chest and had the rough frown of a man—or beast—who not only knew death, but was fairly chummy with it too.

Mahrute managed to get off a single shot before the beast—or man—slapped the weapon from his grasp. He knocked Warren halfway across the room with an indifferent backhand, and then returned his attention to Mahrute. He picked up the bodyguard's bodyguard by his tailored jacket (Savile Row) and shook him vigorously.

And that's when the action really started.

Bullets, lots and lots of bullets, danced around the room. They shot up the vaulted ceiling, the drapes, the kitchenette and another Victorian pastoral print Warren had been somewhat fond of.

When the dust had finally cleared, the four brawlers crawled out from their respective hiding places and lifted their heads to ascertain the source of the artillery fire.

Henrietta Bragg was standing on the threshold, holding her Glock. She had strolled back over to bring the luggageless Mahrute a change of clothing—some pleasant garments that had belonged to her grandfather—but had found the gentleman more in need of firepower than haberdashery.

So she had provided this too.

Basil and friend did not remain long after. If this hadn't roused the entire Kilobyte police force, nothing would. They weren't taking any chances. They made their exit expeditiously, leaving Warren to kick himself for not asking if they were registered for the upcoming election. Every vote counted.

He stepped over the scraps of what remained of his cottage and helped Mahrute to his feet. He then thanked the pistol-packing Henrietta.

"Nice Glock," he said.

And that concluded the evening.

11 — Overhead, Overheard
and Overridden

O r so one might have supposed. But this was Kilobyte, the town that never slept, and at the chirp of midnight on the old church clock (digital quartz movement), Frederick Abbott, his arm now free of its sling, arrived on Warren Kingsley's doorstep. (Henrietta Bragg and her charcoal-resin baby had retired for the evening half an hour earlier, as had Deputy Lance, awoken by the ruckus.)

It had been a stressful few days for the mayor of Kilobyte. Listing these one by one, he'd had a gunman enter his office uninvited, causing all sorts of hassle; he'd had a corporate stooge fall to his death, involving all sorts of headaches; he'd had a wife, Sheryl, for reasons she didn't care to explain, take six overnight bags and her dog Butterscotch for an extended stay with friends outside of town; and now, on top of it all, he had some mysterious new candidate preparing to enter the election. This man, whoever he was, would appear to be a true dark horse—not a thing was known about him, not even his identity.

Those had been Frederick Abbott's last few days. It was ironic that his secret opponent, Warren, had recently lain awake asking himself what the life of a mayor might entail. Had he asked Abbott instead, the other man could have cautioned him that it was one kick in the shorts after another.

So, having been kicked four times this week (and thrice today), why come to Warren Kingsley's tiny cottage now? Thus far, Abbott had been getting a twofer with his employee: a speechwriter who refused to write his speeches and a bodyguard who had no interest in guarding his body. What balm could Warren, or his cottage, offer a man beyond that? The answer was none, no balm, but there was a simple explanation for Abbott's arrival, nonetheless. In this life, it has been well said that we desire the things the most that we cannot have, and while Abbott continued to be snubbed by Warren at every turn and in every position he arranged for him, he still found himself inexplicably drawn to the man. He was like a large, baffling magnet. The mayor had become obsessed with Warren's mystique, his utter contempt for following orders, and upon Abbott's word, he would have this Kingsley's assistance!—whether he had an "in/inn" with him or not.

The assistance he required tonight was bodyguarding assistance. Leaving his house at around nine that evening—or a little after because he had to stop and take a phone call from the pest Telly, apparently intoxicated and demanding a celebratory bobblehead for some creature named Kiki—Abbott had reached the bodyguard's neighborhood at half past ten p.m. Although owned and operated by the Abbott Enterprises concern, the cottages in the area were not any Abbott had ever visited personally. (In that way, they were no concern of his.) As a result of this absentee ownership, he got hopelessly lost on the drive there.

At five minutes past twelve, after he had seen the lake four times and the field of corn six, he drifted up in front of Warren's address, nowhere near where the GPS had said it was, and emerged into the humid night air.

He had no idea what to expect from a bodyguard's dwelling. Aside from the occasional romance novel his wife might have left lying out, depicting hunky bodyguards and the women who loved them, Abbott had nothing to go on with regard to the profession.

If the world of fiction was any indication, a bodyguard's home life involved a lot of standing around with your shirt off, glaring warily—these moments interposed with time spent cleaning and honing your weapons at the kitchen table, also warily but sometimes grave, the way one looks pondering a dark and violent past.

Up until now, the mayor had only known the genteel office version of Warren Kingsley, the Warren who was supposed to write his speeches but never did. Abbott presumed, in this virile and less refined environment, he would either get something shirtless and wary, or something shirtless and grave. What he did not expect was the small, respectful older gentleman—completely shirted—who opened the door to him.

"Good evening, Mayor," said this shirted man.

Abbott was surprised. He hadn't realized that bodyguards had butlers. "Have we met?"

"Borodin Mahrute," said Borodin Mahrute. "We met at the sheriff's office. I am Mr. Kingsley's bodyguard."

Abbott remembered him now. The man he thought was to be his bonus bodyguard but wasn't. "I'm here to see Kingsley," he said curtly. "He up?"

Mahrute replied in the affirmative. Mr. Kingsley was up and exploring the crawl spaces above the house. He stated this with such ready aplomb that Abbott had no reason to question it. Apparently, this was a perfectly natural thing for Kingsley to be doing at ten minutes after midnight.

"Would you care to come in?" Mahrute asked.

The mayor crossed the threshold swiftly.

Most of the obvious debris from earlier had been cleaned up, but the cottage still presented a subtle, lived-in look. Abbott couldn't be sure, but the Victorian print over the mantelpiece appeared to have a fist hole in it. "Expect him down any time soon?"

Mahrute nodded. Unless he was mistaken, the resounding thump from the bedroom, followed by the subsequent grumbling and swearing, would be Mr. Kingsley now.

It was. Warren came in, brushing cobwebs from his hair and sucking on the thumb he had smushed in the crawl-space door. He removed a handful of cigarette butts from his pajama pocket. "I think I see how he did it, Mahrute—oh hi, Mayor. Care for a smoke?"

The mayor shook his head at the kindly offer, and Warren continued to talk to Mahrute:

"After I locked him in the closet, Basil must have crawled up through the attic and back down again into the kitchenette. He dropped cigarette butts all along the way. You'd think the little bastard could have curbed his habit for five minutes. And that wasn't the only thing I found—" He paused, regarding their visitor in more critical vein. "Why are you here, Mayor?"

Abbott cleared his throat and stepped forward. "I've come to speak with you, Kingsley."

Warren had gathered as much. He didn't think the mayor was here to help him sweep up butts. "What can we do for you?"

Abbott told him. "As you may have heard, things have come to a head in town. There has been another death. My wife has packed up and left, out of concern for her safety, and I can't say I blame her. I have reason to believe that my life is still in danger."

Warren had gathered this as well. Gunmen don't take potshots at you if it's not. "What would you like me to do about it?"

Abbott turned a shade of purple to match the stripe in Warren's pajamas. "I would like you to offer some kind of protection, that's what! I require your services as a bodyguard, Kingsley. I tried calling you this evening, but you never answered."

"My cell doesn't seem to be working right now. I think someone stepped on its gizzard in all the hubbub."

Abbott hadn't come here to discuss hubbubs or phone gizzards. "You can pack a bag and come back to my mansion right now—"

Warren nipped this attractive plan in the bud. "I told you, Mayor, I don't bodyguard anymore—I'm retired."

Abbott couldn't recall Warren telling him anything of the sort. "Mr. Mahrute then—"

"Mahrute's my bodyguard."

"But there must be something you can do!" The mayor was desperate. He couldn't go back and ask the sheriff and her idiotic deputies for help now. He just couldn't.

Warren was not without compassion. "I suppose I can take you on part-time. Freelance."

"Thank you, Kingsley."

"But I don't like the idea of leaving the cottage just now. I'm expecting some return guests, and if I'm not here to receive them, they might make a ruckus. Not good for the neighbors, ruckuses. You can stay here, if you like."

While Abbott gazed around the room in shock and awe, Warren concluded:

"And speaking of ruckuses, I still have a few small matters to discuss with Mahrute. Excuse us a moment." He showed Mahrute into the sitting room.

They might as well get some more use out of it.

**

Once enclosed—*enclosed* being a relative term, with a large, gaping hole in the back wall—Warren reached in his non-cigarette-butt pocket and produced a couple of apple cores and a banana skin. "I found these up there too."

"Indeed?"

"I don't think Basil was here long enough to eat a pair of apples and a banana. If he had been, I would have smelled his characteristic bouquet long before then." Warren was basing this on the Telly Blake principle of distinctive smoker aroma. "No, the fruit was clearly left by some other uninvited guest."

"Who?"

"I don't know, but he's been here for a while. You recall me mentioning the peach pits? I think these are more of the same. We have a fruit lover squatting on the premises, Mahrute. But how violent a fruit lover is he? That's what we need to ask ourselves."

That was certainly a vital question, but Mahrute had more pressing matters on his mind.

"You believe Basil will return?"

"Perhaps. He and his ginormous friend might not believe we know everything, but we're in deep enough to cause them concern. I don't think they're satisfied that we're as clueless about the Colony and Javier Clark and the rest of it as we actually are."

"If you are concerned, we could move our base of operations to the mayor's house, as Mr. Abbott suggested."

"And leave Maria and Gladys and the rest of them on their own? Where do you think Basil and his chunk-of-oak will go looking if we're not here?" He shook his head. "This isn't like you, Mahrute. I thought you always looked out for the little guy—and the little gal. The Stengel household has about sixteen of them."

Mahrute accepted the rebuff with a gentle smile. It was nice to see Warren exhibiting some signs of the bodyguard's doctrine.

Warren paced the sitting room. He arrived at the gaping hole, broke off a piece of Sheetrock that was dangling and tossed it on the pile. "I can't help thinking that Hank Busby knows more than he said."

"Perhaps we should meet with him again."

"Perhaps. Or, better yet, I could spring it on him during the debate. Make him squirm a little. It might kill two birds with one stone, that."

Mahrute appeared skeptical of this as a political maneuver. Warren, however, had already moved on to a new subject. "I found this too," he said, reaching in his top pocket.

He showed him.

* *

Upon their return to the living room, they discovered the mayor tinkering with a broken vase on the mantel shelf.

He was looking casual. Very casual.

An instant before, he had been compelled to move faster and more sprightly than his old pins were accustomed to carrying him.

He had been listening to their talk, or was trying to, and for those curious if this was how politicians typically comported themselves, it was not. Sixty percent of the elected officials in the surrounding counties would have frowned at this skullduggery, while roughly two-thirds in the state legislature would have formed a committee to do it.

Fred Abbott had no qualms about eavesdropping. He had once leveraged the buyout of a really nice asphalt-repaving company after listening at a bathroom stall.

In any event, it didn't matter. He could barely make out the conversation anyway. As he scampered away from the wall, he could only say with any real certainty that Warren and Mahrute had recently met with the snake Busby, possibly over a refreshing apple-and-peach cobbler, and someone had suggested adding basil to the recipe.

Abbott continued to look casual. He broke up the larger pieces of the vase between his fingers—casually—and eventually swept the remains into the fireplace. "You're back, Kingsley. Excellent, excellent."

Warren frowned. "Were you listening at the door, Mayor?"

The mayor puffed out his chest importantly. Listening at the door! The very idea! He was listening at the wall (he might have said), which was much thinner than the door.

Warren said, "Well, it's not important. As I was saying before, if you'd like to bunk down here for the night, you're welc—"

Abbott cut him off mid-invitation. "How could you meet with Hank Busby?!" he bellowed, "my political and personal rival! My sworn enemy!"

Two days earlier, it would have been Abbott's wife the mayor suspected Warren of engaging in funny business with. He hadn't cared for that exchange of glances the two had shared at the house; he still didn't. This, however, was far worse.

"How could you meet with the man behind my back? Have you been giving him pointers on how to defeat me? Is that it?"

Mahrute took it upon himself to soothe the savage mayor. "I can assure you, sir, that the meeting was conducted with the purist of motives. Mr. Blake, Mr. Kingsley and myself have been looking into recent events to assist the sheriff. Mr. Busby, as a person of interest, seemed a logical place to start, especially since he had been actively avoiding the authorities. As far as divulging any secrets, you may have my word that the last thing on Mr. Kingsley's mind is giving Mr. Busby any undue advantage in the election. That would be contrary to his"—how could Mahrute put this?—"personal goals."

Abbott was indeed soothed. "Oh, I see. Yes, that makes sense." He slapped Warren on his pajamaed shoulder. It felt firm yet silky. "You were sizing up the competition for me, is that it? Nicely done, Kingsley, nicely done. Sorry I doubted you."

Warren waved aside the apology. It was a mistake anyone could make.

The mayor continued to savor his bodyguard's guile. Who knows? Maybe he could make a decent press secretary yet. "So that's what you meant by asking him a telling question during the debate tomorrow? I couldn't catch all of it through the wall, but that's what it sounded like you said. Good idea, Kingsley, good idea. Throw off his timing, make him stumble over his words. But you should know it's not only Busby we have to worry about. There's some new candidate looking to enter the contest. I don't know a thing about him yet, but he's obviously some cocky young upstart."

The mayor smirked unpleasantly, making him look like a cocky old downstart. "Well, I have a surprise for him. He can only run as a write-in candidate—it's too late to get on the ballot. But that's not all; they won't tabulate any of his votes, should he get any, unless he files Form 64-K. It's pretty obscure—many jurisdictions in the state will count any substantial number of write-in votes, but not Kilobyte. We have a different set of regulations here. Basically, the charter states that you can have no official candidacy, write-in or otherwise, unless Form 64-K is at the clerk's office no later than twelve p.m. five months prior to the Monday before Election Day. Five months prior is tomorrow. He's going to show up at the debate, expecting to throw his hat in the ring, but it's going to be too late. No matter how many write-in votes he gets, they won't count. I bet no one has told him this. Ha-ha."

Warren was more amused by the mayor's admission than the other could know. "Has any candidate ever won with the write-in vote?" he asked.

"Twice," said Abbott. "We're a plucky town, and we tend to favor the underdog. The way things have gone for my administration lately, I wouldn't have counted this guy out. Hank Busby is just a poser, but this dark horse might have had a shot, were it not for that form."

Warren concurred completely. "Form 64-K?" he clarified.

"Form 64-K. Notarized."

Warren nodded. "You're a notary, aren't you, Mahrute?"

Mahrute agreed that he was.

* *

Soon after that, Warren showed Abbott to his accommodations for that evening: the famous sitting room. "If you have some time," he said, "try actually sitting in it. Somehow, it would make me feel better."

The mayor stepped back from the battered parlor and blinked. "There's a hole in the wall!"

Warren did not deny this. "Which reminds me—try not to snore. I'm right through the opening, and I need my sleep. Big day tomorrow."

Abbott still hesitated. After Warren had departed, the mayor hollered to his host through their talking portal. "You never did say what you found out grilling Busby?"

Warren appeared at the crevice and said, "We didn't find out much, aside from some mention of the Colony and how to hit a fastball, low and away. I don't think he's the one behind the attempt on your life."

"Oh, no? And why do you say that?"

"Busby said it himself. If he wanted to shoot you, he would have done it personally, and with pleasure. He's not the hiring kind."

Abbott bobbed his head slowly. "What's this about an artist colony?" he asked. "You're not telling me that Hank has gone all hippy-dippy on us?"

"Not an artist colony—the *Nudist Colony*."

"You're not saying Busby has been swanking about in the buff?!"

"Not him—others." Warren explained that when he said nudist colony, he meant *Nudist Colony*.

"Oh, yes. *That* place." The mayor had heard some of the fellows at the council meetings mentioning it. Not a place he frequented himself. "And Busby is a customer?"

Warren yawned. "Not Busby. One his protégés was—Javy Clark. Hank mentioned that Daryl Blue also paid them a visit every once in a while. According to one of the waitresses, the Colony is the secret den of a secret society. Blue and Clark might have had some connection with this society, and now Blue is dead, and Clark is missing. Both ex-ballplayers."

Abbott reviewed this morsel. A secret den of a secret society. That was two secrets, by his count. Abbott didn't much like secret societies. Damned difficult to canvass their votes. "You've given me a lot to think about, Kingsley."

Warren was glad. That was what a bodyguard was for.

"And I tend to agree with you. Hank Busby is probably not the man behind the assassin. I can cross him off the list and rest easy tonight."

"You'll be safe here, alright," said Warren, shoving a chest of drawers across the hole so he could get some rest himself. There was a slight impact on the slide—a grunt and a bonk, followed by the sound of an overly talkative man reeling back. Warren called around the corner, "Did I clip you in the head, Mayor? My fault. Good night."

* *

Up above them, in a crawl space now cleared out of fruit and cigarette butts, a man emerged from his clever hiding space under a pile of painting tarps.

The would-be assassin, for it was he, had heard everything that had transpired that night. He didn't quite follow why it had transpired, who Basil was and why they had to be so noisy about it—but he knew one thing. His target, the mayor, was here. He could finally get at him.

He had failed at the mayor's office, at the mayor's house and in the street, but now he had him where he wanted him (Plan D). He could get him finally, and it would be precise (Plan D Plus).

He crawled back under his tarps and slept contentedly.

12 — DO I HAVE TO DRAW YOU A PICTURE?

B y eight a.m., Sheriff Jenny Blake was in her office downtown, pondering the case(s) again.

She began by pondering David Wincher, whose death she did not put down to suicide or an accident. As the evening news had reported at five, and then again at ten, the authorities—Sheriff Jenny and her deputies—were still investigating the matter, but the assumption would seem to be that Mr. Wincher had perished through misadventure. Jenny did not string along with this assumption. It was too coincidental, calling to confess something and then dying before anyone could get there to hear it. She wasn't buying it.

She had no suspects in the Wincher case. David might not have lived in a glamorous building, but it was a secure one, and no strangers had been seen entering the premises. No one connected with the assault on the mayor had been anywhere near the scene—other than the mayor himself. It had been Mayor Abbott, strolling by at the time of the incident, who had spotted the body in the alley and alerted the attendant, thus immersing the street in a swarm of ghoulish onlookers. The whole affair had been very unpleasant for the poor man (Fred Abbott). It couldn't have been very fun for David Wincher either.

Moving on from Wincher, the sheriff pondered Hank Busby. Hank had finally come in for questioning yesterday, care of her deputy Tony. After all the hype, the meeting was something of a letdown. Hank's answers to their questions had brought them no new information or insight at all.

Dismissing Hank from her mind, Jenny pondered Sheryl Abbott, now absent without leave. She had disappeared fairly rapidly, had Sheryl; Jenny wondered why. The woman must be up to something.

Finally, just to complete the entire range of investigative contemplation, the sheriff spent a moment pondering Daryl Blue. What with the happenings since, the late press secretary had been shunted off to the side in her mind, but in some way his accidental murder—if it was accidental—was still at the core of everything else she was pondering. She was certain of that.

Off to the side of Jenny's desk, although never shunted, lay Deputy Lance's daughter Gladys, scribbling away furiously on her art pad. She was on her stomach, her tiny legs wiggling in the air as she finished the final few touches on her latest drawing. She was a dedicated artist, and the last details were always the most important to her.

At last, she popped up and presented the canvas to her father, standing at the water cooler and doing a touch of pondering himself.

With four other daughters, you might think that Deputy Lance would have a hard time conjuring up enthusiasm at a moment's notice—oo-ing and ah-ing with the proper zest at each new art submission he received and keeping track of who had entered their Blue Period recently and who leaned more toward the Post-Modernist school.

Lance, however, was more than equal to the challenge. He oo-ed with just the right emphasis at the bright parts, ah-ed at the faces of the subjects depicted, and did not miss the use of azure and turquoise in the sky, across the landscape and inside what looked like a bowl of bluish-green pudding.

The bowl of pudding, explained Gladys, was a bowl of money. She had run out of green in her crayon box.

Lance liked the picture very much. "Is that me?" he asked, pointing to a curious figure with a large, gleaming head, a brown uniform and something along the lines of a Gatling gun in his hand.

Gladys nodded. She would have thought that much was obvious. He was guarding the bowl of pudding-money.

"And who is that, up on the cage?" asked her father. "Is he at the zoo?"

Gladys explained that it was Warren Kingsley up on the cage. And it was not a cage; it was a balcony. There were some animals present, because Warren liked animals, but it was not a zoo he was at. It was at a house, the mayor's house, and he was on a balcony.

Lance understood. He was on a balcony. Either way, he thought it a lovely depiction. Her character study made Warren look like Adolf Hitler, but it was a lovely depiction. "Why is he up so high?"

"Because it's a balcony," Gladys replied. "He's dressing the people," she said simply. "At the mayor's house. He dressed them at the conference meeting because the mayor did not want to talk to any of them or dress them or anything. He is not a very good mayor, or that's what Mommy says. It's because he never dresses anybody."

"*Ad*dresses them," Lance corrected—unless Warren and the mayor had taken up a sideline in the clothing industry (he wouldn't have put it past Abbott, the man with a finger in every pie).

Non-addresser or not, the mayor was an important man, and Lance would have preferred his wife didn't speak about him that way. While not technically Lance's boss, Abbott could still make life very unpleasant for him and his comrades.

He finished his survey of the drawing. So those were *people* Warren was addressing, behind the small animals. Lance had thought they were caribou. "It's a nice likeness, darling. Although, it looks like the balcony is a little tall to me. I was at the mayor's house, you know, and he has a terrace, not a balcony. Terraces are much lower."

Gladys Stengel waved aside these petty disparagements. She had heard tell of a balcony, and that was how she had drawn it. She hurried over to show the sheriff—hopefully a less censorious critic.

Jenny smiled brightly, though slightly distractedly. She wasn't sure why Lance's daughter had drawn Mussolini shouting down at a herd of confused-looking elk, but she liked the use of color. Especially the field of blue snakes.

Gladys puffed. She explained that the snakes were grass, blades of blue grass. Jenny said of course they were. She would have spoken more about her appreciation of Gladys's snake grass, but Deputy Albert interrupted their salon discussion. He had just returned from an errand.

Jenny hadn't realized he had stepped out. Albert so seldom left his desk that she always took it for granted that he would be there.

"I got something for you, Sheriff," said the wandering deputy.

She set down the picture and gave him her full attention.

"There was something in the ballistics test I didn't care for, so I went back and checked with them."

"And?"

"I was right to check," said the mustachioed one.

Jenny nodded. It was a great story so far, she thought, but it could use some improvement in the third act.

"And the reason why I was right to check," proceeded Deputy Albert, "is the bullets weren't the same."

"What bullets?"

"The bullets in the gun that killed Daryl Blue."

The sheriff said oh. Those bullets. "How not the same?" she wondered.

"The bullets in the gun, and the one that got Daryl in the noggin, were pretty typical; guess you'd call them round-point bullets. But the one that hit the mayor in the titanium was hollow point."

"That's odd."

"It is, right? Guess the gunman really wanted to do in Fred with that first shot. Hollow points make a helluva mess."

"Yes…" said his superior. "They do, but…" She trailed off. She was pondering again.

Lance came over to join their discussion. "That political rally is starting up soon," he reminded them. "After what happened when the governor came through last year, we should get there early."

It was not something Kilobyte was proud of, but most official extravaganzas in town had a habit of turning ugly. No one likes to use the term "riot," but a sort of *riot lite* was more or less what always occurred.

People had their theories—a certain element of lawlessness in the area, a modern-day predilection toward outspokenness and public displays—but a more obvious explanation should have probably suggested itself: half-price beer and politics were not a good combination.

"And with the hubbub last night, we should be extra careful," Lance continued.

Jenny looked up. "Hubbub?"

"At Warren Kingsley's place. Remember Warren telling me about a couple of roughhousing out-of-towners breaking into his cottage?"

Jenny did remember now, yes. Warren and that friend of his, Mahrute, had played it very cagey when asked about the incident.

"If we leave now," said Lance, "I should still have time to drop off Gladdy at her dance class."

This announcement prompted an interested stare from Deputy Albert. As a student of the arts himself, he wondered if the little one was confining herself to dance, or had she considered other theatrical disciplines?

Gladys replied that she was keeping her options open. She was wise for her four years.

Jenny, for her twenty-eight, did not feel very wise. She picked up the astute one's drawing again. Warren Kingsley...a crowd of onlookers (who still looked like bison)...a balcony up in the sky...other balconies Jenny knew of...David Wincher's balcony...a balcony somewhere else she had seen recently...

She peered down at the doodle and frowned.

It was the age-old question. What was wrong with this picture?

* *

Mayor Frederick Abbott—for he was still mayor the last time he checked—returned home to Warren Kingsley's cottage at noon and slammed the door behind him. Warren and Mahrute followed a few seconds later, not slamming.

Warren was dressed in his best Armani, somewhat tobacco-smoked from Basil's closet cohabitation last night. Mahrute had donned an attractive Hawaiian shirt and baggy Bermuda shorts (Henrietta Bragg's grandfather's garments).

"You seem upset, Mayor," Warren suggested.

"Upset?!" exclaimed Abbott. He picked up a vase and dashed it on the floor. Who needed roughhousing thugs when you had politicians? "Upset?! Upset?! You bet I'm upset! You whamboozled me."

Warren wasn't certain of the precise definition of the term *whamboozled*, but he got the gist. He reached down and steadied Captain Drayton, who was having another holiday from Henrietta's barn. The mayor's behavior was visibly disturbing him. "Is this about the rally?" Warren asked.

"Is this about the rally?!" exclaimed Abbott. "You bet it's about the rally! You never told me you were running against me."

"You never asked," said Warren.

"Well, you won't win, you hear me? You will never, ever win— you got it?"

Warren didn't know why not. He had filed Form 64-K. Thanks to the mayor.

"It won't matter!" Abbott declared. "You can't hoodwink the entire township of Kilobyte into voting for you. It has taken me years to do that—and you only have four months!"

"Actually, I think it's closer to five, Mayor."

"It won't matter," Abbott repeated. "I say it's a pipe dream. An absolute pipe dream!"

Even as the mayor spoke these words, he didn't really believe them. It might be a pipe dream Kingsley was seeking, but men like Warren had a way of building on the vapors of those pipe dreams and winding up with something quite three-dimensional, quite three-dimensional indeed.

Already, the masses had responded enthusiastically to the announcement of his candidacy. Warren had hardly said anything at the rally—Abbott himself would have stretched it out four times as long—but it had worked. They had loved Warren for it. He was the man Kilobyte had been waiting for their entire lives.

More and more, Abbott was finding what the people wanted was brevity. Brevity and new blood—as if they hadn't had enough blood, new or old, this week already.

"You won't get away with this," said the (current) mayor.

Warren frowned. This sounded like dudgeon to him. "When you say I won't get away with it, what do you mean exactly?" He peered down at the Captain, who didn't know either.

"I mean you won't get away with it. I'll fight it. I'll cancel Form 64-K. Call it a conflict of interest. You—you—*did you* hear that?" asked Mayor Abbott, changing the subject.

Warren had heard it. So had Mahrute. And the Captain. A faint cough from the patio outside. Perhaps Basil, returning, had finally found those cigarettes unbeneficial to his health.

It wasn't Basil who had coughed.

A man in a sleek black suit and sleek black sunglasses—every inch the type of man Abbott had always wanted on his staff—stepped in through the sliding door. He was joined by three clones, each sleeker than the last. They had stepped outside for some air.

Once inside, they parted, like a Broadway dance number, and down the middle a tall, plus-sized woman reentered the cottage. She had a slightly supercilious brow, small, piercing gray eyes and silver streaks in her hair.

Warren and Mahrute had never seen this mysterious endomorph before now, but they couldn't help but be captivated by her. She had a presence. Abbott, meanwhile, had no difficulty identifying her.

He should have known her from her posse alone.

"Hi, Clarisse," he said. He turned to Warren and Mahrute and sighed. "It's Clarisse," he explained.

**

"So this is how my brother conducts his affairs as the mayor of Kilobyte," said his steadfast sister. She was sitting in one of Warren's easy chairs, a cup of freshly brewed tea at her elbow and a raspberry scone in her hand. "This is good," she remarked, referring to the scone.

"Made them fresh this morning," said Warren, who was not ashamed to admit that he was a man who baked. He was in the kitchenette, attending to the rest of the refreshments. This included whacking aside the hand of one of the Clarisse Royal Guard as he reached for a roasted Brazil nut that had not yet properly cooled.

"Well, they're damn good," chewed their special guest. "Too good, really. If you run for mayor half as well as you cook, you will win this election from my brother in a snap. You can have my write-in vote right now."

"Clarisse—" bleated Fred Abbott.

He was perched on a stool by the counter, the other three guards a stone's throw away—just in case any detrimental sibling "horseplay" should break out. They were watching him closely.

"Clarisse—"

His sister's remarks swept over him. "Of course, I might have a word with your decorator, if I were you," she said to Warren. She peered over at a pile of what appeared to be the remnants of a coffee table. "That wasn't your doing, was it, Fred? I heard you smashing something when you came in."

"Clarisse—"

"Fred was always breaking things when he was a kid," said Clarisse. "Setting off firecrackers in the house, busting up my dollies with a hammer and then squeezing himself under our parents' bed to hear what they were going to do about it. He was a slithering, thug of a boy, and now look at him."

"Clarisse—"

"I'm not saying I don't love him, mind you. You have to love your family. As a mayor, on the other hand—now that's another story."

Abbott attempted another tack. "How did you find me, Clarisse?"

Clarisse set down her scone. "Your office told me you were skulking at home. As good a place as any for a politician to skulk, I suppose. I checked at your house, though, and your butler said you weren't there. You were here. This is your home now apparently—a tiny ramshackle in the woods. Not that I'm disparaging your place or anything," she told Warren.

Warren wasn't concerned. It *was* a tiny ramshackle in the woods. He had never heard *ramshackle* used as a noun before. He liked it.

What he didn't like was the condition of this ramshackle. He didn't mind the broken coffee table and the rest of the damage—they added character—but he did have an issue with his bookshelf. It was this bookshelf, oddly unaffected by last night's brawl, that had attracted his attention.

The unit ran up the wall, a full fifteen feet in the air, toward the tip of the cathedral ceiling. (What his cottage lacked in horizontal dimensions, it made up for in the vertical.) Abandoning the Brazils for the time being, Warren stepped to this shelving and scowled up at it. Captain Drayton joined him. Something about the shelf seemed off to man and dog, as off as a peach pit in a non-peach-eater's garbage.

"The town council is talking," continued Clarisse behind them.

"Let them talk," spat Fred Abbott. Councils talked too much anyway.

"They're saying you've deserted your post, that you're hiding out. Is it any surprise that this fine, upstanding young—or I suppose we better say *middle-aged*—man has taken it upon himself to run against you in the election? I'm not surprised. Are we?"

"It's an affront to all I have done for him!" said Abbott, whose *we* was. "The man is supposed to be my bodyguard. My temporary press secretary…also my speechwriter. That's what I hired him for—those are the things, I should say."

Clarisse shook her gray-streaked head. "You probably hired him to be your political opponent too and simply forgot about it. It sounds like you've hired him for everything else."

"If I had realized this underhanded skullduggery was going on—"

"But why didn't you realize it?" she asked. "According to your butler, you knew that a dark-horse candidate was entering the election."

"I knew a dark horse was entering," agreed Abbott. "I heard a rumor. Nonetheless, I didn't put everything together until later on. Well, not until the rally this morning, if you want the truth, when Kingsley stood up next to me and announced his candidacy. But I've been distracted. We do have a murderer on the loose, you know?"

Clarisse frowned. "You must always put things together, Freddy, even when there are murderers on the loose. If you'd simply get with the program, you could prevent these disasters. Not that I'm calling you a disaster," she told Warren.

Warren didn't mind. He *was* a disaster. A disaster and a ramshackle. Always had been. He continued to scowl at his bookshelf.

"If you hadn't ignored this man," Clarisse carried on, "assigning him new responsibilities every thirty seconds, he might not have risen up against you. First that baseball man, Hank Busby-Hat, or whatever his name is, and now this gentleman. You oppress the little people, Fred, and then the little people push back on you."

Abbott puffed, much like little Gladys had in the discussion about her drawing. "You don't understand, Clarisse; everyone has numerous occupations in town. That's—"

"How things are done in Kilobyte. Yes, I know," she said. "I think that's why I started summering in Boston."

Fred Abbott took a deep breath. He tried a third tack. "What do you *want*, Clarisse?"

Clarisse appreciated the question. Down to the nitty-gritty, and only twenty minutes late. She liked it. "As I said, the council has been talking. If you are going to persist in hiding out—"

"I'm not hiding out; I'm planning."

"If you're going to persist in hiding out and shirking your duty, we, the council, have no choice but to assign your office to a provisional mayor. It's in the bylaws."

Abbott had heard enough about bylaws for one afternoon. If they weren't going to bar a man's bodyguard from running against him, what good were they?

"We have to do it, Freddy," said Clarisse.

Freddy snorted. "Oh, you do, do you? And whom, might I ask, will you be assigning these mayoral duties to—*my* mayoral duties—if I decide to continue my sabbatical?"

Warren was curious about this himself. He wondered if it was him. If it was, it would save him a lot of trouble and annoyance running for office.

Unfortunately, Councilwoman Clarisse didn't know the answer to that question. "I have Hugo calling the paper-pushers right now." She pointed to one of her sleek young men, holding a phone to his stolid ear. "This is a good thing, Freddy," she told her brother. "It'll give you time to finish all this wonderful planning of yours and maybe, eventually, beat back the Huns from the gate. Not that I'm calling you a—well, you know," she said to Warren.

Warren didn't know, because Warren wasn't listening. He had finally arrived at a conclusion regarding his bookshelf. "Has someone been reading my H. W. Janson's *History of Art?*" he asked. Warren's little furnished cottage hadn't come with much, but it had more than its share of books, and as long as he was a renter here, he took a proprietary interest in them. He glanced around the room, posing the question of the amazing, shifting Janson to those assembled.

Mahrute said he had not had the pleasure of perusing H. W.'s work, no; the guards in the kitchen shook their heads; and Abbott glared and asked, "The What's *History of Who?*"

Prompted for her statement, Clarisse asked Warren if she looked like the sort of gal who would mess with a complete stranger's Janson, and Warren scowled a third time. The guard Hugo, still waiting on hold with the Kilobyte Administration Offices, also shook his head.

He hadn't boned up on classical art since he took that master's degree on Greek and Roman studies a few years back.

Warren wasn't satisfied. The fact remained that someone had replaced the Janson on the wrong shelf. *The Poetical Works of Byron* was also out of place, as was the *International Bartender's Guide* (with a new introduction by the editor). He slid them off the bookshelf and stacked them neatly on the counter, adding to the mix *Bartlett's Familiar Quotations*, *Joy of Cooking* and three books of English estates—none of which were where they were this morning. For some reason, Warren always noticed these things.

Disinterested in her host's shelves, Clarisse asked if anyone else was cold.

"It does seem a little chilly in here," Mahrute agreed.

"I'd call it a tad nippy," said Warren, still distracted.

"It's freezing," maintained Clarisse.

Warren went to attend to the thermostat. He departed from the shelf with the Captain in tow, the latter apparently under the impression that the journey would end in the doling out of doggy treats.

Happy for the reprieve from his sister's criticism, Abbott flipped open the cover of the *Bartlett's* with his finger, twisted his face in contemplation of some quotation and grunted. "What are these doing here?" he wondered.

"Those are all the books that were out of order on the shelf," Warren answered from the thermostat. "I'm trying to detect a pattern."

The mayor never went in for patterns, unless they were voting patterns, and those just made his head throb. He picked up a fig wrapped in bacon and chowed down somberly. Say what you will about this Kingsley, he knew his way around a fig.

"Well, that explains one mystery," said the cottageholder, returning from his temperature adjustment. "Someone had the A/C set on fifty. No wonder it's chilly in here."

"Glacial," insisted Clarisse. If she wanted this kind of cold, she could have stayed in Boston. She returned to the subject of her brother's inadequate mayoring. The poor man's respite hadn't lasted more than a few minutes. "Have you thought about stepping down permanently?" she asked him.

"Never!" said Abbott.

"But you don't seem to enjoy politics very much."

"I'm crazy about it!—or is that *them?* I'm crazy about politics," said Fred Abbott. "The power play, the spirited debates. It's a hoot. Besides, Sheryl never would have married me had I not been mayor."

"Yes. Sheryl..." said Clarisse. "And where is my sister-in-law? She wasn't at the house."

"Shut up," snapped Fred Abbott, like any lover of spirited debate, and Clarisse sniffed at the comment.

"Well, I don't know what else to say," she concluded. She looked over at Mahrute, standing quietly in the corner beside the coffee-table mound. "You haven't said very much, have you? You look like an intelligent, brightly dressed sort of fellow. Perhaps you can talk some sense into my sibling?"

Unfortunately, Mahrute did not have the luxury of talking sense to anyone just now. He had his client to concern himself with; a client who had long since passed the sense-talking stage.

When you considered how many years Borodin Mahrute had known Warren Kingsley—many strange and wonderful years—it would seem inconceivable that the latter could do anything now that would astonish the former. But when one peers across the room and finds even a strange and wonderful client climbing up the side of a bookshelf like some literary tarantula, one—which is to say Mahrute—might feel entitled to a little astonishment. (Gladys wouldn't have been surprised, accustomed as she was to depicting Warren at soaring heights, but Mahrute was.)

He stared up at Warren, as did Clarisse and her four guards—Hugo last of all, because he had just gotten through to the town clerk.

Abbott also stared. Captain Drayton took the opportunity to bound up and snag the last fig from the politician's astonished fingers.

Up above them all, in the swirling haze of the cathedral ceiling, Warren had pried open the A/C vent from the wall and was even now, as they gaped up at him, fishing his hand inside, his foot slowly slipping from its placement on the highest shelf.

He addressed the room. "I'm going to need a box," he said. "About yay big—a space on the kitchen counter, also yay, and a bag of something cold from the freezer. Glacial, if we have it. Frozen peas would do nicely, but I'm not married to them. In the meantime," he went on, "if anyone knows how to defuse a small, intricate explosive, speak up now."

He threw this out as a topic of discussion.

13 — Icy Commentary

They had surrounded the kitchen counter—eight stern and determined faces, all staring down at Warren's grab bag. Removed from the vent, it now lay at the bottom of a shoebox surrounded by a sack of Erma's Freshly Frozen Peas—"Just Heat and Enjoy!"

Abbott's stern and determined face was the first to speak. "What the f—?"

Clarisse held up a hand. "Keep it clean, Freddy. Your raucous language won't help matters." She paused. "So who wants to poke it first?"

Mahrute was happy to lend a hand, if not a poke.

"It's all yours," said Warren. "I have one of those folding pocket tools in the kitchen drawer, if you need it. I assume you'll want some kind of cutters?"

Abbott broke in with a heated "Har!" He didn't know why he said *Har*. *Har* just came out. "Someone has been putting explosives in your vents?"

"Just one vent," Warren replied. "A small explosive."

"Is it going to go off?" Abbott asked.

"Not unless the M-man makes a hash of it. The explosive appears to have an intricate temperature control, set to go off once it rises above a certain temp—fifty-five in this instance. I saw a device like this in Omaha once, or possibly it was Kansas City. Anyway, as I say, it uses an intricate temperature control. A rather ingenious way of guaranteeing that your target is home when it goes off. It works pretty well. The target is cold, they turn up the A/C and *blam!*"

"Kingsley?"

"Yes, Mayor?"

"What about now?"

"Oh, it's quite safe now. Erma is seeing to that. Eh, Mahrute?"

Mahrute nodded, but not emphatically.

For all his brave talk, Warren was beginning to feel a little uncertain himself. Still, if you are going to die, you might as well die among friends. Or, that is to say, one friend, a mild canine acquaintance, five strangers and a staunch political opponent.

The staunch political opponent could only gaze away as in a dream. "How did you know?" he muttered.

Warren was delighted to explain. It was the misfiled books, he explained—or, to be precise, the vacancies the misfiled books created once they were taken off the shelf.

"It's funny," he said, "I always thought they should have installed a ladder in here, just like those fancy old mahogany libraries you see in movies or books of English estates. It appears our mysterious arsonist has provided one pro bono. Look at the spaces; they form a perfect ladder up the shelves, all the way up to the vent. Pretty resourceful. Although, I have to say, our visiting acrobat would have done better replacing the books in the same order he or she found them in."

"Shouldn't we call the police?" Abbott blurted out.

"Probably not time. Erma won't last forever."

"Maybe we should just run for it!"

Warren scorned this craven behavior. "Nonsense. Mahrute is on it. Correct, Mahrute?"

Mahrute went on tinkering.

"Besides," said Warren, frowning, "any sudden movements or change in barometric pressure in here, and the whole thing could go—"

"Blam?" asked Abbott.

"Blam," agreed Warren. "And then, if it hits the gas line, *blam, blam, BLAM.*"

"Anything we can do?" asked Clarisse, waiting for the full catalog of *blams.*

Warren considered the question. "I'm sure Mahrute could use some room to move around better. And perhaps a little less noise."

Clarisse attended to these matters instanter. With the help of Hugo, she cleared everyone back. Abbott would have been happiest clearing back all the way to his house (in Rhode Island).

"I don't get it," he whispered. "Who could have done this?"

"A good question," whispered Warren. "You want my theory?"

Abbott didn't care one way or the other. He shivered, and it had nothing to do with the A/C temperature.

"Whoever they were, they must have been pretty agile," whispered Warren. "It's not everyone who can scale that shelf the way I did. It took amazing concentration and reflexes." He took a moment out to ponder his amazing concentration and reflexes. "That points to either Basil, the little rapscallion, or our mysterious squatter, whoever he or she is."

"Who is Basil?" whispered the mayor.

"Yes," whispered Warren.

"And who is this squatter?"

"Exactly." Warren went to the fridge and pulled out the exhibits he had shown Mahrute the previous night. Some old apple cores and a banana skin.

There was one other thing, a piece of electronics. "It's some kind of bug," Warren said. "A bugging device," he added—not to be confused with the little critters who float around your face when you're trying to mix up a scone batter. "I found it during my attic crawl."

Clarisse looked reflective. "Someone has been bugging you?"

"Like gangbusters."

"And eating fruit and planting plastique in your vent?" She was fascinated by this, especially the *blam* angle. "Don't we have a nephew who's some kind of explosives expert?" she whispered to her brother. Hugo could get him on the line right now, if they did.

Abbott knew of no such relative. "We have a nephew who's a lay-about," he whispered.

"Yes, I know that. Not him. Another nephew."

"We have a nephew who's a mailman," Abbott whispered.

"Why'd I think he was a munitions expert?" Clarisse whispered.

"Don't know," Abbott whispered.

There was a short pause.

"I've always been fascinated by that profession," said Warren, joining in on the discussion.

"Explosives?" asked Clarisse (at a whisper).

"Postmen. It seems very diverting, that line of work. Out in the fresh air, dogs nipping playfully at your heels—"

"Shh!" whispered Abbott, as a dog nipped playfully at his. "The Muldoon fellow is doing something."

He was correct. The Muldoon fellow, a.k.a. Mahrute, *was* doing something. He drew back the clippers and shook his head. No, they wouldn't want to cut that one...

The Captain, bored with tugging on Abbott's pant leg, jumped up on a chair and stuck his paws on the kitchen counter, offering his assistance. Mahrute scooted him aside, preventing him from chewing the plastique or chomping the orange wire out of turn. "Perhaps it would be best," he announced, "if everyone cleared the area."

Unlike with Abbott, when Mahrute suggested this, Warren did not deem it craven. "You heard the man," he said. "Everyone out."

You didn't have to tell Fred Abbott twice. He was at the door, damning the barometric pressure in a matter of seconds. "Aren't you coming, Clarisse?" he called back, but not before he was already halfway outside.

Clarisse was less resolute. She didn't like the idea of leaving anyone behind, especially this nice Don Ho man and his large friend who baked so well.

But if there wasn't anything they could do...

"Good luck," she said, walking swiftly in the direction of her Freddy. "Boys," she gestured.

If you didn't have to tell Fred Abbott twice, you didn't have to tell her sleek guards once. Before the word had left her lips, they had assembled in a beeline for the door. They still looked like a fancy Broadway musical, but now like one after someone had called it a wrap.

Captain Drayton joined them in their exodus. It wasn't that he lacked courage, but—well, you know.

Alone at last, Warren turned to Mahrute. "Maybe now we can hear ourselves think."

Mahrute looked up from the box long enough for a kindly smile. "You should go as well."

Warren wasn't going to dignify that with a reply. Mahrute was his bodyguard, and sometimes bodyguards have to be checked on. You have to make sure these specialists are worth the money. "I'm not going anywhere," he said.

Mahrute nodded appreciatively, straightening the lay of his Hawaiian shirt, and returned his attention to the box.

Warren joined the scrutiny at the counter.

"So anyway," he remarked, returning to more important topics, "I haven't noticed, do mailboxes around here have those little thingies on them?"

"Thingies?" asked Mahrute.

"The little thingies on the side. You put them up or down."

"The flag?"

"I'm sure you're right. The flag. Do mailboxes here have those?" he asked.

"I am not certain," said Mahrute.

"You don't see them around much anymore," Warren commented.

"I'm sorry?"

"The flags."

"Oh. The flags."

Warren nodded. Yes, the flags. A.k.a., the thingies. Everyone seemed to have those community mailboxes now. They don't have the same panache as the old ones with the thingies, he opined. "You place them up to indicate to the postman that you have outgoing mail, correct?"

"Pardon?" whispered Mahrute, squeezing his fingers deeper into Erma's frozen cauldron.

"The flag thingy," said Warren.

"Oh, the flag thingy." Mahrute supposed you did. Place them up.

"But what if you place yours up, but don't stick any mail in the box? If the postman comes and he has no mail for you, does he place it down or leave it up?"

"I suppose he places it down," said Mahrute.

"But then the person thinks the man took mail that never existed."

"Then I suppose he leaves it up."

"Then he thinks the postman hasn't come. It's sort of a paradox, isn't it?"

"I suppose," Mahrute whispered, and ran a hand over his mustache, attempting to derive comfort from the gesture. It was one of the few times he wished he had a beard.

"Guess it's open to artistic interpretation," Warren asserted about the mailboxes, at which point Mahrute reached for a wire, held his breath and snipped.

* *

Outside, on Warren Kingsley's front lawn, Fred Abbott and his sister Clarisse were pondering the heroic behavior of Warren and his vibrantly dressed friend, the latter of whom Abbott was beginning to think may have been called "Mazoo" or possibly "Rutabaga," not "Muldoon."

The minutes ticked by. Abbott was asking himself how, if Warren blew himself up, this might affect the polls (he had known things of this sort to swing in a candidate's favor); Clarisse was asking herself why she hadn't requested Warren's scone recipe before leaving; and the Captain was asking himself what became of his doggy treat. During this communal meditation, the door opened, and their host emerged. He appeared unscathed.

"We're good to go," said Warren. He spoke with total confidence now. Not getting sprayed all over the wall in a flurry of plastic explosive and frozen peas will do that to a man.

"It's safe?" asked Clarisse.

"The thing's a spent force. I'd stake Mahrute's reputation on it."

"What about our lives?" demanded Abbott.

"That too," Warren agreed, but he seemed to feel Mahrute's reputation was enough.

* *

The sheriff had been called, and things were returning to normal. (Most importantly, the Captain had been sent home with his doggy treat, and Clarisse had secured that scone recipe.)

Fred Abbott still couldn't bring himself to rejoin Warren and Mahrute inside. While his sister discussed some matters with her men in the driveway, the mayor lingered at the entrance, running his finger-tips up and down the doorframe.

Warren was in no mood for extended good-byes or whatever it was Abbott was doing. "Watch the digits," he warned. "Don't want to smush any fingers in the door."

Abbott did not watch the digits and was not concerned with any-thing getting smushed. He continued to draw invisible doodles in the wood, like a giant, aged Gladys Stengel. "I still can't believe how close we came," he whispered. "So close to death, always so close to death."

"It's a real poser," said Warren. "In or out, Mayor?" he asked. "In or out?"

The mayor was remaining *out* for now, with an option on an *in* at some point in the near future. "Could this have been one of your ene-mies, Kingsley?"

This? wondered the other man. Oh, the explosive. Warren hadn't really thought about it. He did have lots of enemies—too many, really. He should probably do something about that. "Actually, Mayor, I would say this was more likely one of your enemies than one of mine. Think about it. We never did track down that attempted assassin. I would bet that he, in this instance, tracked you down."

"Tracked…me…down… You mean to here?"

"Why not?"

Abbott mouthed, *Why not?* Kingsley was correct. Why not? "Well, I'm definitely not going back inside now!"

"What about your own home or office?" Warren suggested.

Abbott wasn't going there either. His enemies were everywhere, *everywhere!* "I'm taking that leave of absence," he decided.

"That's convenient," said Clarisse, appearing on the porch behind him, "because I've learned who your successor is. That is, should you continue this 'sabbatical' of yours."

The mayor was continuing his sabbatical and then some. "Who is it?" he asked.

"I am," she replied coolly.

Abbott stared at her. "You?"

"I. According to Hugo, since Kilobyte has no elected deputy mayor, that duty, however temporary, falls to the most senior member of the town council. I am that member."

Abbott continued to gape. "You?"

"Yes, little brother, me."

"But...but...I won't allow it!" he sputtered.

"So you won't be taking a sabbatical, after all?"

"Yes...I mean, no...I mean, *you?!*"

Warren could see things were well in hand on the mayor question. He, meanwhile, had other fishes to fricassee, not the least of which was becoming mayor himself. "Well, looks like you got everything under control," he said. "I suppose I'll be seeing you both at the debate tonight. Take care of yourselves, Mayors. And if that explosive was meant for you, Mayor Abbott, keep your wits about you. You can never be too sure where danger might lurk."

With these happy words, he shut the door on the man.

Rejoining Mahrute in the kitchenette, he did pause to wonder if that muffled yelp he had heard had anything to do with smushed fingers.

14 — INCOMMUNICADO

t had.

An hour later, Abbott sat brooding over his bandaged hand. Kingsley had been correct: danger truly did lurk everywhere.

The mayor (possibly current and perhaps—or perhaps not—on sabbatical) was sitting at a booth in the back of a very dark room.

He was drinking and scowling, scowling and drinking.

He wasn't especially worried about his fingers. Smashed fingers were the least of Fred Abbott's troubles at this point. After his afternoon with his sister and Warren, the dejected politician needed to go somewhere and think: about assassins, about Clarisse and about the future of his career.

It struck him, just before Warren Kingsley's door had struck his fingers, that it didn't matter whether he disassociated himself from his elected office or not. As a full-fledged mayor or as a mayor on leave, he was in constant jeopardy.

He needed a plan.

And such was why, some sixty minutes after he had left the home of his bodyguard, Frederick Abbott could be seen sitting and glaring at his watch in the back of the Nudist Colony—home of the "Early Diner's Big Man's Seafood Buffet: $8.99, Hush Puppies Included."

He had come here because he needed a place where he wasn't known, where he was a nobody. Not Mayor Frederick Abbott. Just plain, old Fred.

Also, he really liked buffets.

He hadn't been to the Colony in years. The last time he was here, it wasn't even called the Colony. It was the Raunchy Coconut then. In some ways, Abbott had come here looking for the Coconut of his past. He enjoyed those days; they were simpler times. Now, everything was all assassins, bodyguards and sisters—not to mention strip clubs that held out on you when you asked for more hush puppies. In short, everything was all effed up.

He gazed out across the darkened room and snorted. Even though he was the one who had arranged this summit, he still viewed the upcoming meeting sourly. And when, shortly after he put in a new drink order, a shadowy figure emerged from the darkened aisle and took a seat at his booth, Abbott greeted this figure with all the sourness at his disposal. "You're late," he told him. "Sixteen minutes, four seconds."

Telly said onk? and knocked over the tartar sauce. He was surprised the boss had called him this afternoon—the boss never called him—and he was even more surprised that the old man frequented joints like the Colony.

He must have hidden depths, the boss.

You'd think, after leaving this establishment not fourteen hours earlier, the youth would be suffering from a hangover. He was not. The Blakes did not get hangovers. (Just ask his sister Jen or Warren's close, personal friend Harvard Blake.) As for Telly's tardiness, the intern might have explained that he was late because he had been told to come to "that filth haven" off Route 4 at two o'clock sharp, and as anyone could see, this wholesome establishment was off Route 6 and was anything but filthy. (You could confirm the latter detail with the eager young woman up on stage, currently twirling away on the cleanest stripper pole you have ever seen.)

But these didn't seem like plausible excuses to Telly anyway, and it didn't matter, because Abbott had already started yelping to no one in particular about a dearth of Big Man Hush Puppies. "You were too obvious," he growled.

"Obvious?" Telly spoke with astonishment and, in spite of the general atmosphere of the place, brightly. "How do you mean obvious, boss?"

"I mean obvious," said Abbott, sipping from a sidecar cocktail. He had already had three. "Scooting over to the table like that. You were too obvious. What I want from you is subtlety and guile. Guile, guile, guile."

"You bet," Telly replied. Guile was the intern motto. "You sounded pretty agitated on the phone. What's up? Hey, your fingers are all bandaged. Is that why you're agitated? Bandaged fingers?"

Abbott said it wasn't bandaged fingers, no. "I need your help."

"You need *my* help, boss?"

"I need your help," Abbott said. "I'm a marked man."

"Marked?" So that's what happened to his fingers—someone marked them. "Marked how?" he wondered.

"I had yet another narrow escape this afternoon," said the mayor. "The killer is edging ever closer."

Telly hated when killers did that. "What do you want me to do, boss?" He couldn't have been more eager if he had been up on stage, winding around a polished stripper pole.

"I need protection."

Telly said ah. "Warren—"

"Don't talk to me about Warren!" exclaimed Mayor Abbott. "I need better protection than Warren Friggin' Kingsley." He paused to drink and nod intelligently to himself. "Do you still have that Doberman pinscher you're always babbling about?"

"Kitten?" Telly couldn't remember ever mentioning his dog, Kitten, but it didn't matter. "Actually, she's more Jen's dog than mine. Why do you want to know about Kitten?"

"I need to borrow it."

"You want to borrow Kitten? Why do you want to borrow Kitten, boss?"

Abbott smacked the table and said not to ask so many dumb questions. "Just go and bring the mutt here. And stop gaping at me! You're gonna do me a *flavor*," he said, setting down his drink. "A favor," he corrected.

Telly was happy to oblige. "I—let me make a call," he said, standing.

Abbott waved his drink. His intern could phone all the dogs he wished, as long as he got results.

Telly said he'd be right back. He could speak better outside without all the music playing. Something still bothered him, though: "Did
you cut yourself shaving?" he asked, peering back at the bandaged
hand.

Abbott asked if he was likely to have been shaving his knuckles,
and Telly said no, he supposed not.

"You haven't been bar brawling, have you?"

Abbott didn't answer. "Just make your call," he said, sipping.

* *

Things were finally coming together for Abbott, or so it appeared to
his inebriated mind. He was finally getting the protection he deserved.
Once he had that protection, he would get his wife back, wherever she
might be. And once he had his wife, he would get re-elected—and no
Clarisse or Warren or giant lizard was going to keep him from it.

He drank his drink happily.

Then again, this all hinged on the idiot Telly bringing the necessary dog, and as the minutes passed and the cocktails came and went,
this became more and more questionable.

"To elect or not to elect," Abbott announced, staring down at a
cold hush puppy like Hamlet pondering the skull. He regarded it
sadly. "It's always about dogs," he sighed.

He didn't usually talk to himself, but sitting alone in the Nudist
Colony, slowly becoming soused on sidecar cocktails, anyone is apt
to start soliloquizing at some point. This Abbott did, and it seemed
to him, listening to himself speak it, that it was pretty good stuff too.
Pithy, with a boldness that amused you.

He was just regretting not bringing along a scrap of paper, for it's
always best to get these observations down as soon as you think of
them, when Telly poured back into the booth.

"You're late!" Abbott gurgled. "Fourteen midgets, six sextons!"

Telly said sorry, and squeaked forlornly across the vinyl seat.

Abbott gazed at him. "Did you call your duck?" he asked.

"My duck?"

"Your *duck-dog*," Abbott amended.

Telly shifted in his seat. "Yeah…about that."

"You didn't call your dog-duck?"

"Jen gave her to our aunt."

Abbott's head jerked up. He could hardly believe his ears. "Clarisse—"

"No, not that aunt. Our other aunt. Your non-sister aunt."

Abbott began counting aunts. He had run the total up to about nineteen when he slammed the table again. "Where's your duck?"

Telly explained, "Jen let our aunt borrow her—borrow Kitten. She's not in town, boss. Kitten isn't."

Abbott stared. He sputtered and stared, and then sputtered some more. Everyone was leaving town on him. "You gave your druck to your aunt! Why! Why! You don't see me giving my aunt drucks!"

"Jen had to—she has weasels; our aunt does."

"She has weasels," Abbott repeated. *She has weasels,* he repeated again, once more doing his rendition of a one-man back-up chorus. "What do you mean she has weasels? What's your aunt doing with weasels?"

"She's not doing anything with them. They're overrunning her farm, getting into her livestock and making a mess of things. Jen gave her Kitten to run them off."

Abbott comprehended. He drank. "Oh, yes. Yes, I see. She has a weasel problem. For a minute there, I thought she had some kind of act."

"Act?"

"Like Mississippi Mona and her python. Do you remember Mona? Used to work a club called the Raunchy Coconut. Did her routines with a python wrapped around her shoulders."

Telly didn't remember. He wondered if wearing a python could have been all that comfortable for her. Abbott had no data on this. All he knew was she had one in her act and it did wonders for her popularity.

"That's what I thought you meant when you said your aunt had woodchucks."

"Weasels. She's trying to scare them off."

"No, I understand that now. I am abreast. Speaking of a breast, did you ever catch Mona's act? No? Well, it was pretty racy stuff, let me tell you."

He spoke wistfully. Mona and her python had always been one of his favorite topics. Good ol' Mona. Abbott might have asked her to marry him all those years ago had it not been for that bouncer. Big girl, that bouncer.

Telly leaned in eagerly. He loved racy talk.

Unfortunately, before they could delve into the subject further, his employer burbled, "Damn nuisance, you not having your wood-chuck!" And just like that the warmth and joviality of the man discussing Mississippi Mona all but evaporated.

Telly tried a conciliatory smile. "Actually, chief, I think I can get something better."

"Better?"

"Another dog, a runaway Jen picked up the other day. I like to call her 'Chomper.' "

"Chomper," repeated Abbott, to whom the name sounded promising.

"Yup, good ol' Chomper. She's a real firecracker. Jen was going to take her over to Henrietta's farm, but then all this stuff came up. If you need a dog, this one is the goods. Fierce and loyal. I can go grab her, if you like."

A vague grin had crept across Abbott's face. He nodded slowly and slapped his assistant on the back. He had always liked this kid. "Good work, boy. Now then, here's the flan. Or, that is, when I say *flan*, I mean *flan*. Did I mention I'm a manned mark?"

Telly agreed that the boss had mentioned something to that effect.

"Well, we all know who this mark is," said Abbott. "Or rather, who marked the man. I'm the man." He leaned in. "And I know what's behind it." He paused, staring up at the young woman spinning round and round on the stage. "*Soparla,*" he whispered.

Telly repeated the word with the necessary awe. "So you *do* think it's Soparla after you?" He wouldn't have thought a guy like the boss would go in for old folk legends. "You think *the lizard* is trying to kill you?"

"Must be," sipped Abbott. "But he's no lizard. Or a duck either. Maybe not even a weasel. He's a man, and he is everywhere. But he's made an error," said Abbott. He reached in his pocket and pulled out an item he had swiped from Warren Kingsley's countertop. "He left this behind at Kingy's house."

Telly blinked at it. "It looks like an apple core, boss."

It was an apple core. Abbott was happy the kid was following along. "Soparla left it. And we're going to use it to find Soparla."

"How?"

How? It was an excellent question. Abbott wished he had an answer to it.

Actually, he did have an answer. "We're going to take this dog, this Whopper or whatever you call her, and have her sniff the core, and then we turn her loose."

Telly stared a moment, trying to comprehend. "You want to turn Chomper loose on Kilobyte?"

Abbott sloshed his drink in agreement. "It occurred to me that Butterscotch—that was my wife's dog before they both left—it occurred to me that Scotch Butter had run off Soparla once, just like your aunt and the werewolves in her garden. Your dog can do the same. The man doesn't seem to like dogs. It's his Achilles heel." Abbott mused on this. They recently had a catcher go down with an Achilles heel. Very painful.

Telly reviewed his boss's remarks. "You want Chomper to run off an assassin?"

Abbott waved and sloshed again. "Run off. Chew the gizzard out of. It's immaterial."

"It's an interesting idea," Telly admitted, taking a pensive bite of something he thought was a scallop but wasn't. "You want a sort of combination watchdog and tracker?"

"A *commendation*, yes," Abbott agreed, applying his cocktail again. Setting down the goblet, he picked up one of the stray hush puppies, looked at it as if he wondered what it thought it was doing there, and then flicked it onto the floor, freeing it into the wild. "Okay, here's the plan," he said. "You're going to take this dog, uh, Marmaduke did you say?"

"Chomper."

"Right, Chomper. Even better. You're going to take this dog Chomper—or, as you say, Marmaduke—and…"

He related his plan.

He concluded, saying, "The important thing is to unearth this man Soparla before he makes one last deadly liaison with yours truly."

Telly nodded. "Is liaison the stuff they put on dogs' fur to make it look smoother?"

Abbott gave his intern another encouraging slap. Now the kid was getting it.

Telly still had a couple questions. "What do I do with Chomper again?" he asked.

Fred Abbott carefully re-explained everything.

Telly nibbled on a hush puppy and from time to time said, "K."

15 — ROLLING IN THE AISLES

From Fred Abbott's private office window, Warren Kingsley could see that the town had come out in droves for the debate between the mayoral candidates. All around, they had crowded into the stadium, awaiting something more thrilling than the typical Kilobyte K game.

Warren hadn't expected such a showing. When he stepped out onto the mayor's balcony a moment later, he felt a little like a Roman emperor about to address the populace—or, if not the emperor himself, one of the warm-up acts for the emperor, rattling off witty anecdotes (in Latin) and recommending the best place to get your toga cleaned. It wasn't the worst feeling.

Frederick Abbott—Kilobyte's answer to a Roman emperor—still had not appeared. The debate was due to begin at five o'clock, but so far only Warren and Hank Busby had graced the scene with their presence. Hank was still down on the field; Warren, as noted, was up in the mayor's office, stretching his legs.

Originally, Warren was not to be admitted to the debate. Though thoroughly up to date on Form 64-K, he had not gone through the primaries and therefore, according to the town bylaws, had no claim to any public debates.

Mob rule changed all that. While their man discussed the matter with the council, a chant of *"Kinnng-sssleyyy"* could be heard emanating from around the park. This kept up for some time, and eventually the moderator, who was retiring next month anyway, called for another podium to be added to the diamond. It couldn't make this spectacle any more ridiculous than it already was.

The moderator did not approve of conducting the debate in the middle of a baseball diamond—many moderators are funny that way—nor did most of the town council endorse it. The exception was Councilwoman Clarisse, who thought it had a certain something. She was easily amused.

Warren came inside from the balcony and cracked his knuckles. Mahrute, standing respectfully in the background, had not seen this much nervous energy on the part of the client since the last sixteen times he was somewhat certain someone was out to get him.

"I need a walk, Mahrute," he said, and Mahrute bowed his head. "I think I'll stop in my office for a moment. Haven't been in there for days."

Mahrute bowed again. He recommended Warren think positively. With any luck, he observed, this would be his office soon enough.

Warren gave it a cursory glance. He supposed it would be. If so, he would have to do something about the wall color. And the bullet holes behind the desk. All wrong.

He went for his walk.

The first thing he did upon arriving at his pleasantly colored, unshot-up workspace was check his voicemail. Warren had not checked his voicemail in over a week.

He did not get much of a thrill out of it now. There was one interesting message, however. He played it:

"Kingsley, this is the mayor! A gunman has just taken a shot at me … call for help, Kingsley … he may still be in the building … this is Mayor Abbott speaking …"

The message ended there. Warren gathered it was from the mayor.

No doubt this was the message he had left during the kerfuffle the other morning. Warren remembered hearing something about it at the time. The mayor had evidently called the guard Earl first, then Warren and finally Telly. It made sense that there would be a message.

Warren looked at the time stamp: *9:41 AM FRIDAY.* He frowned at it. Something about this stamp did not make sense. Warren couldn't say what precisely, but like the decorative touch of a bullet-hole fresco, it was all wrong.

Something went clunk against his office door. Warren frowned at this too. He didn't like clunks. Hanging up from his voicemail, he stepped to the door and opened it.

In a perfect reenactment of Friday's discovery of a lurking David Wincher, a body tumbled in, revealing itself to be Frederick Abbott's estranged wife, Sheryl. Her body was a lot more pleasing than Wincher's, though Warren still had his reservations.

"Oh!" she exclaimed. She stared up at Warren. Warren stared down at her.

Perceptive observers, particularly those with a knack for picking up on vibes between the sexes, might have picked up on one such vibe here. A sort of sexual tension, without the sex. It had existed for some time. Abbott had noticed it himself on many occasions, as had his intern, Telly. There seemed to be a real animosity between the mayor's wife and his sometime employee, Warren—so much so that the natural assumption would have been that they were secretly and/or unconsciously in love with one another.

This was not the case. They simply disliked each other.

From the moment Sheryl met Warren, she thought him a giant lunkhead. And from the moment Warren met Sheryl, he thought her a tawdry fortune hunter projecting no sexual desirability whatsoever. More like a crass imitation of sexuality than anything. Warren liked his women soft, pert and reasonably intelligent. Or, if nothing else, not quite so sneering.

"Can I help you?" he asked. The last he had heard, she had left town. Unless his office existed in some alternate dimension, he was fairly sure this was still Kilobyte.

Sheryl bounded up and took a seat in his chair. "I wanted to see you."

"Through my door?"

No, not through his door, she retorted. "I was trying to hear if you were in here. I thought I heard Abby talking."

Warren said that was his voicemail. "I just got a message, belatedly, from your husband. It's funny, too, because—"

Sheryl said never mind funny voicemails. "Have you had any more visits from THEM?" she asked.

" 'Them'?"

"*Them*—the people who came to see you at your cottage."

Warren said ah. Them. No, he had not had any more visits from *them*. "Friends of yours?"

"I wouldn't call them friends, no," said Sheryl.

Warren wouldn't call them friends either. It was one of the few things he and Sheryl could agree upon. "But you know something about them?" he asked.

Sheryl nodded her head slowly, surprised by the perspicacity of his question. Yeah, she knew about them. She knew *all* about them. "There's this...I guess you would call it a 'society.' "

"A secret society?"

Sheryl nodded again. She supposed you would call it secret, yes. "I first came across them at the Colony—"

"The *Nudist* Colony," clarified Warren.

Yes, the *Nudist*, responded Sheryl sharply. "I used to work there. Don't look at me like that. I wasn't a dancer. I was the hostess. Although, with what they had me wearing most days, I might as well have been a performer."

Warren understood, and he sympathized. He had seen the outfits at the club. He personally didn't mind the tailoring, but, on the other hand, he hadn't tried to shimmy into any of these garments on a reg-ular basis. "So you worked at the club?" he prompted.

"I worked there," she said. "And I found out things. Things about the management. There is something off about these dudes—off in a big way."

Warren hadn't seen many men at the Nudist Colony, other than paying customers like himself, so he had no way of judging how *off* Sheryl's dudes may or may not have been.

She went on with her admission. "It wasn't long after I started my job that I met Abby. I knew he would never look at me twice if he found out where I worked, so I quit." She shook her head sadly, little knowing that her Abby would have most certainly looked at her twice after learning of her workplace—perhaps even asked her if she had heard tell of a celebrated performer called Mississippi Mona and whether Sheryl had her phone number or not.

"I quit, and I was free," she said. "It was over. And then I had to go and mess things up again. I never should have reopened that can of worms."

The worm motif was new to Warren. He wondered if this was going to be a fishing story (a favorite pastime among some of the older residents of Kilobyte). He hoped it would not. He hated fishing stories.

Not wishing to appear rude, he waited while Sheryl swallowed thoughtfully and continued:

"You never met Javy Clark, did you? He used to be a ballplayer around here."

Warren had not. He was fairly certain that he and Sheryl *had* been friends, however.

"He and I were what you might call an item. We were in love. I suppose you find that hard to believe, coming from me? Love?"

Very little surprised Warren Kingsley anymore. World-weary and hardened, he had known many strange bonds to form among his fellow human beings. Not especially for him, but some human beings.

"I was in an unhappy marriage," explained Sheryl, trying mightily to defend her actions. "I'm not going to lie to you; I married Fred Abbott for his money. But, through this amazing fluke on our honeymoon, I won a bunch of money of my own. It wasn't a colossal amount, but it was a lot for around here. I could get by on it. I didn't need a rich husband, after all. But that's just what I did have. I had made a huge mistake. When we got back home, I wanted to run away with Javy. He told me it would never work. I didn't understand why, and soon after that, he vanished without me. Apparently, in the middle of a major league game, he went down the tunnel and disappeared. Just like that." She snapped her fingers. "I didn't know what to do. I asked Hank about it—Hank Busby, he's the one who introduced us—and he acted all weird about it. I began to think that Hank knew more than he was saying. I started associating more with him, just to see if I could learn anything about Javy's disappearance. That's when I met Daryl Blue."

Warren was relieved that they had arrived at a more familiar personality. Assuming Sheryl hadn't taken up with any new boyfriends in the last two days, they must be winding down toward the end of her story. He didn't want to rush her, but he had a debate to attend.

"Daryl and I hit it off right away. It wasn't like it was with Javy, but it was nice." She paused. "I don't know what made me do it—what made me say it—"

"Do and say what?" asked Warren.

"We ran into each other at the diner one day, Daryl and I. We couldn't talk long—it wouldn't have looked right—but I pulled him over to a table and told him I couldn't stand another day with Abby. I still had most of my winnings, so I suggested the same thing I had suggested to Javy. We should run away together. Live like bohemians somewhere. Daryl was against it. I think he thought bohemians were some kind of upstart political party. He had a career here, he said— someday he might even run for office himself. He couldn't up and leave. I said I would divorce Abby, then. It had been enough time that people wouldn't talk very much, and even if they did, I didn't care. People were going to talk no matter what."

"People do talk too much," inserted Warren.

"But Daryl didn't like that idea any more than running away. Involvement in a scandal? Adultery with the mayor's wife? It would never do. He had his career—his stupid, stupid career. That's when I said it. I told him I knew *people*."

"Colony people?"

"Yes, Colony people," said Sheryl. "I told Daryl that these people were 'available.' For the right price, they could get rid of our problem."

"Rid of it with a high-powered rifle?"

"Something like that. I mentioned an email address I had overheard when I worked at the club. *Soparla*'s address."

Warren nodded. He wondered if the legendary assassin and righter of wrongs had his own domain, and whether it was a .com or a .org.

"At first, I thought Daryl wanted nothing to do with it. But he must have, because—" She swallowed deeply again. "Because late one morning, two days ago, Soparla tried to kill my husband and ended up killing Daryl by mistake. Daryl must have arranged for the hit, after all. I had this stash of cash only Daryl and I knew about—running-away money—and the evening before, it was gone. After Daryl's murder, this unpleasant little man I recognized from the club paid me a visit. I knew him as 'Basil.' He told me I never should have stuck my nose in Colony business again. *I remembered what happened to Javy, didn't I?* Javy and I had met at the Colony, so I took it he had gotten mixed up in something there he shouldn't have, and Basil had been involved in his 'disappearance.' I knew then Daryl had died because of me. Javy too, most likely. It was all my fault!" She took a breath and whispered, "It feels good getting this off my chest. I haven't told anyone else any of this."

Evidently, she still hadn't. A few seconds earlier, Warren had quit listening. Had he heard the part about Sheryl shouldering the responsibility for the actions of the hitman Soparla, he most certainly would have agreed with her. It was totally her fault. But he hadn't heard it. He was thinking.

"Ten o'clock," he said, speaking to himself more than Sheryl.

"What about it?"

"That's when the mayor was shot at—at ten o'clock."

"What if he was? Who cares?"

But Warren did care. He glanced back at his office phone and frowned. It was showing a very different time now—4:58. He was going to be late. "Are you going to watch the debate?" he asked.

Sheryl replied brusquely that she was going to put as much distance between herself and this crappy town as she could.

Warren said that was too bad. She would be missing out on a treat. "Well, I must be getting down to the diamond now. Nice seeing you," he lied.

Sheryl held him in place with a surprisingly strong grasp. "I came back to tell you this so you can bring Daryl justice. He didn't deserve to die."

Warren didn't suppose he did. And he would attempt to get him a portion of the justice Sheryl mentioned. It was all about timing, he said.

Nineteen minutes' worth of it.

**

Warren thought about those nineteen minutes for a good nineteen seconds after he had left his office.

Then his mind flitted back to the debate, his speech and how he was going to make mincemeat out of his opponents by saying very little. It was a technique that had served him well so far in his campaign. His slogan was *The less said the better*, and it was working.

The mayor had finally arrived.

"Mayor Abbott," gasped the moderator. He wasn't certain how to react to the other man's disheveled appearance and bandaged fingers or the aroma of sidecar cocktail he exuded. "We assumed—we were concerned you weren't coming, sir."

"Muk," said Fred Abbott staunchly.

"Perhaps you went to the wrong locale? Originally, the debate was to take place at the Kilobyte Inn—"

"*I* dibble *n*," muttered Fred Abbott.

The moderator nodded knowingly. "We moved the location at the last minute—against my wishes, I might add. The candidates for the Kilobyte mayoral race are not the Beatles. That's what I told them—they are not the Beatles."

Abbott didn't mind. He would assume the role of any bug the people wanted. Beetle, gnat, electronic listening…they were all fine, so long as Soparla did not consume them. That would not be fine. "The cast has died," he whispered philosophically, and the moderator said indeed it had.

"You see, we required more room for all this." Moderators, like the jaded wives of town tycoons, occasionally needed to get things off their chests. He waved a hand at the flock of spectators. "It was either here or the town concert hall, and the concert hall is undergoing renovation, as you know."

Abbott peered up at the stands. For safety reasons, occupancy was restricted to the sections behind home plate. This still represented plenty of attendees. Abbott counted about a bazillion of them, all bobbing up and down in their seats like a bobbing boat on the bobbing, bobbing sea. He wished they would all quit bobbing. "Let me at 'em!" he snarled, and had to be restrained.

The moderator liked his enthusiasm. He returned to his seat and began the introductions.

**

In a row of folding chairs alongside the dugout, Sheriff Jennifer Blake was pondering again. She was pondering hollow points and balconies. Some might say she had become obsessed with these two disparate items. (Curiously enough, she thought little about plastic explosives, now that the stuff had been properly disposed of from Warren's cottage. That was *so* two hours ago.)

Next to her sat Henrietta Bragg, accompanied by a complement of dogs from her barn. Captain Drayton was among them, along with a handful of his scruffiest lieutenants. As Henrietta would lean over to explain, the animals had been pining for Warren ever since he left his cottage this afternoon. He had some sort of hold over them.

Jen wasn't surprised; the whole town seemed to have fallen under that hold. In a few short days, the man had become a local phenomenon. Everyone was talking about him: on Twitter, on Facebook, on the *K-town in the Morning* talk-radio broadcast. In person too. From the bar/restaurant to the electronics superstore/laundromat to the dental office/beauty salon, the weird-ass combo-businesses of Kilobyte were abuzz. The man was a living legend. Like Soparla, without the scales.

The sheriff looked up and saw Mahrute standing behind the podiums on the pitcher's mound. Warren was in the center, Hank Busby and Fred Abbott to the right and left. It made the middle candidate look even larger than life than usual.

The bodyguard's bodyguard appeared to be pondering as much as she was. She wondered what about. She also wondered where he had gotten that shirt. She liked it. Very bright. Very festive.

If she could have read his mind, she would have learned that Mahrute was pondering matters very much in line with her own thoughts. Not hollow points or balconies, but tiny, disjointed details that did not fit into his orderly consciousness—things people said and did, how these things contrasted with the other things they said and did, and why he, Mahrute, had ever thought it a good idea to travel without any luggage. Even a solitary overnight bag would have alleviated some of his Hawaiian-shirt chagrin.

A few feet away from the glare of that shirt, the candidates were in full swing. The debate raged on...

For the majority of the event, and despite the nature of the question asked, Hank Busby would spout off about government spending and fiscal responsibility. In response, Fred Abbott would spout off, somewhat less coherently, about fiscal spending and government responsibility, with occasional flights of fancy regarding the hidden hand of violence in their town and the disturbing trend of hush-puppy hoarding at popular entertainment establishments.

When asked how he reacted to these various assertions, Warren would reply in two- or three-word sound bites, and as a result got a big hand for it.

During one of his longer ripostes, he suggested a solution to all of Kilobyte's maladies. It was really very simple, he said: They needed to take it easy. Try not to sweat the small stuff. Much like Kilobyte, he was turning forty himself in a few weeks—this got a big hand—and if he could embrace his middle age, why couldn't this municipality? If the K-man could do it, so too could the K-town.

(Pause for standing ovation.)

Once the cheering had settled, the moderator thanked him for his inspirational comments but wondered what this had to do with the rise of property taxes in the area—to which Warren replied that one's property had no income, so why should it be taxed? Several audience members yelled, "Warren for king! King Kingsley!" and this got a smattering of support as well. (Warren nodded his approval. It was nice to know that he had something to fall back on should the mayor thing not pan out.)

Regarding taxes and other such matters, he went on to say that it was not like the government had any clue what to do with the money. He had seen firsthand that they had no clue. Let the properties keep their money, he remarked.

(Applause.)

Warren, personally, didn't like to carry money—it made your back pocket so bulbous—and he saw no reason why the government should be any different. Why should the government have a chubby buttocks? They couldn't even be troubled to put those little flag thingies on the sides of mailboxes. If the fine people of Kilobyte elected him, that would be the first bullet point on his administration's agenda. Mailbox thingies.

Cheers filled the stadium. Several attendees woofed.

Scholars and pundits like to talk about tipping points in history—those moments when things sway in a new direction. Warren, standing on the rubber behind his mound-podium, nodding out at his supporters and well-wishers, could be said to have landed on the fulcrum of one of these tipping points now, and landed on it perfectly. He couldn't have done better if he had just struck out the side.

The adulation showed no signs of slowing down. He might well have rode these cheers and yaps all the way to victory, had it not been for *the Disturbance.*

It started in the bullpen. It began as a far-off growling, like a throaty rumble of gathering thunder. Then an animalistic grumbling. And finally, a cacophony of otherworldly clamor.

Several of Henrietta Bragg's dogs raised their heads at the commotion, only to lower them again, exactly as their captain had done the previous evening. They were clearly in the presence of something larger than themselves.

Hank Busby was the last to hear it. Attempting to field a question on town violence, he was just saying something about Soparla, and how one cannot give in to superstition and unmanly emotion, when the yowling nearly unmanned his remarks completely.

The whole of the stadium gazed silently toward the bullpen. There was a distant clang, a woof and a snarl, and the gate flew open.

Frederick Abbott turned and stared. It was a dreadful stare, the stare of one who has unleashed a horror on his fellow man. It wasn't Soparla that was upon them—lizards don't woof, nor (most likely) do lizard-men assassins. This was something far more ferocious than that.

"Chumper," he whispered hoarsely.

And he was right (sort of). The beast was loose. The animal came running fiercely down upon them, a flash of white fur and jagged teeth.

It was a six-pound Maltese, and she was angry.

She whooshed onto the field, darting in and out of shoes and boots and other fascinating objects. Starting at Abbott, she dashed in and out, out and in, sniffing and barking, barking and sniffing. She might have started the approach angry, rage over being cooped up in a stuffy truck all afternoon—and after that, a stuffy bullpen—but she was quick to forgive these transgressions.

She was all smiles now.

Making her way to Deputy Tony, finding nothing among Deputy Tony to recommend itself, she bounded up on Mahrute, finding Mahrute's scent dignified and divine. She then shot over to Hank

Busby and Fred Abbott, liking Abbott better than Busby. No, Hank. No, Fred. After that, she gamboled over to Henrietta. She found a true kindred soul there—also the smell of her various animals (those present now running in circles all over the diamond, much the way fans of years gone past had once rushed the field after their team won the pennant).

For perhaps ten seconds, the Maltese applauded the amazing Henrietta aroma, jumping joyously in the air six times, nipping at the dog-woman's waist. Discovering that you can only do this so many times before people start looking at you funny, she ran over to Abbott, then the sheriff, then Warren, then Hank Busby, then Mahrute, before finally getting scooped in by Telly, appearing out of nowhere and in the nick of time. (Sort of.)

It was the old rookie story—she had tried to stretch a single into a double.

"Chomper," Telly explained, holding up the squirming goods.

The moderator attempted to calm down the surging crowd after that. He spoke coolly and concisely, occasionally pausing in his inflection to shoo away a charging dachshund or Chihuahua, care of Henrietta's pack. The dachshund and Chihuahua were being chased by Deputies Tony and Lance, respectively.

"That concludes our debate today, ladies and gentlemen," announced the moderator abruptly. Might as well cut their losses now, he thought. "Please exit in an orderly fashion."

Someone yelled, "Bring back the mascot!" Another hollered, "Warren rocks!" A third asked where the restroom was. The one off Aisle 6 was closed.

While the fans reluctantly departed the stadium, Fred Abbott stumbled over to his intern's side. "Where have you been?" he whispered/hiccupped.

"Oh, you know, hither and thither," answered Telly sullenly.

The mayor harrumphed and said yes—scornfully. He understood *thither* was beautiful this time of year. He also hiccupped again.

"The truth is, boss, I have been through hell."

Fred Abbott goggled. Hell was probably very balmy just now, he would think.

"The collection of the dog proved to be a tad more trouble than I thought," said Telly, struggling to hold on to the dog in question. It was hard to keep a good Maltese down. "Anyway, boss, I'm here now."

This fact was abundantly clear to the sheriff, who came storming over to the spot at the conclusion of Telly's explanation. The shenanigans this evening had her brother's name written all over them.

She now stated this name—in full—with all the pent-up rage of a long-suffering sister.

She only unleashed this version on special occasions. The name Soparla could hardly have rung out with more sinister dimension. "Costello!"

Telly shied behind his employer. The dog in his arms, previously a beast, had become the little woolly lamb it so closely resembled. Recognizing the leader of the pack when she saw it, she nestled against the beta animal's chest, not wanting any trouble.

"It's not my fault," Telly pleaded, not wanting any himself. "The boss asked me to bring the dog and hide in the bullpen with it. Don't talk to me about it; talk to the boss." He stepped aside so she could talk about it with the boss.

She would have no opportunity. The moment Telly cleared a path, Abbott's own oppressor came swooping in from the opposite dugout. "Abbott!"

In their years together, Clarisse had sometimes found it helpful to refer to her brother by their family name. Like the name "Costello," it seemed to resonate with man and boy.

"Yes, Clarisse?" stammered "the man," hiding behind his sidekick.

"What the hell have you done, Abbott?"

"I haven't done anything, Clarisse. Nothing at all. Why do you ask?"

Clarisse asked because her nephew had said he had done something, and she had never known him to be a liar. Her sibling, on the other hand...

"It was all part of my plan," said Fred Abbott with another hiccup.

Those still left on the field gathered closer for his explanation. The sisters Jen and Clarisse led the brigade. Warren and Mahrute had also taken an interest, together with Henrietta Bragg, Deputy Lance and Hank Busby.

The stands had totally emptied out now, with the help of Deputy Tony and the grounds crew, so Abbott could speak freely and openly. He did not speak freely, however, and only spoke openly after Clarisse had kicked him in the shin.

"Ooch! Don't do that. I've had a hard—*ulp*—afternoon, Clarisse."

"You're going to find it a lot harder if you don't talk, you ridiculous sot. Why did you ask this boy to bring a dog here?" She glanced at Henrietta Bragg, a veritable canine whirlwind, and frowned. She would attend to her later.

"It was the plan, Clarisse."

"So you said, Fred."

"I figured the animal would locate Soparla for us. The thing has got to be found, what or whoever it is. We were going to use her as one of those whatchamacallits. A tracker?" He was pretty sure it was tracker. "She was going to sniff out the lizard. Also, protect us from it—him."

Clarisse's hostility had begun to fade with each strained, pathetic word. She didn't know whether to growl like her nephew's little furball or chuckle lightly. Freddy had become so obsessed with his own safety that he had clearly come unhinged. Drink would have also assisted with that. "And exactly how was this going to work, Fred?"

Abbott had to think about that. Then he had it. Telly was to conceal himself in the bullpen before the debate, giving the dog Chumper—excuse him, he meant *Chumper*—the apple core from Warren's cottage to sniff. The apple core with the Soparla scent all over it. At the key moment, before they got started—more key had the boy actually arrived on time—Telly would turn the mutt loose, and she would root out her quarry lickety-split. Assuming that quarry was near at hand—which he no doubt was. He was always near at hand.

This time, Clarisse did chuckle. She turned to her nephew. "And you gave the dog the apple-core clue?"

Telly nodded.

"And?" she asked.

"She ate it."

Clarisse returned to her brother. "She ate it, Freddy. So much for your plan."

"I still think it could have worked, Clarisse. Maltese have very good tracking abilities." Or was he thinking of every other dog breed?

His sister couldn't tell him. "Maybe you're right; it might have worked. In fact, maybe it still can. Hey there!" she said, addressing herself to Mahrute. Mahrute stepped closer. "Do you still have that listening bug you guys found in the baker-bodyguard's cottage?" Mahrute still had the device. "Well, give it to the dog to sniff, and maybe she will lead us on a merry chase across the countryside. If this Soparla is as stealthy as everyone thinks, he's probably not far off."

Mahrute did as instructed. He presented the bug to the Maltese. She had no sooner gotten a whiff of the circuitry than she sprang from her holder's arms. She began running around the field with the thrill of the hunt.

"She does enjoy doing that," observed Warren.

Her antics were more controlled this time around. Having chased after the dachshund and the Chihuahua a moment—also a hoagie wrapper she didn't like the look of—she rejoined her man Abbott.

"What's she bugging me for?" wondered the mayor plaintively, slowly backing away.

Clarisse didn't know for sure, but she suspected it was because he had been at the cottage today. That's where the device had been planted.

Hank Busby had another theory. Perhaps he, Fred Abbott, was the killer Soparla.

Clarisse didn't think so. As a boy, little Fred couldn't stand lizards. He couldn't even keep a turtle as a pet. He said it kept peering out at him from inside its shell. "Oh well, that was a waste—" she started to say.

Warren held up a finger. "Just a moment, please."

The councilwoman was impressed by his commanding aspect. Very mayoral. "Yes, Kingsley?"

He pointed. The dog was on the run again—on a path for a form standing unobtrusively by the rain tarp. No one had noticed him before then. At last count, there had been a regulation nine players on the field—and then this guy appeared. A nondescript, olive-skinned figure in nondescript clothing and hat. The tenth man. Perhaps he was the designated hitter.

"Who's that?" asked Henrietta Bragg, but there was no time for an answer.

Springing out of the way of the Maltese—the new arrival did not care for dogs of any breed—he charged headlong toward the mayor.

From the bill of his hat—they never think to check the hat—he withdrew a steely blade, and before anyone could react, he plunged this blade toward Fred Abbott's chest.

Mahrute disarmed the assailant a split second later—knocking him cold with a single chop to the neck—but it was too late. The knife had struck.

What followed had a certain poignancy to it, poignancy mixed with the ridiculous. There was no blood—as Hank Busby would later comment, you need to be human to have blood—but the scene wasn't pretty.

Abbott teetered. He danced. Grasping the wound, he stumbled backward with his head in the air, like a left fielder looking for a pop fly. Eventually losing his balance altogether, he slipped on a baseball an unhappy attendee had thrown on the field and fell against Telly.

Unequal to the sudden shift in weight, the intern gave way, and they flopped to earth together, a heap of arms and legs and remembered cocktails. If this was how Julius Caesar had gone down in the Roman senate, it was unlikely Shakespeare would have bothered writing about it.

"Ow," said Abbott, for it did not feel good.

"Ow," said Telly, underneath him.

The sheriff reached the tangle first. She got the Abbott and Costello parts sorted out and examined the gash in the mayor. There was no blood because there was no gash. The blade had struck something other than flesh.

"Not his titanium card case again?" asked Lance.

It wasn't anything as outlandish as that. It had hit a flask of cognac, also constructed of titanium. Abbott had found it in the back of his limousine on the drive over. It seemed like a good idea to slip it in his pocket, and a good idea it had proved.

"The man is charmed," said the deputy.

A few yards away, Warren looked on reflectively. He wasn't interested in magic flasks or the men saved by them. He was gazing down at their fallen foe, the latter's furry nemesis also studying him closely.

The Maltese, gracious in victory, licked the prone man's face and scurried off, presumably to hit the showers.

"I know this guy," said Warren.

"You know Soparla?" gasped Henrietta Bragg.

"Not Soparla," answered Warren. "Or that's not what he called himself when I knew him. I encountered him years ago; Mahrute and I both did. His name had a sort of *oo* sound in it."

Outside the stadium walls, a sort of *oo* sound drifted in, together with assorted hooting, some collective shouting and laughter. It was the unmistakable sound of Kilobyte horseplay, possibly drunken horseplay.

"Perhaps we should go inside," suggested Mahrute. Allow a few troublemakers to get wind of their disturbance on the field, and they could have a real scene on their hands.

The sheriff seconded this proposal. Inside was best.

They shared a look. Perhaps inside she and Mahrute could finally combine their respective mental resources and bring about a solution to these enigmas.

They had a lot to talk about.

16 — EASILY EXPLAINED

The hometown clubhouse was vacant. The grounds crew had left for the evening, as had the janitorial staff. The only souls who remained were the two-dimensional talking heads on the mounted television screens in the back and the ghosts of ball clubs past.

With the assistance of Deputy Lance Stengel and Hank Busby, Mayor Abbott was carried in and laid gently on a not-so-gentle wooden bench.

Costello "Telly" Blake followed, limping slightly, alongside his Aunt Clarisse, his sister Jen, his coworker Henrietta Bragg, several dogs and Warren Kingsley. Warren dropped the body of the assassin, still unconscious and now handcuffed, onto a parallel bench. He stared down at him again.

He turned to Mahrute, who was also there, and said, "He was called Knobby or Macaroon or something…"

Mahrute replied that he believed the name was Nibu.

Warren said that was it. "Indian?"

"Japanese," corrected Mahrute. Japanese on his father's side. He was fairly certain his mother was from Mumbai. Warren said that was funny; he had always thought him Indian.

"We'll need to hole up here for a few minutes," said Sheriff Blake. She had just checked the parking lot outside, and there were more loiterers than you could shake a nightstick at—not that they shook many nightsticks at people around here. Most of them were their friends and neighbors. Although, as Lance had suggested earlier, there was a certain tougher element among some of the regulars. That was what had given the sheriff pause. Carting off their perp now would only lead to a mob scene, and mob scenes could quickly become violent, friendly and neighborly or not.

They would have to wait.

Councilwoman Clarisse hoped it would not be for long. During the recent tomfooleries, she had become separated from her men (Hugo et al.) and felt quite underdressed without them. "So you know this man?" she asked Warren in the meantime.

"We did," he said. "Mahrute and I tangled with him a while back. He tried to kill a friend of ours, John Hathaway. Mahrute kicked the stuffing out of him, and then the guy showed up again later, in disguise, and tried to steal a priceless artifact. He's a well-known assassin and occasional thief."

Sheriff Blake nodded from her spot at Fred Abbott's bench. That all squared. "The mayor says he's the man who took a shot at him Friday, so I guess we have our man." She seemed uncertain about this, somehow.

Warren shared her doubt. "I'll tell you this much," he remarked. "He's no Soparla."

Jen looked up inquiringly at the statement, but it was Mahrute who answered for his client. "Based on the reputation of your legendary hitman, Sheriff, and the track record of Mr. Nibu, it would seem unlikely that they are the same person."

"Why's that?"

"Because, to date," said Warren, "he has never had a successful hit." He shook his head empathetically. A clever commentator had once declared, with Warren's lack of expertise at keeping people alive and Nibu's failure to make them dead, a quick switcheroo of clientele would have resulted in a staggering success rate in either of their respective fields. Warren had always found this clever commentator rather cheeky.

Nibu stirred from his wooden sprawl. The sheriff moved in closer. Her deputy had already read him his rights. It was while he was out cold, but the rights had been read. "Who hired you?" she asked him.

The wannabe killer appeared unequal to the interrogation. He could really go for something refreshing to eat first, maybe a tangerine. He had been on the run since early this morning and had forgotten to have breakfast.

Pressed for information now, with tangerines to come later, he ultimately replied, "I do not know who it is who hired Nibu. I was paid with the cash and given the assignment of terminating the good man Mr. Abbott. My employer had the access inside the city hall building and was able, therefore, to sneak Nibu's pistol in within those confines. It was all for naught, however. I attempted my assignment many times, with guns and explosive clay, but never do I succeed." He closed his eyes and sighed.

The sheriff had all she needed for now. "You understand that you will be charged for the attempted murder—many times—of Mayor Frederick Abbott, the attempted murder of Warren Kingsley, Mahrute Borodin—"

"Borodin Mahrute," said Borodin Mahrute.

"Borodin Mahrute," she amended, "Councilwoman Clarisse—"

"Don't forget Captain Drayton," Warren interposed.

The sheriff had not realized any military personnel had been present at his cottage. The list was growing. "And several others," she concluded. "I am also charging you with the accidental death of Daryl Blue."

The assassin's eyes shot open. "Who is this Blue?"

"Daryl Blue," said the busybody Bragg, sitting in the corner, petting her pack of dogs. "Daryl Blue," she uttered, "was the poor, unfortunate man you murdered during your assault. You killed an innocent man, you horrible, slimy beast!"

Warren Kingsley threw her a sympathetic glance. He wasn't so sure how innocent her Daryl had been—according to Sheryl Abbott, he had been the instrument of his own demise—but either way you sliced it, it had certainly been unfortunate for him.

The horrible, slimy beast was staring out at them in disbelief. "Killed? A man called Blue? How can this be? Nibu could not have done this Blue killing" He had a reputation of noncompletion to uphold. "It is not possible. I never—"

...concluded the sentence. Beginning on the syllable *nev*, a not-yet-sober Frederick Abbott declared *Gar!* and sprang onto the man's chest. Not confining himself to simple repartee, he abandoned the decencies of debate and began whapping the assassin's head repeatedly against the wooden plank of the bench.

He had succeeded in knocking him out cold before being dragged off by Deputy Lance. The officer wondered if they should read the unconscious man his rights again. It seemed like a good time.

Fred Abbott was still going strong. "Let me at 'im!" he yelled. "I can take 'im! Let me at 'im!"

The sheriff told him to calm down. This was not how the authorities treated prisoners in Kilobyte. Not with so many witnesses present. "What has gotten into you, Mayor?"

Abbott might easily have responded *a vat of cognac*, but he was not equal to any quips at the moment. "Gar!" he said again. "You mollycoddle this man, ask him questions and, uh, coddle him!" he vociferated, leaving off the *molly*. "It is an outrage, a perversion of, *ulp*, justice. A man lies dead, shot; another man lies dead, fallen from a balcony—and all your department does is stand around and ask questions, questions, questions. Pah! You don't even know that Henry Ford invented the automated *'splembly* line. Phooey on you all!"

The sheriff wasn't aware of these many transgressions. If true, they certainly pointed to a lack of—well, she wasn't sure what—but a lack of something. "Who was talking about Henry Ford?" she asked.

"That would be me," said Deputy Lance. Actually, he and Tony—at the scene of David Wincher's "accident." And Tony was really talking more about Indiana Jones; Lance couldn't remember why. "Hold on a sec. How'd you know about the Indy? We were alone in Wincher's apartment at the time."

"Perhaps you were not as alone as you thought," said Mahrute. Like the failed assassin Nibu, he had a knack for blending in until he was needed. "I hope I am not stepping on any toes by speaking up—"

"You are!" snarled the mayor, but was immediately shushed by his sister.

"However, there is quite a lot about these incidents that does not add up."

Jen had observed a lot of fuzzy math herself recently, discrepancies she would also enjoy discussing. She told Mahrute to go first. He could smush all the tootsies he wished.

He thanked her. "You will pardon me for mentioning it, Mayor—"

"I won't!"

"...but you seem to have a vast knowledge about the town you have been elected to lead, as well as the things that go on inside that town."

"Thanks," said the mayor. If the man was going to compliment him, he supposed that was okay.

"But I am at a loss to understand how you came about most of this knowledge. As a case in point, you arrived at Mr. Kingsley's cottage last night distressed that a dark-horse candidate had entered the mayoral race. You did not yet know his identity. What I would like to know is how you knew anything about it?"

"Common knowledge! Came down the grapevine."

"But it had not. Mr. Kingsley had not yet made his announcement; he had filed no forms." As far as Mahrute was aware, he, Mahrute, was the only person with whom Warren had shared his intentions. So, again, how did Mayor Abbott know? What was the source of this Kilobyte grapevine that had been so informative? Mahrute was beginning to believe it had a more clandestine existence.

He produced the infamous electronic listening device from his Hawaiian pocket. "I theorize that when Mr. Nibu reawakes, he can confirm, among other things, that he has never seen this device before. You, Mayor, have seen it, however—or know of it, at any rate. I would suggest that a network of these devices are present throughout the town of Kilobyte, planted in cottages and restaurants—such as the one Mr. Kingsley and I discussed his plans in—cottages and restaurants that your Abbott corporation constructed."

Abbott said *pah!* then *gar!* then *pah!* again.

The sheriff wanted to be clear on this: "So you believe Mayor Abbott heard Lance and Tony talking at Wincher's place through one of these bugs?"

Mahrute did not. Bugging Mr. Wincher's residence would not have been necessary. "I believe he heard them talking because he was hiding in the next room."

"You mean—" began Hank Busby.

"I mean he killed Mr. David Wincher," said Mahrute.

"But how?" asked Lance. No one had been seen entering the apartment building.

"Not before the murder was supposedly committed," conceded Mahrute.

"Well, he hardly could have killed him *after* the murder was committed," said Lance. He paused. "Could he?"

Mahrute agreed he could not. "You will recall that it was the mayor who first drew the apartment-building attendant's notice to the fallen body in the alley. Ostensibly strolling by and noticing it, he brought the attendant out from his post. By the time the guard arrived, however, a crowd had already gathered—also the mayor's doing. A word spoken to a passerby here, a harried gesture to a passerby there, it would not take long before a mob assembled. But no one knew what they were looking at—quite simply, because there was nothing to see. Figuratively speaking, the mayor had raised the flag on the mailbox, but there was no mail in the slot."

Warren was the only spectator who appreciated the reference. He gave Mahrute a knowing finger point and wink, and the acting inspector continued:

"While the attendant struggled to sort out the commotion, the mayor, having established his alibi, slipped upstairs and shoved Mr. Wincher to his death. My guess is he asked to speak with his employee, perhaps come to an arrangement regarding Wincher's blackmail attempts. I don't think Mr. Wincher knew the extent of Mr. Abbott's treachery; he only knew that Abbott was hiding something. This ignorance was his undoing. Once inside the apartment, the mayor would only have to lull the man into a false sense of security before luring him out onto the balcony. An ironic place for the corporate stooge's last hurrah."

The details were coming over the plate a little fast for the sheriff. She had suspected something was up, but never to this degree—lulls, lures, hurrahs…it was becoming too much. "So that's what Wincher wanted to fess up about? Blackmail? And that's why he had to die?"

"Indeed. He had seen something he should not have on Friday. As I say, ironically enough, he saw this looking at a very different balcony."

The sheriff snapped her fingers. *The balcony.* The very item she wanted to discuss. Well, one of two items.

It was all coming together in her mind. Little Gladys's picture. The tyke had drawn Warren on a balcony at the mayor's house—but he should have been on a terrace. So why had Gladys drawn it that way? The answer—Warren had said *balcony*, and Gladys must have overheard him saying it. Lance had not mentioned the press conference to his daughters, so the only place she could have heard about it was the night she had stowed away in Henrietta Bragg's barn. (Henrietta had told Jenny the entire saga of the Stengel-children infiltration while the two women waited for the debate to start.)

The sheriff put her hypothesis to the candidate forthwith:

"When you told Henrietta about the threatening phone call after your first press conference, did you say *balcony* or *terrace*?"

Warren thought about it. He supposed he had said balcony. The caller had said balcony, so Warren had said balcony. Was there a difference?

Jen felt there was. A balcony is high up, a terrace low.

Warren said no kidding. "What's a veranda, then?"

"Another word for terrace."

"And a veran*dah*?" he asked.

The sheriff had moved on from the definitions of *veranda* and *verandah*. "When Wincher called and Warren picked up, the former mistakenly believed he was speaking to the mayor."

A natural assumption, said Warren. If everything went according to plan—

The sheriff rolled over him. "He told Warren, who he thought was Mr. Abbott, that he had seen him *on the balcony*, meaning the mayor's *office balcony*, the morning of the mayor's attempted murder. But what had he seen the mayor doing on his balcony that was worth getting himself killed over?"

The question was more or less rhetorical. She had a pretty good idea about the answer there too, but she was not one to hog the spotlight.

Mahrute took up the baton. "From the window of his own office, I believe Mr. Wincher saw the mayor drop one or two items over the railing of his balcony. He dropped these into a potted plant on the balcony below. The lower balcony protrudes from the building more than the one above it, so hitting the target of the pot would not be a difficult feat. The first item he dropped, the murder weapon, would later be found by Mr. Nibu, as per their instructions in email. The second, dropped sometime later, was a burner phone—this retrieved by

David Wincher. It's possible he had never seen the mayor dispose of the pistol. He may have only seen the phone drop and knew everything was not as the mayor had described it."

The sheriff was getting excited now. "You're saying the mayor had the murder weapon *before* Nibu arrived to shoot him"—everything was happening out of order on this case—"and he also had the phone used to call Daryl before he was shot? So Mayor Abbott's the one who stole the burner phone from his wife, after she stole it from Mrs. Klondike?"

"The clip!" exclaimed Deputy Lance. Everyone stared at him. "The plastic clip thingy we found under the mayor's desk. It goes to a cheap mobile phone!" He looked around. "Sorry, just thought I'd mention that. Go on—you were saying something about the mayor and the gun and the phone?"

Mahrute was saying that and more. "Mayor Abbott required both these items to kill Daryl Blue himself."

Henrietta Bragg gasped. The rest of the room was too transfixed for such an outburst themselves, with the exception of Hank Busby, who said *son of a bitch*. He then looked straight at Fred Abbott and repeated, "You're son of a bitch."

Telly added, "Say it isn't so, boss," and Henrietta, fresh off her gasping, agreed with Hank Busby that the mayor was a son of a bitch.

The accused Abbott, arguably a son of a bitch, sat back on his bench and lowered his head slowly into his hands. Unlike Telly, who never experienced hangovers, he seemed to be getting his a tad prematurely. Murder accusations and brandy cocktails did not mix.

Warren contributed a thought to the conversation. "So that's why it was off by nineteen minutes."

The sheriff looked up. She had forgotten there was anyone else in the room but her, Mr. Mahrute and two horrible, slimy beasts. "What was?"

"The mayor. He left me a message after getting shot—or fibbing about getting shot, as it turns out. The message was at 9:41, but according to all the evidence, Nibu didn't even arrive upstairs until 10:00 a.m.—a time supported by the mayor's other call to Telly at 10:05. The 'victim' called in his first SOS nineteen minutes early."

"Hollow point," said the sheriff.

Warren Kingsley sniffed. He thought his point was pretty solid himself. He was only trying to help—

"No, the hollow-point bullet," she said. "My deputy Albert discovered that the bullet that supposedly struck Mr. Abbott's card case was a hollow point. All the rest were standard. Don't you get it? A standard bullet will slice through cheap drywall easily. That was the type that killed Daryl. But the first one, the one that hit the mayor's case, had a soft tip. Hollow points typically won't pierce hard surfaces; that's how they're designed."

Warren thought he understood. "So the mayor took the gun and shot himself in the chest—"

"He wouldn't have to; he would only have to sling the jacket over a chair and fire into the case, which he put in the pocket. No one would hear, because it had a silencer. He couldn't risk the bullet piercing the case, because people would wonder why it hadn't pierced him, hence the hollow point."

Warren definitely understood now. "And he could have bruised his chest earlier, running himself into a bureau or something. Yes, that works. But how did he do the rest? I mean, the odds of hitting Daryl smack dab in the skull through a sheet of drywall must be astronomical. How'd he see through the wall and hit his target with such precision?" He peered over at Mahrute, but for once the well-informed one had no answer.

"I have not yet worked that out, I am afraid."

Warren looked to the sheriff, who said she was relying on Mahrute. No one else in the room got any consideration.

Gradually, the mayor lifted his head from his hands. Soused or not, he could still recognize a failed filibuster. This Mahrute fellow and the sheriff, they had talked and talked, but they had nothing. They were just stalling, hoping something would come to light; hoping that Abbott would crack. But he hadn't cracked. He reached up and held his head again. It felt like it might crack. "Ho, ho!" he laughed, then wished he hadn't.

Warren was not prepared to admit defeat so soon. He just needed to brood a little. You can't beat a little brooding. He picked up a baseball from the floor and began tossing it idly in the air to assist thought.

It wasn't helping. This was probably why very few major league pitchers had ever solved an important murder investigation.

Truthfully, it wasn't the ball's fault. It was the noise from the TV in the back. He couldn't hear himself think over all the idiotic talking heads.

If Warren despaired of normal talk, he despaired of TV talk all the more. He abhorred it. The faces on the screen, local media from the looks of them, were discussing various matters of alleged relevance, rattling away on one topic after another—the debate this afternoon, the Kilobyte K's chances in the playoff race and a load of other useless crap.

Warren had had enough. He poked his face around the set and tried to locate the volume on the side. He would have also settled for the power button or the self-destruct key.

None of these were immediately apparent. He saw some inputs. The serial number. Several buttons that only made funny overlay menus appear on-screen. But no volume.

Finally he spotted it. It was labeled *Volume*. He held it down firmly and, finally, silence, marvelous silence.

"Now then," he said, returning to the discussion, "how did he do it?" He gave his opponent his best debate-honed stare. "How did you do it, Mayor?"

Abbott chuckled again and then went *oo*. He grasped his head.

Warren glared at him and went back to flipping his baseball. After a while, the sheriff ambled over and snatched it from him mid fling. The up-and-down motion was giving her a headache.

"Hey, no grabsies," said Warren. Now that the TV sound was off, he found it too quiet; he could hear himself think almost *too well*. His thoughts were coming through loud and clear, and they startled him.

Suddenly, he froze, gazing down at the conniving killer gripping his giant, conniving head. Something was percolating in Warren's own head. He peered at the mayor, then back at the TV, then, finally, back at the mayor and his head one more time.

He had it. It was so obvious.

"Hey!" he shouted to Telly, and Telly said yo. "That report you have been preparing for the boss man—it's an inventory for the office, right? Equipment in storage, equipment in use? That sort of thing?"

"Yup."

"Are there serial numbers on this list?"

Telly said there were. Tons of them.

Warren thanked him. "That will be all, Telly."

Telly said K.

Warren strolled up one end of the clubhouse and then back again. He was going to enjoy this. "I know how he did it," he said. "I know how the mayor shot through the wall and hit the Daryl prize with such accuracy."

It had finally come together—the phone, the gun, the clip—well, actually, the clip didn't seem to have any use to Warren at all, other than incriminating the man who had dropped it.

He proceeded with his explanation, sans clip: "There is one immutable way to ensure that you can hit your target without first seeing it—you already know where that target is going to be. It's like Wayne Gretzky—" He paused. Actually, it was nothing like Wayne Gretzky. "Forget that part," he remarked. "What the mayor did is this. Using the burner phone he had stolen from his wife, he called Daryl Blue in the office next door, no doubt keeping his voice down so he wouldn't be heard through the same cheap drywall he would shortly be firing through. Purporting to be the intern Telly prepping his inventory reports, he asked Daryl to kindly read him the serial number on the side of his TV.

"As you just saw, there is only one way to read off a serial number on a mounted TV. You stick your face up close to the edge and squint. All the mayor would have to do is measure the distances beforehand, and there you have it. The head of Blue would be locked in place at an exact distance from those measurements. One target, in a precise location. As soon as Daryl read off the first number, Mr. Abbott fired. One target, dead."

He looked up to give the moderator a knowing wink, before realizing that they weren't at the debates and the moderator had long since left them.

Most of the small assembly inside the clubhouse wasn't sure what was more shocking, the brilliance of the mayor's murderous telecommunication or the ease with which Warren Kingsley had uncovered this.

Clarisse came over to the bench. She placed a hand on her sibling's head and frowned. "Does he have it right, Freddy? Is that how you did it?"

The mayor said *erf*.

She gave his hair a gentle pat. "You might as well tell us everything," she whispered.

Mayor Abbott hesitated no longer. They had figured everything out. The game was up, and his credibility with his constituents was shot to hell. Just like his office drywall and Daryl Blue's head. Abbott just wanted to lie down and rest now. Take that sabbatical he kept talking about.

He told them everything.

A few weeks before, through his network of eavesdropping devices, he had overheard his wife and press secretary discussing their affair at the diner. That was bad enough, but then his wife, his beautiful, wonderful wife, had suggested they hire a hitman—for him, Mayor Frederick Abbott! Abbott couldn't believe it. And after he had gone to so much trouble finding and marrying her.

He came to a decision. He would get them before they got him! Or, he would get the snake Daryl Blue, that is. His wife, Abbott was sure, would learn to love him. Give her time, and the idea of hiring a hitman to solve their marital problems would become a distant memory, or not her go-to maneuver at any rate.

Abbott put his plan into effect immediately. He arranged, through the email address he had heard Sheryl mention, to have the assassin take him out—him, Mayor Abbott. He used the cash Sheryl had stowed at the house and told the assassin he would hide the pistol inside the building. The assassin left this under a booth at the diner, and Abbott had no trouble sneaking it past the guards at the office. They never checked *his* goods and chattels. He also suggested the assassin bring Warren and Telly bogus packages to keep them out of the way (not that this kept the pest Telly from almost mucking everything up).

Before dropping the gun into the flowerpot Friday morning, as arranged, the mayor phoned Daryl with the burner phone. Affecting his best idiotic Telly voice—Telly said hey!—he asked Daryl to read off his television's serial number for the inventory report. Daryl read as he was told, Abbott fired through the spot he had previously measured, and it was done.

If the shot had missed, or anything had gone wrong, he could always put it down to the botched hit, and no one would suspect that he, Fred Abbott, had been the one to fire the shot, that he, the mayor, had hired the assassin—*for himself*.

Nothing went wrong—at first. Daryl Blue was dead, and good riddance, said the mayor. Abbott had already fired the bullet into his card case a few minutes before. (The smoky aroma his intern had attributed to Warren's manly musk was actually the residue of that shot.) All Abbott had to do then was slip his jacket back on, with the bullet hole in the pocket, make a call for help and wait for the authorities to arrive. He rather hoped the hitman would not be caught—so much less explaining—but even if he was and he claimed he had fired no shots, whom would they believe? Abbott was the mayor! That most wonderful of human inventions, a politician.

Little did that politician know he had far more pressing problems to contend with than the hitman's escape. The man showed up!—thanks to the imbecile Telly directing him there. (Telly said hey! again.) Abbott was astounded. This had never been part of the plan. The hitman was supposed to go to the wrong office and flee as soon as the heat was on. By then, he would have been seen by a number of witnesses, and Abbott's story would be confirmed.

But here he was, gun and all. Fortunately, Abbott had taken the precaution of jamming the gun before dropping it into the plant pot. When the man pulled the trigger, nothing happened. They struggled, and the assassin fled (a little late, but better than never).

At first, Abbott thought everything would be fine. He had improvised splendidly. But slowly, little details started to leak out from the stuffing of his plan, like a ragged chew toy in the jaws of his wife's dog Butterscotch. David Wincher was the worst leak of all. He had seen the mayor get rid of the phone from his balcony. Who knew what else he had seen? He had to be silenced. Mahrute was correct; the man let him into his apartment without question. The mayor only had to lure him out onto the balcony. He told Wincher he could explain. If he would just step this way, the mayor would show him—it was so simple. He hit Wincher with a brick he had picked up outside, and Wincher took his plunge—to the *other* alley, not the one everyone had gathered around. The deed was one.

Finally, Abbott thought he was safe. But he wasn't! The contemptible assassin would not let up! He had been hired to kill Abbott (by Abbott—but Nibu was not to know that), and he would not rest until he had completed his assignment. It was then that Mayor Abbott was certain that he truly had engaged the legendary killer Soparla, the cold-blooded hitman. He had unleashed a monster, a reptilian monster. He tried emailing him again, calling off the hit, but he received no reply.

The die was cast.

Warren didn't know anything about dice, but he agreed that Internet access in his cottage, where Nibu was secretly hiding out, was not what it should be. He had often had trouble with it himself.

Abbott was sorry to hear this. More sorry than he could say.

He peered up from the bench and gave one final sigh. He fully admitted that he had killed two men, attempted to frame another (Hank Busby), stolen money from his wife and possibly undertipped his waitresses at the Nudist Colony this afternoon. But was he really all that bad? Compared with other politicians?

His answer came swiftly. A pair of handcuffed hands had wrapped themselves around his throat and were choking the everloving rhetoric out of him. As Abbott himself had suggested, the hitman Nibu had been hired for a job, and he intended to finish it.

They tumbled onto the floor and underneath the bench, out of reach of Borodin Mahrute, Deputy Lance Stengel and Sheriff Jenny Blake, all trying to break up these final contractual negotiations. The strength of Nibu was surprisingly fierce for one who had never successfully killed a man. Another few seconds, and his record would have gone to "1" in the win column. But he had not anticipated one last hero plunging into the fray, a military breed, a defender against wanton violence.

The bullmastiff Captain Drayton was there, and he gave Nibu a swift chomp on his hindquarters. Nibu yowled in pain. He released his stranglehold, and it was over (for real). Nibu massaged his buttocks. He really did not care much for dogs. And dogs did not care much for him.

**   **

Warren Kingsley needed some air. Between the ever-present stench of the locker room and the aroma of politicians and assassins rolling around on the floor in anger, the atmosphere had become a little too thick for him.

He needed another walk.

He headed down the dark, cavernous hall of the stadium. Outside, fans continued to hoot and holler. If the sheriff was concerned about walking their perp out before, she definitely didn't wish to walk out two now, one the mayor of their town. Their waiting would be a mite prolonged.

Warren was in no hurry to leave. He didn't mind this place. The interior wasn't as grand as a major league park, but as minor league facilities went, it was pretty impressive. The killer Abbott had certainly spared no expense.

A man could get lost in here. Warren was getting a little lost—in his thoughts. He was brooding again. Once a brooder, always a brooder, he supposed.

He was thinking about the mayor and what he had become, and the assassin Nibu and what he had become, and he was thinking about himself, Warren Kingsley, and what he would become.

Was he really all that different from those two men? he asked himself. He could see what the thirst for power had already done to him, Warren Kingsley. He had thought of nothing else but votes for two days now—and this from a man whose attention span usually lasted a few minutes at the most. Who was to say that he, Warren, wouldn't someday gun down one of his staff? It could happen.

And then there was Nibu. How was Warren all that different from Nibu, really? They were two sides of the personal-security coin, and so far, every time fate flipped that coin, neither side came up. It landed on its edge. It was a funny world.

Warren peered up from his brooding and saw a funny dog.

Chomper, back from her explorations of the stadium, had scampered up the corridor ahead of him. She was beckoning to him. He followed—the darkened halls of Abbott Park were no place for a nice Maltese—and saw her sitting at a dead end, fifty yards away.

He noted the curious expression on her face when he reached her, a look of whimsy combined with sorrow. If Warren read that look correctly—and he was pretty sure he had—it was saying, "I'm awfully sorry to get you into this, big fella. You see, I'm not very bright."

Warren wondered what she was sorry about, and what this *this* was.

Then he knew. A hidden hand, connected to a giant, concealed figure, had come down on the back of his neck, knocking him to the floor—just as Mahrute had done to Nibu outside.

The last thing Warren saw, as his face dragged along the painted concrete, was Chomper's Maltese features peering into his.

She licked him apologetically, and then Warren was out. Just like Nibu. The parallels were eerie.

If only Warren had been conscious to appreciate them.

17 — Audience Participation

Warren was alone again—alone in a pitch-black, chilly hovel, without even a furry little Maltese face to keep him company. He sat up and rubbed his head and neck. A gleam of light was pouring in from the hall outside. He was in some sort of supply cage. All around him lay industrial inventory, baseball inventory and assorted other inventories of the combined businesses of Abbott Enterprises. Warren steadfastly refused to record any serial numbers.

He went to the door. It was made of chain-link, but it had a long sheet of metal welded down it, no doubt to discourage the theft of the combined inventories of Abbott Inc. It also obscured his view out into the hall. There was a small space between the door and wall, a tiny lip of chain-link and air. It was to this tiny lip that Warren applied his own lips and said, "Hello?"

Every good dialogue had to start somewhere.

Happily, someone out in the corridor responded to his conversational gambit. They said, "Woof!"

Warren brightened. "Is that you, you little pipsqueak?"

The Maltese of his downfall replied with another bark. The pipsqueak was she.

Warren was delighted. She might have inadvertently gotten him into this predicament, but as far as he was concerned, all was forgiven.

He reached in his pocket and pulled out a handful of beef jerky he had purchased for Captain Drayton and friends. Holding this through the links, he was presently rewarded with a hearty nibble.

He sat back on the concrete floor. Now, what to do with that doggy in the window?

He had an idea. He went to the shelf of game supplies and selected a baseball from one of the buckets. From his non-beef-jerky pocket, he produced a pen. Warren always had a pen. At one time, years ago, this was to jot down recipes that might occur to him; sometime after that, it was useful for recording his poetic musings. He was a complicated man, our Warren, with many varying interests.

He was decidedly focused now. He quickly scrawled out a note on the ball, signed it "My name is Warren Kingsley, and I approve this message," and took it to the door. Observing the miniature Maltese head and the jaws that went with it, he hesitated. This would never do. Using his own jaws, he chewed the hide loose from the core of the ball, then finished it off by pulling down a flap with his fingertips. That would work. A perfect Maltese handle.

He bent open the chain-link back as far as he could, rolled the ball through and shouted, "Take this to Mahrute! That's right! *Maaahruuute.*" He articulated the name slowly and carefully, so there would be no confusion. "Go get him, girl! Go get, him!"

She snatched up the ball and went to get him (one could only hope). She scurried down the corridor, the precious orb dangling from her mouth. All Warren had to do was wait. The waiting was going to be the tough part.

Or perhaps it wasn't. Seconds after she departed, he heard a rattling at the door, consistent with some foreign hand taking down the locks.

"That was pretty quick service," he said, nodding appreciatively.

He had nodded too soon. The door opened, and the fiend Basil came in. Warren should have known. (When fiends are afoot, who better to represent them than li'l Bas?)

Given that there was no snarling furball in his vicinity, nor was Basil gripping any slobbered-up baseball, it would seem that his canine ally had not, as Warren initially assumed, taken the message to the opposition—a gaffe of enormous scope, even by Maltese standards. Basil had arrived on his own accord.

"Hiya, matey. How you getting on?"

Warren replied that he was getting along just fine. How was Basil?

"Just smashing. Sorry for the accommodations, but after the number we did on your cottage last night, you probably don't mind it all that much, yeah?"

Warren replied that he minded it more than you might think. "Why am I here, Basil?"

His captor leaned on the frame of the cage. "Now, that's a good question, idn't it? The fing is, chum, we need to take you out."

Warren wondered, as he had in the past, if this was *take out* with a stiletto to the guts or *take out* for a wonderful evening on the town. Perhaps it was somewhere in between.

"You should feel privileged," said Basil. "The Society only affords this service to extra special fellows like yourself. Jimmy Hoffa, Javy Clark—all the nibs."

"You're going to make me disappear?" Warren asked.

"That's a pleasant way of putting it—yeah."

Warren had one question. Actually, he had about sixteen, such as what team did this Hoffa play for and what did Magic Marker points have to do with anything, but he would stick with one question for now: "Why?"

Basil said ah. "You see, you didn't heed my advice, now did you? You went on mucking wiff our business, and now we haff to muck wiff you."

"How did I muck?" wondered Warren. He recalled no additional mucking. "I haven't done a thing to find Javy Clark or look into his disappearance. As tempting a mystery as that was, I left it alone."

"Yes, but you didn't leave the political temptation alone, did you? You ran for mayor. We can't haff that, can't haff that at all."

Warren wondered why not. It was a free country (in theory). If Basil didn't like Warren running, he didn't have to vote for him. Warren hoped that he would, but it wasn't required.

Basil was only too happy to explain his position. "There's an intricate system in place here in Kilobyte, my man. A two-party system. You're the third wheel."

Warren didn't like the sound of this. Systems, wheels—it sounded complicated. And crooked. "Are you saying one of the candidates is in your pocket?"

Basil wasn't saying that at all. "They both are. Or they might as well have been. Abbott never knew what was going on, so we had no problem controlling what he said and did. Hank, on the other hand— well, Hank's one of us."

Warren shook his head. Good ol' Buzz. You would think you knew someone you'd met twice for about five minutes each time.

"The Buzz plays for our team, alright," Basil assured him. "But it don't matter now, does it? You're too popular. You might win, and then where will we all be?"

Warren couldn't say. He, personally, was in a dank little closet. "That's it?"

"That's it, chum. You're throwing off the natural order of fings. So we gotta take you out. For the good of *the Society*."

Warren was getting a little tired of hearing about this wondrous secret society. He didn't even like to hear about his own society, and he had to live in it. "What's so special about keeping the town under *Society* control anyway?" he would very much like to know.

"There I can't help you," said Basil. "It would be giving away secrets, wouldn't it now?"

Warred supposed it would. It was a *secret* society, after all. "You won't get away with this, Basil. Whatever it is you're trying to get away with—you won't get away with it. I have people, people who will come looking for me."

Basil said yes—Mahrute. "He's a pippin, that one. I like him. But I regret to inform you that he won't be looking for you—not here any-how. The fine mayor Abbott, you see, is not the only one wiff access to bugs. I hacked his system and got access to some wonderful War-ren Kingsley sound bites. It wasn't difficult putting together a quick mixtape. This, sent to your Mahrute in the form of a voicemail, will lead him far, far away. Once he figures out what happened, you'll be long gone."

Warren knew there was a reason why he hated voicemail. So mis-leading. He supposed Basil had thought of everything. "So what now?" he asked.

"Now, we wait. It seems there's a gang of loiterers outside. Sup-porters for you, it looks like, milling about and making a nuisance of themselves. We'll wait for them to disperse, and then we'll go. They're a charged-up bunch. You're quite the popular pet. Just think how popular you'll be once you're gone. You know the best legends are always in the past."

* *

Strangely enough, Warren did not take comfort in this. He would admit, however, that he did like Basil much better after he had gone.

He paced his humble cage. He still had the doggy dispatch to keep hope alive, but he wasn't optimistic. So much of it, he realized, depended on a tiny Maltese brain. Tiny Maltese brains might have a use somewhere, Warren supposed, but when it came to effecting escapes from ballpark dungeons, they were pretty weak reeds to lean on.

Yelling was pointless. Basil would have thought of that too. No one would hear him from this deep in the stadium. And there was no point in ruining his voice for nothing. Warren might need it later for a victory speech.

Perhaps some intricately constructed paper-clip mechanism would facilitate his release—sort of a reach-around- or hook-the-lock-type maneuver. He went through the boxes of office supplies and found no paper clips. It didn't matter. He didn't feel like unbending a bunch of clips anyway. It would have only made his fingertips sore.

Another clang sounded behind him. Over his shoulder, he saw the door creak open with a diffident swing. Most likely, it was only Basil, returning to impart another gibe at Warren's expense, or possibly call one of his friends a Honeycrisp.

In either event, the captor would find his prisoner ready. Warren had prepared a whole slew of witty comebacks to Basil's cockney slurs. And if these failed to penetrate, he could always kick the twerp in the cojones.

It wasn't Basil at the door; he and his cojones were elsewhere. The man who peered within was much taller, with a pleasant, stubbled face and light brown hair that stood up slightly in the back.

"Hello?" said John Hathaway, for the pleasant, stubbled face was his.

Looking back on it now, Warren regretted flinging a baseball at this face (what you might call a preamble to the witty comebacks). He should have taken the time to identify whose face it was first. He was pleased to see, however, that Hathaway still knew how to duck.

Having evaded Warren's opening remarks, his ex-client glimpsed back into the cell and frowned, as one looking for additional errant pitches. He was holding a Maltese.

It would seem that Chomper had gotten her man, after all. Sure, some critics might argue that a dog sent out for a Mahrute, returning instead with a Hathaway, had some pretty heavy explaining to do. But the young lady had her reasons. As anyone who has ever wandered the halls and passages of a minor league ballpark with a baseball in his or her mouth can attest, these excursions aren't easy. Shadows creep up on you, noises stir in the distance and even the flavor of beef jerky on the ball, so engaging when you started out, begins to lose its appeal. It isn't long before the stoutest emissary will accept a proxy for her assignment, and for the pup this proxy took the form of the J-man now carting her about.

This was no mere substitute, mind you—she knew him. She trusted John Hathaway. Had she known how to speak, she would have called him "Johnny" or possibly even "Hath."

"Is that you, Warren?" asked the Maltese-approved choice.

Warren said of course it was him. Who else would it be? "I'm glad to see you, Hathaway."

Hathaway was delighted. He wondered what Warren Kingsley threw at people he wasn't glad to see.

"What the hell are you doing here?" asked the two men in unison—Warren breasting the tape first.

Hathaway, as the second-place finisher, answered first. "I told you the other day, I'm investigating a case."

"Did you tell me that?"

"Yes!"

Warren was shocked. "Are you an investigator?"

Once again, Hathaway said he was. A PI. "My team and I are looking into the disappearance of Javy Clark."

"You don't say." Warren and his team had frequently *discussed* Javy Clark. "Have you found him yet?"

"No."

Warren said that was too bad. Sounded like he and his team could use a tune-up. Perhaps, if they needed some practice, they could try finding this Jimmy Hoffa person first. Warren understood him to be missing as well. "You got my message, then?"

"Message?"

"On the baseball." He looked closer at their furry envoy. "Where's the baseball, Hathaway?"

Hathaway couldn't say. He had simply picked up Pixie in the corridor and paused outside this storage closet after the dog started squirming at a noise inside.

Warren explained that he was the noise. *"Pixie?"* he repeated.

"That's her name."

"Not Chomper?"

Hathaway said no. Why would it be Chomper?

Warren said no reason. "So you two know each other?"

"She belongs to a friend of mine. She ran away recently, but I tracked her here when someone in town mentioned a crazy-ass Maltese had been running amok at the local ballpark. Several of the townsfolk also mentioned hearing her howling on the great open spaces the last couple nights. I knew it had to be her." And her it had proved.

"Well, I'm really enjoying catching up with you again, Hathaway, but perhaps you wouldn't mind stepping aside so I can make a dash for the great open spaces myself."

Hathaway didn't mind. Following Warren out of the warehouse space and along the dim corridor, not quite the open spaces of Warren's dreams, he said, "What's going on?"

Warren decelerated slightly. Where should he begin? "You wouldn't happen to have met a guy called Basil in your travels, would you? Psychotic little Brit with lightning reflexes?"

Hathaway also slowed his stride. "As a matter of fact, Warren, I have met him. On several occasions, and *never* would have been once too often. He's not actually British, you know?"

"No? What is he?"

"Long story. Is he the one who locked you in here?"

"With relish. Nice work picking the lock, by the way."

Hathaway said it hadn't been too hard, mostly because there was no lock to pick. Someone—presumably Basil—had busted the chain and then shoved a chair underneath the handle to hold it in place. The Kingsley maneuver, in spades.

"Well, nice job picking the chair, then. You're a real lifesaver."

The lifesaver, having picked up his tread again, drew to another halt. He snatched at the bodyguard's brawny arm. "This Basil is not as ridiculous as he looks, Warren. You really don't want to mess with him."

"So he keeps telling me. I think I'll finally take his advice."

They arrived at an intersection. "I guess this is where we part," said Warren. He stuck out his hand. "Good luck on your quest, John."

"Thanks, Warren. Good luck on whatever the hell you're doing."

"Thanks. I hope you find Javy Clark, if he's still alive. You do realize he didn't disappear from *this stadium*, don't you?"

Hathaway realized that, yes.

"Good. I just thought you should know. Be careful out there. There's a lot of evil about in this little town this evening."

Hathaway replied that he would certainly keep his wits about him. As long as he didn't have Warren there, protecting him, he should probably be fine.

* *

Warren must have taken a couple of wrong turns after the hot-dog emporium, because he never did find his way back to the hometown clubhouse. He wound up on the other side of the stadium. Still, there was a door here, and an exit was an exit.

He launched through this door and heard it seal shut behind him with a decisive click. Immediately following that click, he was greeted by a chorus of drunken voices and the sound of shattering windows. The possessors of the drunken voices were throwing bricks through the windows.

Unlike Hathaway, Warren was not especially adept at ducking. He stood there, glaring disapprovingly, before another of those unseen hands reached up and dragged him to safety.

He hit the concrete barely ahead of a second volley.

"Gotcha," said the intern Telly (and bodyguard in training). Warren had been somewhat lax in the other's instruction up till now, but the student exhibited excellent natural instincts.

Warren asked what he was doing here. He was asking that a lot this evening.

Telly's explanation was less cryptic than Hathaway's. "I was heading out and found these punks sitting on my truck, drinking. I told them I just wanted to get in my vehicle, and they told me to eff off and showered me in bottle caps. I've been hiding behind this dumpster ever since."

Warren didn't think this a very honorable way for a bodyguard in training to act. The kid must not have had much of a teacher. "We'll see about this," he said, and Telly wished he wouldn't. They'd move along eventually, he argued—as soon as they finished pelting the stadium with rocks and bricks, or got done drinking the rest of their beer, whichever of these things came first.

"Speaking of moving along," asked Telly, "why are you here? Your friend Mahrute said you'd gone back to your cottage to pack. Something about an important case out of town."

That was all off now, Warren replied. He wasn't going anywhere except home to bed. And on that note, he stood up. He'd had enough of the Kilobyte youth movement. "Attention, dumbasses," he proclaimed.

The dumbasses froze en masse.

Warren addressed himself to the hooligan leader, a freckled-faced boy with red hair and an impish disregard for public property. "You, chief moron, what do you think you're doing?"

The chief was busting up the stadium, and what business was it of his (insert opprobrious description of Warren here)?

Warren didn't mind. They were just words. "Well, knock it off. I want to pass through."

The chief didn't care what the guy wanted. "We're busting up this building until they tell us what they did with Warren Kingsley!" His crew cheered him on.

Warren used to get this kind of adulation himself. "What they did with Warren?" he repeated. "What *have* they done?" he wondered.

"They won't say! We think they've gotten rid of him—one of those backroom deals politicians are always doing. They didn't like him because he was one of us—a voice of the people. They want to stick us with those other two old coots."

Warren could understand their objection to coots, but they appeared to be overlooking the obvious. "I'm Warren Kingsley," he announced.

The boy laughed. "You? You don't look a thing like Warren!" Warren Kingsley, he might have pointed out, was dope. "You're not dope; you're just an aging pretty boy. Outta our way, pretty boy!"

On this occasion, Warren did duck, but not before getting winged by a jagged rock, flung by the lead hooligan's second in command.

He dropped down next to Telly again and rubbed his shoulder resentfully. It was only a flesh wound, but it still smarted.

His trainee had been right. They just needed to wait this out.

Amusingly enough, that was just what Telly thought they should *not* do. Warren was right; they needed to take a stand, show these guys who was boss. He reached for a garbage-can shield and charged out into the breach.

The clang-clang-clanging of Telly's lid getting strafed with bricks and rocks echoed through the alley. Warren shook his head and frowned. He supposed he would have to go rescue the boy now. He had to do everything around here.

Except he didn't. Rising up from the dumpster, he saw Telly huddled behind his misshapen buffer and the whole of the brick-throwing squad lying unconscious in the alley.

None other than Hank Busby stood hunched over the human wreckage, a look of satisfaction on his wrinkled face. Just like the good old days—he had gone through the opposition like a buzz saw. "You okay, kid?" he asked Telly.

Telly said he was just ducky. "What did you do?"

Hank said nothing much, just knocked some heads together. "I gotta go, kid. Never say I'm not looking out for you."

He took off down the street before Warren could ask, just out of curiosity, if the Buzz was a card-carrying member of a murderous secret society. He supposed he would have to leave that question for a later political discussion.

"Telly!" gasped Sheriff Blake, arriving with Mahrute.

The bodyguard's bodyguard looked mildly interested to see Warren here instead of home packing. But he was not shocked. Very little shocked Mahrute.

"You okay?" the sheriff asked her brother.

Telly said he was just fine. "Did you see Hank?"

"No, why?"

"He kicked ass!"

"Really, where?" She glanced around and saw the plethora of hoodlum asses—kicked. "Oh."

"Why'd you come back?" Telly wondered.

"Tony took the mayor and that other weirdo in to process, and I realized you weren't with us. You just disappeared."

"I had disappeared too," said Warren. Almost permanently, he might add.

Telly smiled. "You worried about me, sis?"

"Always."

Telly said that was nice. He worried about her too.

Warren wasn't all that anxious, personally. They seemed fine to him. "In case anyone would like to know," he said, "I was nearly kidnapped tonight."

"Kidnapped?" asked the Blake siblings.

"Kidnapped," agreed Warren Kingsley. "Or possibly worse. My captor's intentions were somewhat ambiguous. Basil," he said to Mahrute, and the other man nodded.

Mahrute had thought something was off with the voicemail he received. The communication itself was perfectly reasonable and well disseminated, but it didn't fit. Even if Warren had Mahrute's new phone number, which he didn't, Warren hated voicemail. Rather than leave a message, and risk all that talking, he would have simply kept calling Mahrute over and over (and over) until he reached him. Either that, or sent an email. Warren didn't mind email.

"I am relieved you escaped," said Mahrute.

"I am too. An old friend of ours helped out. Hathaway."

Mahrute was pleased. He had always thought very highly of John Hathaway.

Warren too. More so now. "But we can't stand out here all night talking about how great John Hathaway is. As another not-really friend of mine said recently, I'd like to put as much distance as possible between myself and this crappy place."

The sheriff thought him wise. "You guys head back. You too, Telly. Lance is on his way in the other squad car, and I think we'll look into things a little. If this Basil person is still on the stadium premises, we'll nab him for sure. Meanwhile, we need to start breaking up these rabble-rousers. Things are getting out of hand."

On this cue, the rabble-rousers in the alley began to struggle to their feet. Most of them staggered away, but one RR, the gang's red-haired boy, had a parting remark to make. This remark was, "Die, fascists!"

He punctuated this observation with a flung beer bottle. It was one of the bulkier varieties, twenty ounces, and it struck Jenny Blake solidly on the head.

"Ouch!" said the sheriff, and went down like a mistreated doll after playtime had gotten too rough.

"Jen!" Telly reached to pick her up, but she had already bounced up again.

"I saw you throw that, Timmy Jenkins!" she yelled after the fleeing delinquent. "I know your mom!"

These adrenaline-powered declarations now concluded, Jenny started to feel a touch woozy. She gripped at Warren's jacket and just missed taking another plunge. "My goodness, I'm short," she said, wavering between the vertical and horizontal.

"We need to get you to a doctor," said Telly. He took his sister from one side, Mahrute took the other, and they hobbled up the alley.

And straight into the path of Basil's ginormous friend from the previous evening.

* *

He appeared taller than he had at Warren's cottage, but that could have been because he was outside now and the buildings looked smaller in comparison.

He did not speak. He was much more hands-on. He grabbed Warren by the necktie and yanked viciously.

Mahrute furrowed his brow. This was exactly the brand of client treatment bodyguards like himself objected to and condemned. Regrettably, he had a split-second decision to make—a split-second decision between lending his assistance and keeping Sheriff Blake from toppling back against the concrete. (Though her brother Telly's will to win was strong, his capacity as a pillar of support was an even slenderer reed upon which to lean than a tiny Maltese brain.)

Mahrute chose the more gentlemanly, non-sheriff-dropping approach and, as a result, was forced to stand by and watch his client whipped this way and that by the imported silk.

Warren would have had something to say about this treatment eventually, but once more there was no need. A fast-acting guardian of the law, shaved of head, had bounded onto the scene. He bounded to the spot, bounded this way and that in harmony with the Warren Kingsley slingshot, and then, ultimately, bounded onto the back of slinger of that shot.

"Go!" Deputy Lance Stengel hollered down to them, specifically Mahrute and Telly. "Get Kingsley and the sheriff out of here! I got this!" He had always wanted to say that—*he had this*—and even though he categorically did not *have it*, he had said it, and it felt good.

Warren, Telly, Mahrute and Jen had reached the far parking lot, where Lance had parked the squad car, when Jen wrestled herself free of her two human crutches. "I...have...to go back for my deputy," she said.

Telly wouldn't hear of it. "You got a busted cantaloupe, sis. You're not going anywhere. Warren and I will handle it."

"Not...trained...goofy kid," she insisted. "Couldn't...even... catch ball...without knocking self silly..."

Telly waved all that aside. Knocking himself silly was all in the past. "Warren has been training me. We'll be fine. Get her out of here, Mahrute."

Mahrute carried Jenny away with a flourish, leaving the ex-bodyguard Warren and the never-was bodyguard Telly alone in the dusky lot.

"Shall we do this?" asked the never-was.

Warren had no idea. Speaking for himself, he had volunteered for nothing. "You go, guy," he said.

Telly was incredulous. "You're kidding, right? You're not seriously going to leave good old Lance to get beaten to a pulp after he saved your butt?"

Warren did not feel his butt had ever really been in jeopardy. Not real jeopardy. His necktie, on the other hand, would probably never be the same.

"Well, I'm going," stated Telly grimly. He paused. "I thought you had a bodyguard's code," he remarked. "Leave no man behind. Junk like that."

Warren was pretty sure that was the marines. Although, he did recall a combat instructor, who had been a marine, once explaining the art of the human shield to him—"*You're* the human shield, Kingsley, *you*"—and describing it as *leave no man in front.*

"I thought you had honor," said Telly.

Warren frowned. He had helped save a Maltese this evening. Did that count for nothing? Apparently, it did not. A collie or something, maybe, but not a Maltese.

Warren watched Telly's departure with a puzzled expression on his granite brow. His former apprentice's final words still echoed in his ears. *"I thought you were a hero."*

Warren wondered what ever gave the kid that idea.

* *

Having found no squad car in *Lot F*, Mahrute carried Sheriff Blake down a flight of concrete stairs to an asphalt plateau known as *Lot E*, and then across that lot and up another two flights to a lot designated *G*. Lance had hidden the car brilliantly.

"I can walk, you know," said Jenny.

"I do not mind, Sheriff. You are not heavy."

She didn't suppose she was. But she would still hate for her men to see her this way. "Set me down, will you? I think I saw the car over there." Mahrute set her down, and Jenny squinted. "Am I seeing things, or are there about a thousand skinheads assembled around it?"

Mahrute counted six—six skinheads—but the answer to her question, in spirit, was yes. It was not a night for the Blake family to enter their vehicles unencumbered.

Normally, Sheriff Jenny Blake's commanding attitude and rosy cheeks would have been enough to diffuse the fracas. But she wasn't feeling all that commanding at the moment, and the only thing rosy about her was the scarlet-colored gash in her forehead.

"I guess it would be wrong to shoot them?" she asked.

Mahrute felt that was a question for the philosophers. "I believe I can handle this," he offered, which was the cultured way of saying *he got this*. "Pardon me, gentlemen, but we have an injured officer here. Please step aside."

The gentlemen did not step. One flicked a cigarette in Mahrute's direction. Another made an inappropriate comment about Sheriff's Blake's physique, which, while perfectly correct, was still inappropriate. A third one belched. They were clearly of a tougher breed than Timmy Jenkins's crew.

"Be careful," whispered the sheriff. "I don't know any of their moms."

Mahrute was always careful. "We have had a trying evening, gentlemen. Kindly disperse. I will not ask a third time."

The gentlemen did not disperse, kindly or in any other way. The man who had flicked his cig lit up again. The outspoken objectifier of the female body took out his phone and began tweeting his observations. A fourth, heretofore unheard member, said, "Nice shirt."

Mahrute was once again reminded of his folly with his luggage. This kind of mockery would never have occurred had he accoutered himself in his quiet charcoal herringbone with the red pinstripes. No one could mock herringbone.

"Gentlemen—" he began.

A fifth man, the largest of the bunch, spoke now. He said, "I wish I could grow a mustache like that. Reminds me of my grandma, only hers is thicker."

The ribbing had gone too far. A cold-blooded stare formed on Mahrute's stony visage. He rolled his head slowly, loosening the sinews in his neck. "Excuse me a moment, Sheriff."

The sheriff said he was excused. She dabbed at her gash and asked, "You got this?"

Mahrute nodded in the affirmative. *This* was undeniably a thing that he had.

* *

Costello Blake arrived back at the alley, slightly out of breath and full of apprehension. He could see no sign of the man they had left behind.

"La—" he piped, when a shot rang out from behind his favorite dumpster.

The shot was proceeded by a handful more shots, however many a standard-issue magazine holds—Telly lost count. The first shot nearly made him jump out of his skin; the ones that followed turned his bones to water.

Somehow, in some way, he managed to compel himself down the alley.

He spotted the giant. He was looming over a battered-about Lance. The latter hadn't even had an opportunity to read the former his rights yet.

The perp was holding the officer's gun up to the night sky and had just finished firing off the remaining ammunition in the air. These bare-knuckle brawls were basically sport to him; he had no need for superfluous weaponry. Having signaled for a dozen races no one would ever run, he flicked the pistol to the side, closed his gigantic hand into an even more gigantic fist and drew back his tree trunk of a forearm—

"Hee—" said Telly now, attempting the word *Hey*. He was having a real problem with follow-through tonight. "H-hey," he said again—a little better. "Kn-knock that off. K?"

The colossus straightened up. He smiled a sick smile; Telly wished he wouldn't. His bones had already gone all loopy; he didn't need his spine wriggling about as well.

"Stop. Beating. Lance," said Telly, growing bolder with each word. "He's a father of nine—"

"Five," corrected the deputy.

"A father of five. Are you sure it's five?" asked Telly. He really could have sworn it was more. He supposed Lance would know. "A father of five, with a really hot wife. I mean, not supermodel hot, more of a girl-next-door-in-the-Eastern-European-edition-of-*Playboy* kinda way. I mean, pretty hot." Telly had noticed Mrs. Stengel at the rally today and truly appreciated what Warren Kingsley—and her husband—saw in her.

Lance blinked at him.

The cottage-crusher blinked as well. He was pleased to have the fresh meat. Abandoning Lance for the moment, he glided down the alley toward his new quail.

Telly didn't stir. This was not bravado. He couldn't move, not even a little. The other guy could. He moved real good. How could a thing so large move so fast?

The fist arrived—that enormous, paw-like fist. It came at Telly's face—his tiny, fragile face—

And missed.

A pair of hands, pretty beefy in their own right, had grasped Telly around the shoulders and twirled him out of the way.

Pirouetting into a pile of fruit crates, he half-expected to see Hank Busby on deck again, but Hank was not in the lineup tonight. Warren Kingsley was the man. His heroic preserver. He was just like Polaner All Fruit and Smucker's jam, all rolled into one.

His heroic preserver had taken a fist to the jaw—a proxy jaw to Telly's, but every ballot counted. It sent him staggering back, slightly down in the polls, but he wasn't out. There were still precincts to be heard from.

Instinctively, Telly went to Lance and helped him up. "Let's get out of here!"

"What about Kingsley?"

"Warren will be fine," said his everlasting fan. "He's got this."

Warren supposed he did, but it's still nice to be asked. He watched as the two-sided Lance-and-Telly monstrosity lumbered from view—Telly asking the deputy to get a move on; Lance asking Telly to clarify what he had said about his wife.

Like Mahrute before him, Warren rolled his neck. He looked his opponent up and down. He saw the man for what he was, not a man at all, but a beast. A wild animal that needed to be put down. Soparla? The guy could be Soparla.

Warren didn't mind. He was good with animals.

* *

Ask Borodin Mahrute, and he will tell you: the first three outs are always the toughest. After that, you can more or less relax and blow through your innings. He was working on the second half now.

The sheriff stayed at his side the whole time. Mahrute saw to that. Now and then, between slapping aside some inartistic lunge and administering an effective clout of his own, that brightly colored, Hawaiian-shirted blur would nudge her out of the danger, usually without even pausing in the battle.

On their third go-around, she found herself face-to-face with her outspoken tweeter. He was punch-drunk and woozy—woozier than any tossed bottle could have accomplished—and yet she could not resist the urge to knock the wind out of him with a perfectly timed chop to the throat. She then finished the job with a kick to the cojones. She probably could have left it at the chop, but she hadn't liked what he had said about her boobs.

The scuffle had ended.

Climbing over their collective skinhead pile, Mahrute helped the sheriff into the car and then paused, as Telly and Lance crested the horizon ahead of them.

Mahrute did not like this. If Telly and the deputy were here, where was Warren?

* *

Warren was exactly where they had left him: in a back alley behind the ballpark, engaged in fisticuffs with a deranged henchman, possibly supernatural.

Other than the whap he had received shifting Telly out of the way, Warren had remained relatively unscathed since last seen. Soparla, if he was Soparla, had yet to land another clean shot.

Warren was onto the guy's technique now; he had the *Society* method all pegged. The Society method, he realized, revolved around waiting for your opponent to come to you. It used the other man's aggression against him. In short, it was a system of patience and avoidance. Patience, avoidance and, eventually, the deathblow.

Warren couldn't tell you much about deathblows—not that he'd ever dispensed. And he had always been one who could take patience or leave it alone. But avoidance—now there was something he could get excited about. Very few knew more about a healthy avoidance than Warren Kingsley. It was in his wheelhouse.

Before too long, the alley could no longer contain their mighty struggle. They fought up Chesterfield, turned the corner at Chesterfield and Sixth, and fought their way down Alcott. (Fortunately, traffic heading southbound was light this evening, and very few drivers were delayed.)

It was an epic brawl, one for the ages. *Quiet Man* star John Wayne couldn't have put on a better display himself—only, whereas a resurrected Duke would have enthralled audiences with his dukes, Warren was mesmerizing them with his bobbing and weaving and occasional full-body dodge—like a man agreeing, tentatively, to a limbo dance, but wishing to establish some personal boundaries between himself and the stick first.

They drew a crowd on Chesterfield and solicited several new onlookers after Sixth. By the time they passed from Alcott to Main Street, their entourage had become a seething throng of admirers, full of verve and ready to follow.

Unlike Timmy Jenkins and his crew, this throng had recognized Warren (for the most part) and vigorously applauded the candidate's publicity stunt. (For, what else could it be?) They hooted and hollered as if the fight were for real.

The contenders had reached the town square, and it was here that Warren let himself go. With all the pent-up rage of a forty-year-old man who has never quite clicked with life, he landed blow after blow on Soparla's exhausted frame (he was pretty sure the man was Soparla). The hits kept coming, one after another. *One* for a life spent alone and miserable. *One* for being born with a magnificent, brawny physique, forcing him into a career of elite security work (whereas he would have been much happier as a poet or philosopher). Finally, he connected with two punches to his opponent's face, one for not meeting Maria Stengel before Lance (now annoyingly alive and well) and one for the starch Warren's dry cleaner had put in his Armani against Warren's wishes, making the garment very scratchy in the thighs.

It was the last blow, the scratchy-thigh blow, that floored Soparla for good. (Warren was just going to assume he was Soparla.)

It was a frozen-rope drive to the enemy's jaw. The lizard assassin landed in a fluid cascade at the foot of the stairs of the founder's statue. One of Warren's supporters popped out from the crowd and held the contestant's arm up in triumph. The little town of Kilobyte went *hurray!*

Best. Political ad. Ever.

18 — After Words

One particular spectator had not found it the best ever. He had glared out from his spot in the crowd, approximately ninety feet away, two dark, piercing eyes under a rigid little forehead. Warren had observed the Basil death stare then, and even after the man had shaken his head with resignation and melted into the crowd, Warren could still feel it boring into him. He was one creepy little dude, that Basil.

Twelve hours later, Warren was no longer thinking about the creepy Basil, not exclusively anyway. There were so many other things to think about—and ponder—and brood upon.

The midlife crisis the town of Kilobyte had experienced last night had come to an end. Everything was back to normal now, and with that normalcy came more Kingsley rumination.

He ruminated, first and foremost, on Deputy Lance, sitting at his desk a few minutes ago, happily buried in a horde of golden-haired daughters. They had been climbing and giggling and dangling off Mount Stengel, as their mother looked on.

Maria was not the only one with the glad eye. Telly was standing across from the deputy's wife, his mouth hanging open and his face atwitter. Unless Warren was very much mistaken, that boy had a crush. Better Maria than Warren.

And better Lance than him, thought Warren. Lance was the better man. Warren was glad he hadn't died; he was a good egg. He even looked a little like an egg, around the head. Perhaps that was Warren's problem; he had too much hair. Magnificent, luxuriant hair.

Taking a moment to admire his coif in the window of the police station, he peered down at the drawing Gladys had given him—Warren presiding over the town of Kilobyte. He looked on this pic fondly before returning it to its protective envelope and this envelope to his pocket. He forced his thoughts on to a new topic.

This new topic was Councilwoman Clarisse, now Acting-Mayor Clarisse, soon to be Campaigning-Mayor Clarisse. Warren had met with her before stepping outside for some air. He wanted her to know that he would not be pursuing the office of mayor himself. He had changed his mind.

It was not simply the threats to his safety, the long hours or the starchy suits—he had become burned out, disillusioned. If Timmy Jenkins could fail to recognize his favorite candidate in the flesh, what was the point? People fell in love with the idea of a man like Warren Kingsley, but they did not love Warren himself. They never would. Use you up and spit you out—that was politics.

Perhaps that was at the heart of Basil's behavior last night. Perhaps the little guy was only trying to scare Warren straight. Run him out of town for his own good.

Basil had mentioned liking Mahrute; perhaps he secretly liked and admired Warren as well and wished to save him from a life of corruption and secret-society club dues.

Warren might never know the answer to that question, but he liked to give people the benefit of the doubt. Even if they were creepy little dudes.

On that theme, he had thought it only fitting to give the new town leader a heads-up about what she was saddling herself with. Taking Clarisse aside, he had told her about Basil and the Colony (keeping it clean) and ended with the dramatic reveal that Hank Busby was very possibly one of these Colony Society folks.

She had responded with her best supercilious smirk—so supercilious and smirky that he was momentarily put in mind of Basil. Lowering her voice just above a whisper, she had asked Warren what made him think *she* wasn't part of this society too.

That was when he had stepped outside for air. As he left, he could hear Telly imparting advice to his aunt about her upcoming campaign-announcement speech:

"If you have to speak [imparted Costello Blake], remind your audience that silence is golden. Explain that there is nothing you can say that they can't discover themselves through basic self-exploration. Close with a simple, manly statement pointing out that most things are better left—"

It had been a weird election year, Warren realized.

In the midst of these reflections, Mahrute appeared. Warren welcomed the interruption. With the return of the courier companies in town, his bodyguard had received his belongings and was back in his black pinstripe. Not quite as cheerful as the herringbone with the red stripe, but the yellow waistcoat made it work.

"You done yet, Mahrute?"

Mahrute was finished. He had said goodbye to Henrietta Bragg at her office.

He had wanted to thank her for her company and hospitality, as well as return her shirt. He'd had it dry-cleaned.

"They probably put in too much starch," said Warren, as they walked up Chesterfield Avenue on their way out of town. "Did I see you talking to Nibu in his cell this morning?"

Mahrute nodded. The attempted assassin was in next to Timmy Jenkins, Kilobyte's other public enemy. "Mr. Nibu wanted me to pass along a message to you congratulating you on your resounding defeat of the beast Soparla. He also wanted to apologize for almost blowing you up. It was nothing personal," he said.

Warren had never thought it was. It was all about getting the mayor. The go-getter spirit. "Amazing, him being in the cottage the whole time. Crazy old Nibu. He always was a good blender. We could take some pointers from him."

"Could we?"

"Well, I could," said Warren. "Did he explain how he got mistaken for Soparla himself?"

"He did. He had ingratiated himself with the crime syndicate at the Colony, and one thing led to another. When a vacancy appeared, he assumed his role under the name of Soparla. The real Soparla hadn't been heard from for years, so Nibu didn't think he would mind."

"More blending in," muttered Warren. Everyone was good at something. He paused. "I just realized I forgot to say goodbye to the sheriff."

"I made your farewells for you."

"Thanks, Mahrute. You're a lifesaver."

They had reached the top of Chesterfield, at the pinnacle of which you could see the entire town of Kilobyte. Warren shaded his eyes in observation. He thought they would be walking off into the sunset, but you can't have everything.

"It's funny," Warren observed. "You'd think I would have fallen in love with the sheriff before we left." Normally, on any given junket, he limited himself to mooning over one unattainable woman at a time. Now that Maria Stengel was out of his sights, he could have easily switched gears.

Ah well, too late to start walking back to town now.

"You seem pensive, Mahrute. What's up?"

The bodyguard's bodyguard frowned. "I was only brooding."

"Bad habit."

"It's about Soparla. I am not convinced that the man you vanquished last night is that mythical assassin."

"You *would* try to rob me of that," said Warren sourly. "Why couldn't he be Soparla?"

"Well, for one, he seemed much too young."

"Perhaps he has a good skin regiment. A lizard-man would need one. What else you got?"

"Only that I had another candidate in mind."

Warren would prefer not to hear the word *candidate* again, in this life or the next. "Who else could be him?"

"Hank Busby."

Warren stumbled. "The Buzz Saw? How?"

"It all fits. His age is correct; he has demonstrated exceptional physical skill both on the ballfield and off; and Basil claims he is part of the Society. Also, I asked him."

Warren froze. "You asked him?! What did he say?"

"He dissembled."

"Like any good politician."

"Yes. Although, he did say something curious. On the subject of nicknames, he told me it was lucky that his other sobriquet, the one he had when he was coming up through the minors, never stuck."

"And what was Hank Busby's first sobriquet?"

"The Hit Man."

Warren had no energy left to argue. Maybe Hank was Soparla. Warren could see him as a hitman. The lizard part he wasn't so sure about. No doubt that was only a Romanian figure of speech. *Or was it?*

"What do you think it's all about, Mahrute? This secret society?"

"I can't imagine. Although, I will say that someone, perhaps Mr. Hathaway and his team, will someday pierce that enigma."

Warren wished them the best. Assuming Hathaway didn't spend all his time chasing after errant Maltese, he might have a shot. "If I had known Hank was such a prominent fixture in this society, I would have asked him a few questions. For instance, what do you think 'Opie' means? Basil called me that the night of our first brawl, and it's really been bugging me."

Mahrute, as usual, had an answer (almost). "According to Hank, the word 'Opie' is, in fact, the phonetic pronunciation of the letters *OP*."

"*OP.* Like an abbreviation?" Warren thought about it. *Overdressed Pirates? Outlandish Pears?* He shook his head. "I got nothing. You?"

Mahrute did not.

Warren was resigned to his happy ignorance. "I guess it's up to Hathaway, then. Him and his little dog, what's her name. Better them than us."

Mahrute supposed it was.

Their journey had taken them to the Kilobyte Bus Station. "I guess this is where we part again," said Warren.

Mahrute said indeed. "Have you decided where you are going?"

"Never have before. For now, I suppose I'll head back up to Maine to have a word with Sir Roger Banbury."

Mahrute was astonished. "Sir Roger—"

"Banbury. That's right."

"You mean—he's alive?"

Warren didn't know why, but he resented the question. "I do have more than one surviving client, you know, Mahrute?" He had three.

Mahrute couldn't have been happier. "Then the unpleasantness you mentioned…"

Warren frowned. "It seemed I got a tad above myself at a cocktail party, trying to protect the old codger. I may or may not have shoved him into the orchestra pit of the Bath Chamber Orchestra, trying to save his life from what turned out to be a particularly cacophonous champagne bottle opening. Not a gunshot, you understand?"

Mahrute understood.

"We had a huge argument, and I said a few things I probably shouldn't have. I guess my only crime was overthinking things, trying to do my job *too well*."

Mahrute found it difficult to believe…

…that Sir Roger would dismiss him over such a trivial matter.

Warren wasn't all that surprised. "You know how the man likes his space and hates a fuss. I should have played to my strength and continued to ignore him. Still, he may have cooled off by now."

Mahrute wouldn't be surprised. "If you like, I could accompany you to Rangeley Manor and put in a good word on your behalf."

Warren would like that very much. "You don't have anywhere else to be—any villages or civilizations that need rescuing?"

Mahrute replied that the world's civilizations could wait. They weren't going anywhere.

Warren said excellent. Mahrute could reason with Banbury, while he, Warren, could do what he did best. Not overthink. That was what was wrong with the world.

We all think too much.

FURTHER READING

If you enjoyed Double Talk, you can also cheer on Warren and Mahrute in *Five Star Detour* and its prequel, *Double Cover*.

And for those curious about the cryptic details left unanswered in *Talk*, all we can say is everything will be explained, care of John Hathaway and Enescu Fleet, in *Fleeting Encounter* (TBA).

CPSIA information can be obtained
at www.ICGtesting.com
Printed in the USA
LVOW11*1915030517

533129LV00006B/67/P